CHILD
OF
DUST

CHILD
OF
DUST

A DOTAN NAOR THRILLER

YIGAL ZUR

LEVEL
BEST BOOKS

First edition

ISBN: 978-1-68512-686-5

Cover art by Level Best Designs

This book was professionally typeset on Reedsy.
Find out more at reedsy.com

To Karin

If the sky could cry, there would never be drought in Cambodia.

—CAMBODIAN PROVERB

Contents

II   Part II

III   Part III

Praise for Child of Dust

"Sometimes funny, sometimes thrilling, but always realistic and engaging, *Child of Dust* is another gritty and utterly enjoyable Yigal Zur novel you'll want to devour in a single sitting."—Alan Jacobson, USA Today bestselling author of *The Lost Girl*

"Spanning Tel-Aviv to Thailand to Cambodia, *Child of Dust* tells the story of lechery and greed and every shade of foul in between. There's no shortage of sexual tension, physical aggressions, and unrelenting danger to keep the pages turning. But at the center of this story of a missing girl and a family's secrets is the great big beating heart of its hero, Dotan Noar, an unflinching man from a forgotten time when honor meant more than money and dignity was worth dying for."—Joe Clifford, author of *The Shadow People* and the Jay Porter thriller series

"Betrayal, greed, and depravity collide when a child is taken. Zur's breakneck pacing and memorable characters will have you holding your breath to the final, satisfying conclusion."—James L'Etoile, award-winning author of *Dead Drop* and the Detective Emily Hunter series

Prologue

THREE MONTHS EARLIER

Koh Samui, Thailand

The girl was lying on her back. The first rays of morning light filtered in through the window. She opened her eyes, keen not to miss a moment of the spectacle. She watched the shiny motes of dust floating through the air, following them as they came in on the light and disappeared into the shadow. Pursing her lips, she blew toward them, as if by creating an eddy in the air, she could bring back the tiny particles that had vanished.

Nothing disappears forever. Everything leaves behind an essence that comes and goes. From time to time, it glows brightly, but mostly, its existence is spectral. Whatever disappears leaves a wake, a path, an unmarked trail. A tiny gecko crawled across the ceiling. Hanging upside down, its head pointing to the floor, it made its way slowly into the shadows. It blinked. The girl blinked back, mimicking it. They blinked at each other for several minutes, and then the girl smiled, and the gecko disappeared into the corner.

She had been introduced to many unfamiliar creatures lately. Huge cockroaches that meandered leisurely under her bed, stopping for a moment to wiggle their antennae and then continuing on their way in an amazingly coordinated movement of multiple joints; round beetles that fell from the trees onto the sand, where they found a sumptuous buffet; noisy geckos, like the little one on the ceiling, whose voices were heard at dusk. She was always surprised by the sound, almost like a lion's roar. She was in a new and fascinating world, but one filled with fears that slithered out from the shadows. Sometimes, when she curled up under the thin sheet in the dark, she wondered if everyone was scared of the same things, or if it was just her. A single ray of light danced across the room. She threw off the sheet and walked barefoot to the window, pulling open the richly colored curtain. Instantly, she was blinded by the bright light. She shut her eyes and then opened them again. Before her was a wonderful sight, the most beautiful scenery she had ever seen. She knew she would never forget it, that it would always bring back memories of her bat mitzvah trip. The long white beach was like a strip of gleaming light that stretched down to the water. Tall palm trees grew along it, casting dark patches of shade that expanded the higher the sun rose in the sky. Glittering puddles of water were scattered here and there, created overnight by the high tide. In the distance, she could see the tall statue of Buddha covered in a mosaic of tiny multicolored glass tiles. He sat cross-legged inside a huge stone lotus flower, his hands raised in a gesture of meditation, his ears hanging down like elephant ears, and seagulls perched on his curls. The statue glowed orange and yellow in the sun. The girl could usually make out a gentle smile, but today, a morning cloud seemed to cast a pall over his face.

At this hour of the morning, the sand was still brittle and cool. There was no one by the water. She thought of the treasures she would find when she went down to the beach. She decided to walk to the Buddha, which was as far as her parents allowed her to go alone. The statue stood at the edge of a little spit of land. Palm trees and mangroves reached down to where the beach became rocky. Sand and shells collected in the cracks between the stones. The girl would sit there for hours, cross-legged like the Buddha, cleaning, sorting, and examining the prizes she had gathered. The change in the light falling on the face of the Buddha was her only sign that time was passing. She found shells that looked like ears or tops and flat ones she spread out like shiny little plates, setting a table for the mermaids.

But her favorites were the colorful conch shells, long pointy cones in red, orange, and yellow that collected in large piles. She would choose the biggest and most perfect ones, arranging them in a circle around her on the sand, pointing outward. Sitting inside the circle surrounded by her wreath of thorns, she felt safe. No one could get in.

The girl was tall for her age. Sometimes, she thought she looked like a noodle. The sleeveless shirt she was wearing was much too big on her, an old fraying undershirt of her father's. Her parents had repeatedly begged her to throw it out and put on a normal blouse. But she liked it. She was probably unaware that the deep neckline revealed the borders of her tiny budding breasts, whose existence she tried hard to deny. The light played in the hollows created by her slightly protruding shoulder blades. The only thing she actually liked about her body was the small beauty mark high on the left side of her chest. She took pleasure in the thought that no matter how much she grew, it would always be there, her personal trademark. Hidden by the rocks, she would take off her shirt, knowing that no one could see her, and pretend that she was still a little girl.

Her changing body was already attracting attention, but she wasn't sure if she liked it or not. She could tell that the men lying on the sunbeds on the beach, their bodies gleaming from coconut oil, were watching her from behind their designer sunglasses. When they looked at her, she could sometimes feel herself moving differently, swaying her body slowly like the ray of light dancing on the walls of her room. She could sense the effect she had on the staring eyes.

The girl didn't think she was pretty. There were plenty of prettier, more appealing girls among her friends. Her face hadn't fully settled into shape yet. She had gray-green eyes, greener in the morning and grayer in the shadows and the dark. Her long, straight hair was naturally blond and fell generously on her shoulders. She liked to swing her head quickly to make it swirl around her face, pretending to be invisible, hidden from the world by a golden veil.

Her hair was now held back by a *mala*, a string of Buddhist prayer beads. Yesterday, when she went out shopping with her mother, a group of Buddhist monks in their orange robes passed through the main street of Chaweng Beach. One of them came up to her and put the beads around her neck. Gazing at her with smiling eyes, he said, "For protection," and then rejoined the other monks with their shaven heads. When they returned to the hotel, she examined the beads closely. They were made of reddish sandalwood. After considerable thought, she slipped on the blue and purple bracelet with her name—Eden—stitched into the middle. She had bought it from one of the little girls who sat on the sidewalk dressed in the traditional garb of the Akha tribe of northern Thailand, their quick fingers nimbly embroidering bracelets to order.

A young Thai woman in skimpy denim hot pants and a white T-shirt bearing the logo of the Banana Beach Café was walking down the beach. She was holding her flip-flops in her hand, striding barefoot along the waterline where the waves lapped the sand before receding. Eden recognized her: Nit Noi, "little Noi," the braid maker. Since they had arrived on the island, she often sat beside her, watching as she deftly braided the hair of young Western women. Eden was constantly amazed by how masterfully she plaited the tight, thin braids, weaving bright colored beads into them.

She was surprised to see Nit Noi on the beach so early in the morning. No one else was around. The hotel guests were still asleep. Like Eden's parents, most of them got up late after dancing until the early hours of the morning at one of the Chaweng Beach discos. She watched as Nit Noi came closer. Seeing Eden, she stopped.

Eden smiled and waved.

Nit Noi waved back, a big grin on her face. It seemed to Eden that smiling came naturally to the Thai people.

She left the rocks behind and ran back to the hotel. Taking off her flip-flops, she tiptoed barefoot to her parents' room. The door was ajar. She stuck her head in and looked inside. Immediately, she was overcome by a thick, repulsive odor that stuck to the walls of her twitching nostrils. She'd smelled it before. A heavy ashtray on the glass table was filled with cigarette butts. A line of white powder had been drawn on the edge of the table and was slowly being blown away by the cold blast coming from the quiet air conditioner.

Her father was curled up under the sheet, snoring loudly. She could see his white hairy thigh sticking out. Staring at him, she remembered the sounds she had heard during the night. She had been woken up by giggling when her parents returned to the villa. They fell quiet, and she had almost gone back to sleep when she heard the strident ringing of the telephone and her father shouting into it. She remembered word for word what he had said: "What do you want? Isn't it enough? I gave you enough." Silence. She kept listening. "You want to squeeze me dry? Are you fucking with me?" Silence. "We'll see. You don't scare me." She heard her father disconnect the call and then exchange a few halting words with her mother. The conversation wound down, and Eden fell asleep again. She didn't hear the end.

Her mother opened her eyes and looked at her daughter. "I'm going to the beach," Eden mouthed soundlessly.

"Don't go far," her mother said quietly, stressing each word, unaware that Eden had already spent an hour on the beach.

"Okay, okay," the girl mouthed, adding a gesture that meant, "Don't worry."

Her mother put a finger on her lips, telling her to be quiet. As she turned to leave, Eden thought she saw a flicker of fear in her mother's eyes.

The porch of their villa faced the broad beach, the trunk of a huge mangrove tree twisting around it so that it seemed to merge with the landscape. Eden stood there for a moment, breathing in the odor she was now getting used to, although, at first, it had repulsed her, pinching her nose. It was a mixture of salt, rotting seaweed, and dead fish. Shiny fat flies buzzed around the compost heap from the early hours of the morning.

She ran back to Little Noi on the beach. "Hi, Nit Noi, *sawadee ka*," she said, practicing her Thai.

As usual, the young Thai woman returned the greeting courteously, the only way she knew to behave.

Eden carefully uttered the sentence she had been rehearsing for several days, "*Yin dee tee dai ruu jak*," pleased to meet you.

Little Noi smiled. "Now you get it right."

Eden was thrilled. "Do you want to braid my hair?"

"You want it Rasta style?" the petite Thai woman asked nervously.

"Yes, can you do it?" Eden asked, excited.

Little Noi scanned the area. "Sure," she said. "But we have to go into town. I can't do here."

Eden lowered her eyes, embarrassed. She drew circles in the sand with her big toe. Raising her head, she replied shyly, "My mother will be mad at me."

"No ploblem," Little Noi answered, using the heavily accented expression heard everywhere in Thailand.

The calm was broken by the sound of a motorcycle bumping along the beach. It was coming from the direction of the Buddha. Eden wondered how it had gotten over the rocks and the sand. Was there some secret track she didn't know about? The Yamaha bike zigzagged toward them, taking advantage of the hard-packed morning sand. The eyes of the rider, a skinny young Thai, were hidden behind mirror-lensed sunglasses. A red bandana with white stars was tied around his head. His hands, resting on the handlebars, sported dark fading tattoos of a structure with graduated cones and a waving flag.

Eden could see her reflection in the young man's metallic glasses.

"This my friend, Sonchai," Little Noi said, glancing at him.

"Hi, Sonchai," Eden said happily.

The man didn't reply. Instead, he turned to little Noi and said in Thai, "The white girl is big."

Noi shrugged.

The rider continued to look at Eden while he spoke to Noi. "She'll stand out too much. She'll be trouble, no?"

"No," Noi answered, wary of his aggressive tone. "She's a good girl."

"She better be. I'll kill her if she makes trouble. And you, too. Fuck the money."

He probably got high on *ya ba* last night, Noi thought, worried. For many Thais, the crazy pills, amphetamines, were the only way to feel *sabai*, to chill. Just don't let him mess this up, she prayed. He has to stay calm, or we won't be able to do it.

Little Noi was frightened. There was no need for him to threaten her. There was no question that she would do as she'd been told. They all did. Everyone who made a living on the beach or in the bars worked for them, or other men like them, she didn't know and didn't wish to know. She was very well aware of what they'd do to her if she didn't obey: skin her like a pig after slaughter.

Two days ago, they'd told her exactly what to do to persuade this girl, this particular one, to come with her to a predetermined pick-up spot. Noi knew where they would take her. She'd heard the rumors. She tried to put the disturbing thoughts out of her mind, repeating to herself, "I'm sorry, Nit Eden, so sorry."

"She won't make trouble," she said confidently in an effort to calm Sonchai and get him to focus on the task at hand.

"We go and come back before your mother wake up," she said to Eden, hoping she sounded credible.

"Wait a minute," Eden said. "I'll take my hair down."

Pulling off the string of beads, she ran to the mangrove tree beside her favorite hiding place, and carefully hung it on one of the branches above the rocks. "Wait here," she ordered, pointing at the beads, "I'll be back soon." Then she ran back to Little Noi and the man on the motorcycle.

She hopped onto the bike, hesitating for a moment before she placed her hands against the young man's thin back. Nit Noi got on behind her, gently clasping her hands around her.

Eden could feel the adrenaline flowing through her body. Grinning, she thought of the adventure in store for her and the smile on her mother's face when she saw what she had done.

The man leaned on the gas throttle, raising a cloud of fine sand. The front tire dug a deep rut across the beach, which would disappear with the next wave, together with every other trace of the motorcycle and its passengers. The waves rose and fell, smoothing out the sand in the narrow track between the water and the rocks near the large statue of Buddha, still gazing out to sea as he always had. Nothing was changed.

And then the girl was gone.

I

Part I

Chapter One

Tel Aviv

I was totally drained, exhausted, and that was both good and bad. Good, because I felt great after two hours of a grueling spinning session; bad, because I knew it wasn't enough. Whenever I close a case, it takes me a long time to get back to what I like to call my "routine life."

But what's routine for me seems strange, to put it mildly, to other people. As soon as I begin to talk about what I've been doing for the past month or so, the questions inevitably start coming: "How can you live like that?"; "What are you complaining about? You have a dream life." And then, of course, there's "Now I understand why none of your relationships ever last." That was Mira, my ex-wife, who added, "Not only ours." I sensed a note of concern in her voice, or at least I imagined I did. They all want to take care of me. Just not for very long.

They don't know about the lonely nights in a strange, often dirty, bed in some fleabag hotel on the other side of the world. Lying there for hours on end, staring at the rusty ceiling fan that barely moves the air, doing little more than collecting dust. The heat and humidity clog up my head, and the sweat streams down my chest despite feeble attempts to cool off. Nights when I struggle to get the aging computer called my mind, a late '70s model, to process all the new events and information collected in its memory during the day. Appalling images are engraved on my soul, leaving permanent scars. The nights are spent fixated on the memories that never die, like maggots

3

eating at my brain.

I was striving hard for routine. Making a real effort. A simple, untroubled Tel Aviv life: the gym, my local café, a good book, an occasional business meeting. Not too much business. And even less sex. Nothing overly demanding. I'd pressed "delete" on all my latest investigations, hoping for a little peace and quiet.

I should have known not to ask for anything. Peace and quiet isn't exactly my natural habitat.

I was standing in front of the gym. Small drops of rain had begun falling from the dark sky. The gray winter light of Tel Aviv. It matched my mood. Still, my mouth turned up in a smile. In my world, rain is usually a sign that, once again, I've arrived in a place where the shit is about to hit the fan. But now I was in Tel Aviv, and it was raining, and everything was just fine. I didn't know how much shit was yet to come. Heaps, rivers of the stuff. The average winter crud washed into the Mediterranean was nothing compared to what was waiting for me. If I'd paid attention to the changes in the climate in the past few years, I'd have noticed that there was less precipitation and the lakes were drying up. But the amount of shit rising to the surface was steadily increasing.

The rain picked up as I entered the café next door. Heavy drops splashed on the sidewalk. I sat at my regular table by the wide glass window and wondered why it always rained when I was in this ambivalent mood. My soul was at peace, but my body yearned for an adrenaline rush, for an urgent shot of invigorating action.

The rain flowed down the window like flat waves. The waitress brought my espresso with a smile. Maybe because I was the only man in the place, who looked up at her.

"How're you doing?" I asked.

"Great," she said.

I didn't believe her, but I appreciated the effort. She looked like it was the rainy season in her world, too. That was surprising, because she had all the right qualifications for springtime: a firm butt and perky breasts pushing up against her tight T-shirt.

I was taking a second sip of the bitter coffee when the phone in the pocket of my gym bag chirped. I didn't answer. I knew who was calling. That's why you use different ringtones, isn't it? So you know when not to answer the phone.

I meant it literally when I said "chirped." That's the ringtone I chose for my business partner, David.

I pulled the phone out on the sixth ring.

"You're a moron," he said. "What's up with you?"

"I'm having coffee."

"You kill me, man. What do you have a phone for? Not to answer it? What do you think it means when it rings?"

"That you're going to fuck with my head and ruin my day."

David let out a sigh. He's been doing that for as long as I've known him, and that's a long time. Our partnership became rocky years ago. What keeps it going is the fact that we're always on the verge of dissolving it.

"Now I know you're in a good mood. How long were you on the bike?"

"A couple of hours."

"Any hot chicks?"

"Nothing special. Most of them are anorexic."

He laughed. "Okay, so let me cheer you up. Iris Ben-Lev is looking for you. The name mean anything to you?"

"Not really." I didn't want to tell him that the best thing about spinning is that it clears my mind completely. I wondered if my brain cells were dead or just in a coma.

"Come on, make an effort," David said. "It used to be Blumenthal. Does that help?"

"Okay, fine," I said, reciting what everyone in Israel knows. "One of the ten wealthy families that have the country by the balls. So what?"

The rain started beating fiercely against the glass. The coffee was deliciously bitter. The waitress smiled as she passed my table. This time, the smile seemed genuine. I was beginning to feel a lot better. It wasn't just the caffeine. I could sense something starting to blossom. One case isn't really over until the next one turns up. That's when you file it away in the special cabinet in your brain. The place where you put the files that leave the scars, not the official files that end with a written summary and a list of expenses.

"Big money," David said.

Remarks like that make it very hard for me to tolerate him. It's not like he was a pauper. "Fuck the rich. They make me sick," I said, partly to get at him and partly because it was the truth.

"I guess you're going to have to drink a lot of chamomile tea. That's what my grandma used to give me for a stomach ache. Anyway, you're about to get up close, and maybe even personal, with one of the wealthiest families in the country. You know Sammy Ben-Lev, the attorney?"

"A rising star in international law and high finance. A part-owner of some of Tel Aviv's most popular clubs. A self-made man. Likes to see his name in the gossip columns."

"Precisely. It seems he also has a wife, or an ex-wife, their status isn't clear at the moment. At least, that's what the gossip columns say. In any case, she's supposed to be a real bombshell, and you're about to get a rare opportunity to check her out for yourself."

"What are you talking about?"

"She's on her way there."

"Now?" I was caught off-guard, which is unusual for me.

David laughed again. He knew he'd shaken me up, and he was reveling in it. "Please give her your full attention."

"What's it about?" The truth is I was getting a flash of memory. But with so much adrenaline pumping through my body, I didn't want to jump into anything. Certainly not anything David brought me, which meant work, or in other words, trouble.

"Patience, pal. She'll be there soon." Laughing, he disconnected.

Chapter Two

A black Mercedes SUV pulled up onto the sidewalk outside the window. The door opened, and I saw a long feminine leg in sheer black tights above a black leather knee-high boot with a stiletto heel. It was followed by a tight raincoat with a wide belt. Finally, a head of flowing blond hair emerged, looking like it had just come from the beauty salon. Every hair was in place, ready for inspection. The woman who slammed the door behind her rose to a height of five foot nine at least, not including the heels. And she was worth every inch, including the heels.

The umbrella in her hand sprung open. In three long strides, she was at the door. The waitress opened it for her. She walked in, took a quick look around, and marched straight toward me. All the male eyes in the café followed this shining example of determined femininity. I was the only one who felt like ducking down and crawling away. Who needed this? I must sound like an idiot, but at least I have enough experience to know when a hurricane is coming, and I know the destruction it leaves behind. "Dotan," she stated. It wasn't a question.

I wondered if a woman like her even knew what a question mark was for. I didn't respond. I'm a tough guy, six foot one of muscle, a solid mass, 183 pounds naked and clean-shaven, but I couldn't get a word out of my mouth. She sat down opposite me and tucked her hair behind her right ear. Great. There was a diamond stud in her ear, a single gem, but the kind that requires a conglomerate to insure.

Holding out her hand, she announced, "Iris."

I was surprised by the masculine gesture. I shook her hand, feeling like my own was more a sponge than an appendage. And I've got a hand that has crushed more than one despicable face.

We spent the next few minutes checking each other out. It reminded me of the staring contests we used to have when we were kids. She'd make a formidable opponent. Good start, I thought.

"Can I get you something?" I asked.

"Iced coffee, two shots of caffeine-free espresso, a drop of soy milk, no sugar, and a lot of ice."

Ice in the winter? I wondered as I passed the order on to the waitress. Her throat must be made of steel.

She got her bag from the chair where she had set it down. Black leather to match her skirt and coat, undoubtedly from some famous Italian designer. A lot of black. A lot of metal. She pulled out a thick plastic file.

"This is what I found on you on the Internet."

"A waste of paper," I said.

She examined me, considering, and fired back, "Never mind. I can shred it."

I didn't reply.

"Give me fifteen minutes," she said, glancing at her watch. "If you decide I'm wasting your time, I'll pay for the coffee, and you'll never hear from me again."

"I'm listening."

"My daughter disappeared. Three months ago. Vanished into thin air." I took another sip of coffee. I must have made a wry face, because she said, "I thought I'd find you here drinking wheatgrass juice, not coffee."

She wasn't the first to think she would be meeting some spaced-out yogi, muscle-bound and enlightened. I wondered how else I was going to disappoint her.

"How much time do I have left?"

All the time in the world, I wanted to say. Instead, I answered with a nod in her direction, "As much as you need."

We sat in silence, scrutinizing each other. We both understood. We had formed a pact. Two complete strangers sending out antennae like insects, testing the air to see how far we could go with all our personal constraints and reservations. Did I imagine she was my soulmate? Maybe. But those are the kind of thoughts it's best to nip in the bud. Nothing good ever comes from them. Just trouble. If I'd been smarter, I would have squashed the idea immediately, beaten it over the head, given it a good kick in the guts. But I wasn't smart enough, and she had a captivating smile.

Her coffee arrived. She took a sip and placed the glass back down on the saucer, her hand shaking slightly. She was miles away. Then, she pulled herself together and went on with her story. She told me about her daughter, Eden.

"I can't forgive myself," she said. "I picked my head up off the pillow when she came into our room, but I was mostly concerned that she might wake Sammy."

A cloud passed over her eyes when she mentioned the name of her husband, like the monsoon cloud that appears suddenly, and within minutes, the whole world is dark. And just as quickly as it pours out its rain and goes away, so she sloughed it off and went on. "I thought Eden went out to play on the beach like she did every morning. She'd spend hours on the beach, collecting shells, daydreaming, sitting in her little hiding place. I thought girls her age needed their independence. I tried to ignore my apprehensions, but that morning in the hotel, something seized up inside me."

Her long fingers played with the glass in front of her, twisting it back and forth nervously, wiping off the cold drops dripping down the sides. It was obvious to me that the story she was telling me was one she had repeated to herself over and over again. Time after time, she had gone over the facts as she remembered them, and time after time, she had blamed herself. Her guilt was carved into her face, guilt for not taking good enough care of her child, for letting her wander the beach on her own, for not making her sufficiently aware of the danger of perverts, maniacs, and pedophiles. She blamed herself as a mother for letting this happen to her daughter. She should have known. The news was full of stories about girls being abducted.

But those weren't facts. "Tell me again," I instructed.

She stared at me, not understanding.

"Try to put the events in order. Just the straight facts. Not what you thought or what you felt. We're going to go over it again and again until I get all the details. Right now, I want to get a picture of the specific times and places."

"You mean I got up, took a shower, and went out?" she asked drily.

"Exactly. Spell it out for me."

"The night before Eden disappeared, we held a big event. The launching of our new resort in Koh Samui in Thailand."

"Do you have a list of the guests?"

"No," she said hesitantly. "But I suppose I could get it. We went to bed very late. Before we went into our room I looked in on Eden. She was sleeping. As usual, the night light was on, and she was surrounded by all the stuffed animals she'd brought with her."

"When was the next time you saw here? What time was it?" I could imagine what she was seeing in her head: the last image of her daughter before she disappeared.

"Around seven in the morning. Not before that. It doesn't get light before six, six fifteen."

"How do you know what time it was?"

"The curtain was open. It was light in the room. We'd had a lot to drink that night. I forgot to close the curtain." Again, I heard a hint of hesitation in her voice. I knew she was hiding something. Drugs? An orgy?

"When did you start looking for her? When did you start to get worried?"

"We got up late. We could have ordered breakfast from room service, but I felt like sitting outside. Clearing my head. We were wasted after the event. The restaurant looks out at the sea. The most beautiful place in the world. It looks like the cliché of a tourist poster, but it's real. Palm trees, a long beach, white sand, birds. You think you're in paradise."

She paused for a long time before going on. "We were having breakfast. I looked along the beach, and she wasn't there. I asked one of the waitresses if she'd seen her, but she said she hadn't. I asked another one and got the same answer. It was odd, because Eden was..." She stopped and corrected herself, "I mean, Eden is always around somewhere. She loves talking to people. She'll talk to anyone. She thinks it's one of the most meaningful things in life. And that was a very important day for her."

"Why?"

"It was her birthday. I promised her a special day. We were going to spend it together, just mother and daughter. The whole day together. It isn't like her to forget something like that."

"What did you do?"

"I went down and walked the whole length of the beach. I asked the hotel staff, the vendors. They all knew her, even though we'd only been there for two weeks."

"And?"

"Nothing. I went back to the hotel and called Sammy. He said there was nothing to worry about. She's a big girl, very independent, very responsible, and she wouldn't do anything that would give us cause for concern. He said he'd check. Maybe she went to Chaweng Beach with someone from the hotel. That's the main beach on Koh Samui. It's where most of the shops and restaurants are."

"I know it."

"We waited a while. Sammy checked with the hotel staff, and when it turned out that no one knew anything, we drove to Chaweng. No one had seen her. Everyone we asked just gave us a blank look. I began to see a Thailand I didn't know. That's when the first wave of panic hit me. When I knew something was wrong. I stood there in the middle of the shopping street in Chaweng, and I couldn't move. I was frozen by fear. It was like a nightmare. It *was* a nightmare. I even prayed to God to keep my little girl safe, and I'm not a religious person."

A tear formed in the corner of her eye and slid slowly down her cheek, leaving a shiny stripe. She regained her composure, got a packet of tissues from her bag, and dried her eyes. "I wanted to scream," she went on, fighting back the tears.

"When did you call the police?"

"In the late afternoon. Two local cops showed up in a patrol car. They interviewed Sammy and me. Then another cop came on a motorcycle, but he only spoke with Sammy. I don't know why. All I remember are his mirrored sunglasses and expressionless face."

"What do the local police say?"

"They don't have a single lead." I could hear the bitterness in her voice. "Nothing at all to go on."

"Did you check the hospitals?"

"Of course. We called them all. We checked if there'd been an accident or a drowning, heaven forbid."

"Who else did you notify?"

"Everyone. As soon as we realized she was missing. The Israeli police, Interpol. We used every connection we have. The Foreign Ministry promised to help, the Chief of Police himself called and promised to get involved in the case personally. But nothing. As if she were swallowed up by the ground."

"Witnesses?"

"None. It was early in the morning."

Strange, I thought to myself. The East is crowded. No place is totally empty. There's always someone around. Particularly if you're a Westerner. There are invariably dozens of eyes following you without you having the slightest inkling you're being watched. A Westerner in the East is like an elephant in an anthill, a bull in a china shop. And they're a walking bank, even if they don't know it. They represent an infinite range of income opportunities for an infinite number of locals. Like a coral reef everyone feeds off of, from predator sharks to cleaner fish. If there were no witnesses, it means no one wanted to see.

"I lost control that night. Sammy said I was hysterical. He called a doctor, who gave me a shot to calm me down. I still didn't sleep a wink. I was waiting for her to show up and say, 'Hi, Mommy. I fell asleep on the beach. I didn't notice the time.' I was hoping for that desperately."

"What happened next?" I asked

"I don't really know. It's like time lost all meaning. Every hour was like the next. A lot of people came and went."

I didn't like that. "Israelis?"

"Israelis and others. I don't remember them all. I know for sure the Israeli consul came from Bangkok. It's part of his job to report the disappearance of an Israeli citizen to the Foreign Ministry. He came, spent a little time talking to Sammy and me, promised to use his connections in the highest places, and left. Even in my state, I could see that what he liked to use most of all was his mouth. I knew he wasn't going to be any help to us."

"What about the Israeli police liaison officer in Bangkok?"

"You mean Eli Mazor?"

Naturally, I didn't know his name, but I nodded.

"Equally useless," she said bitterly.

I repressed a smile.

"An overgrown gorilla with a brain running on energy drinks. Every other word out of his mouth was 'motherfucker,' and every third word 'asshole.' Other than that, all he did was tell us about the Krav Maga competition he won, how he took down one rival and made another one pay. From what I understood, he never lost a match. He came, checked out the hotel, asked a few questions, and disappeared. When I went looking for him, one of the hotel staff told me he was in the spa getting a massage. I went to find him. He was there with three girls. One was massaging his feet, another was attacking the fur on his back, and the third was cleaning his nails. Can you believe it? That was the cop the Israeli police sent to find my daughter."

I pretended not to hear her, but I did. I heard every word. Barnea, the head of the International Crime Unit, had some serious housecleaning to do, and he'd better do it soon. If his guy was asleep at the wheel, all the other Israelis were flying high. In places like Thailand and Cambodia, Israelis are like frozen mosquitos. A little heat, and they wake up and start biting and operating their scams. Anyone familiar with the work of the ICU knows they can't take their eyes off the ball for a second. Israelis will immediately set up stalls selling counterfeit watches, open food stands in competition with the local mafia, launder money in fake real estate deals, sell weapons illegally, and anything else they can think of. There was nothing new in what Iris told me. I just wondered why a guy like Eli Mazor was posted to one of the most sensitive centers of Israeli crime overseas.

13

"Was there a ransom request?" I asked.

"No. That was one of the first questions the local police asked. But no. No one contacted us. No letter, no telephone call."

She fixed her blue eyes on me. The pupils were surrounded by narrow glowing haloes. There was nothing cold in her eyes. On the contrary. You could easily sink into them like a hot water spring on a snow-capped mountain. But I could also see how much anguish and pain they reflected.

"I admit I was very agitated. I couldn't think straight. All these people coming and going were like noise in my head. It was keeping me from concentrating on Eden."

"What was her father doing all this time?"

"Talking. Talking on the phone, talking to all the people around us. I don't know exactly." She paused for a moment before adding quietly, "Looking back on it, I think he was just talking."

"What was he talking about?"

"Just words and more words. Pointless advice and suggestions. We grabbed hold of any shred of information, hung our hopes on every rumor. I didn't pay much attention. I only wanted to hear something solid. To know there was a chance of finding Eden."

I didn't want to load her down with statistics. I could have told her, for instance, that in most cases, missing children were found close by, hidden in an abandoned shed or a box buried in the ground where their abductors had held them captive for weeks, months, or even years.

"Everyone else was talking, but I just stood by the window looking out at the beach, praying for her to appear. That night, I slept in her bed, hoping to find her beside me in the morning. I thought maybe it never really happened, maybe it's just a bad dream, and all I have to do is wake up."

She fell silent. I gave her time to breathe.

"For two nights, I didn't sleep. Then, on the third day, I decided I had to do something. I had to start taking action. I had to find Eden."

"What did you do?" I asked

"I organized a search party. I went to Chabad House and the Israeli restaurant next door. There were dozens of Israelis there, kids and older

14

people. I asked them to help look for her. The older ones, the social drop-outs who live in Thailand, are despicable. There was one guy they called the Judge. He gave me a cold look and said, 'Babe', that's what he called me, 'Babe, we're here to chill out'. I wanted to rip his head off. But the youngsters, the backpackers, volunteered right away. One of them, an amazing kid called Daniel, took command and organized them all like an army unit. I could see the compassion in his eyes. He arranged them into four teams, found them each a jeep and driver, and divided the island into four sectors. You know the island. It isn't very big. Then, he assigned each team a different sector to search. I offered to pay them, but Daniel said, 'Forget it. Just pay the drivers. The rest of us are here to help.'"

"Did they find anything? A piece of clothing? Somebody who saw something?"

"Nothing. Not a single trace."

There was such despair in her voice that, despite my wealth of experience, I felt my heart seize up.

"Did you put up notices?"

"Everywhere. All over Koh Samui, on Koh Phangan, all the way to Bangkok. There was a picture of her on the beach with a big smile on her face. It was taken a few days before. We also had it printed in the local papers and the English press, like the *Bangkok Post*, along with a request for information. Nothing came of it."

Again, she fell silent. I could feel her distress. She was being eaten up by the question of whether she had done everything she could, done everything that needed to be done.

"We got a lot of responses, some stranger than others. An Australian tourist said he saw her at the Koh Samui airport with a middle-aged Western man the morning after she disappeared. A British tourist claimed to have seen her in a bar in Patpong in Bangkok. A local medium said she was in a Buddhist monastery on the Thai-Laotian border. Someone at the Israeli embassy thought he had seen her in Phnom Penh, Cambodia. In the beginning, phone calls and emails streamed in with so-called tips. I think there were more than a hundred. They were all investigated, but none of them led anywhere. Gradually, they stopped coming."

"Did you offer a reward?"

"Of course. Ten thousand dollars for any information that led to her discovery. I wanted to offer more, but the Thai police said it was enough. Any more would attract too many nut cases and greedy perverts who would interfere with the investigation."

"And?"

"Nothing. Just a few maniacs who demanded the reward in exchange for phony information."

"How long has it been?"

"Precisely three months."

"That's a long time," I said.

She played with the ice cubes in her glass and sipped on her coffee. I could see her eyes retreating, looking inward, and I knew she'd decided to lay it all out and go for broke.

"Eden is all I think about, twenty-four hours a day. I can't concentrate on anything else. I keep going over it again and again; what did I do wrong? Because I must have done something wrong. I must have made a mistake somewhere along the line, and maybe it's all my fault. Maybe I didn't pay enough attention to her. Sammy seems to have given up. I think he's lost hope." She paused, wondering if she'd said too much. "It's ruined our relationship. Something went wrong; I'm not even sure what. I don't have the energy to think about it. We weren't on the same page anymore. So we split up. Temporarily? For good? I don't know. He says we have to go on with our lives. But what kind of life do I have? There's no life for me without my little girl."

The rain picked up again, the heavy drops striking the café window. It was getting darker by the minute. Tel Aviv in the winter. "I refuse to give up. If there's any chance that Eden is still alive, I won't stop until I find her. Even if it costs me my life. I have to find her. That's my only purpose in this world now, to find Eden."

I understood she was ready to take this to the very end, but she didn't see the journey in the middle, the long road with its infinite ups and downs, questions and fears, trials and disappointments, frustrations and tears, despair, and devastation. I knew this journey intimately. The hardest part of my job is dealing with the parents' emotions. They want results. They want to find their kid, and they won't take no for an answer. They don't see the process, don't understand what it takes. They only look at reality from one perspective. It's like a ray of light: it either shines or it doesn't. And they can't see in the dark. But darkness is what I get most in my profession. It takes a lot of experience to be able to see things in the dark. And that darkness was what I saw ahead of me now.

"Why did you choose me?" I asked. "There are bigger detective agencies with extensive international connections. I could recommend a few."

She pointed at the file in front of her. "This is why. I read everything there is about you. At least everything I could find."

"That's just a stack of paper. A lot of it is worthless."

"I'm sure." She placed her right elbow on the table and rested her head in her hand. "But I chose you because you don't bullshit. Because you know the world. Because for some reason, I trust you. More?"

I answered with a noncommittal gesture of my head.

"It's mainly because you don't care what people think of you."

I smiled, mostly to myself. "That's been true for a long time."

"Why?"

"Do you really want to know?"

"Absolutely."

I sipped at my coffee, deliberating whether to tell her. There are things you don't talk about. Finally, I decided to give her as honest an answer as possible. "That's what happens when you figure out that your relationship with the world is based on half-truths and even outright lies. Caring comes from fear, fear that stems from other people's expectations of you. It starts with your parents, and then it's your job, especially if you work for the Security Agency like I did for a long time. Once you get out from under all those lies, when you stop worrying about how other people see you, you feel cleansed. You see your real self. What people think of you doesn't mean anything anymore."

For the first time, I saw the hint of a playful smile in her eyes. "So you don't really care about money either?"

"That's not entirely true. It'll cost you."

It's hard to talk about money with the parent of a missing child. I usually leave that part to David.

She examined me, considering. "I have a few million in the bank. Will that do?"

Some people would have jumped at the opportunity and agreed immediately. I kept silent. I could see my silence touched a sore spot. They say money attracts money. Maybe it's true. There's no way for me to know. I never had a lot. Every girl I went out with long enough to learn about her finances lived from hand to mouth. More or less like me.

"If it's not enough, there're these too." She fluttered her hand in front of my face, showing me the diamond ring on her finger and the diamond bracelet on her wrist. The gem on the ring was at least eight carats. "If you think these things mean anything to me, you're wrong. I'll give them up in a heartbeat."

"My fee...," I began.

She didn't let me finish. "I know how much you charge per day. David told me. I'll double it, okay."

"No."

She looked confused.

"Whatever David told you goes. That's our fee, not including expenses."

I knew that's what broke people of her status. She couldn't understand a disregard for money, the lack of a desire to accumulate riches. My work costs money, but it's worth what it's worth. No more. As long as I make enough to live on, I don't need any more.

"You want to know why? So that people like you don't think they can buy me."

"Okay. I understand. You're teaching me a lesson."

I smiled.

She fixed her blue eyes on me. "I would like you to help me find Eden."

I said yes. Not because I needed work or money. Not even because of her awesome eyes that I could easily drown in. I said yes because I knew I was her last chance of finding her daughter, or at least finding out what happened to her. And most of all, because a little girl was missing, and since her disappearance she had undoubtedly gotten a heavy dose of the worst this world has to offer.

"Thank you. But there's one condition. I'm coming with you. We're going to do it together."

"I have to think about that."

As she looked at me, I saw her expression turn hesitant. I assumed it came from knowing what can happen when two people of the opposite sex travel together, especially when they are constantly encountering the kind of situations of uncertainty and insecurity that fuel a desire to lean on each other.

"I booked the flight," she said.

I had to admit the woman had balls. "When?"

"Thursday night. Direct flight to Bangkok."

Today was Monday. That didn't leave me much time.

She took out a business card on fine vellum, placed it on the table in front of me, and left.

The rain had almost petered out. I looked out at her car. Its lights shone on the last drops still falling. I could see her silhouette behind the wheel. If I hadn't just been sitting across from her, I might have imagined she was crying.

Across the street, a large, you could even say very large, man in a red cap was standing under the dripping awning of a kiosk. He opened a pack of cigarettes, threw the wrapper into the stream of water carrying garbage into the sewer, and lit up. He glanced indifferently at the sidewalk where Iris's SUV had been parked and quickly got into a black BMW waiting across the street, its lights flashing. The BMW sped off the second red cap got in.

The waitress stopped at my table. "Another coffee?"

"Make it a double shot this time."

She remained standing there, and I could tell she wanted to say something. "What?"

"Any chance there'll ever be a time when you are, like, really alone?"

I smiled at her, but the smile faded as she walked away. Up to that moment, I'd thought I was taking a break. But vacation time was over. No doubt about it.

Chapter Three

I Googled the name Eden Ben-Lev. There were quite a few links, but very little useful information. On the other hand, there was no lack of gossip about her parents, Iris and Sammy. Stories about the fortune they had accumulated, about the mattress empire that belonged to Iris's family, the Blumenthals, about Sammy's wild partying before they were married. But nothing really went beyond the initial information provided by the police to the two English-language papers in Thailand, *Bangkok Post* and *The Nation*.

All the Israeli reports contained the same basic facts: Eden Ben-Lev, the twelve-year-old daughter of Sammy and Iris Ben-Lev, disappeared from Paradise Beach, a family-owned resort on Koh Samui, Thailand. She was last seen by her mother early in the morning. There has been no sign of her since. The Thai police are continuing their search and keeping the Foreign Ministry informed.

I found it somewhat surprising that there was no heart-rending cry for help from the parents in the media, but I could understand why. When the parents of a missing child are big names, they often prefer to operate behind the scenes rather than expose themselves to public scrutiny. The media has a field day, and the parents pay the price. It's actually much harder to keep a story like this under wraps than it is to give the public their pound of flesh.

I was already starting to build in my mind what we call a profile of the missing person. You begin with the time and place of their disappearance, their health and financial status, and any personal items that are missing and might be on them. I made a mental note to ask Iris about that. Then, you examine the possible reasons for their disappearance. Drowning? Abduction? Murder? That's where you start the investigation. Of course, if you think it's an abduction or murder, you compile a list of potential suspects. And like it or not, the parents are always at the top of that list. At least until you can rule them out completely.

The mental gymnastics led me to Jacob. He's an Israeli guy who's been living on Koh Samui for years, long enough to know what's going on. I opened my Facebook page. I bet you didn't think I had one, but I do, with precisely five friends. And Jacob is one of them. Naturally, he doesn't use his real name there. I saw that he was online and wrote a few lines without mentioning names. Jacob responded immediately. "Get off Facebook," he typed. "It's controlled by Big Brother."

"Aren't you stretching it a little," I replied.

"Not at all," he typed, adding a frowning yellow smiley. It was a warning, not a grin. "And don't use your phone to call me. Get a burner."

Jacob is crazy. That's a given. But when did I ever associate with normal folk? Still, this time I thought he was exaggerating. How paranoid can you be? But I guess if you're Jacob, the answer is very. I went to Yoram's shop, the kind that sells everything and anything to foreign workers.

"What's up?" Yoram asked.

"The usual," I said. "I'm still coming and going."

"You still hung up on that nonsense, save a soul, save the world?"

I admitted I was.

"Isn't it time to give it up? I know a gym that's looking for a trainer. Best job in the world, trust me. You don't have to suck up to anyone. It's just guys from Jaffa, from the neighborhood. No fancy tights, no cougars. Maybe a few steroids, but they don't go overboard. You show up, give them a workout, and pedal on home."

"Maybe someday."

"Yeah, sure," he said, not believing a word of it. "You're too fucked up, and that's not going to change." He laughed as he handed me a burner phone and turned to a black guy who had been waiting patiently. They spoke in Hebrish, a new language that had sprung up in south Tel Aviv, where the foreign workers from Africa congregated. I stood there listening to them. It was a joy to hear how they managed to communicate in this weird mix of Hebrew and English.

I went outside and called Jacob on Koh Samui. It rang for a long time. He was probably running some hi-tech scanning program to make sure it was me. Jacob, no last name for obvious reasons, had made a fortune when he sold his startup. He'd developed spyware that was planted in every cellphone sold by a certain American company. Not everyone liked the idea. Especially not the security agencies. Given all the information in his head, he became paranoid, convinced that Big Brother was always watching him. A firm believer in the Orwellian theory, he was never without a tattered copy of *1984* sticking out of his back pocket. He claimed that Israel was a typical dystopian state. Not only was the government corrupt and stupid, but it was so stupid it didn't even know it was a tool in the hands of the defense establishment and the tycoons who controlled the economy. They all made use of sophisticated technology to oversee and manipulate the lives of the citizens. His prime example was the recording and scanning of all cellphone conversations to identify the caller.

"That's when the human element comes into play," he explained whenever we spoke back then before he picked up and left for Koh Samui. "That information becomes currency, and it's worth millions to all sorts of individuals, companies, and organizations. Even the government itself. The temptation is irresistible. People look around and say, I want in on that. Then someone comes along and makes them an offer they can't refuse."

"You don't get it," he used to say to me. "Every one of us is worth something to somebody. Do you remember the exorbitant service charges the banks used to demand before they were outlawed? They never went away. Nowadays it's us, we're the service charges. Each and every one of us. We live in a very cynical world."

That's why he decided to disappear. Erased every record of himself. When he goes online, he uses different identities and changes them frequently. And he only uses the net to check on the organizations he believes are trying to get to him to force him to devise the ultimate security device. The only thing he doesn't know is who'll get there first, Big Brother or the mob. He's scared to death of both of them.

Finally, after about seven rings, he answered.

"Ten seconds. Then hang up and call again."

"That's impossible, Jacob."

"Ten seconds. Then hang up." He wasn't going to budge.

"A Koh Samui hotel, Paradise Beach Resort, a missing girl, Sammy Ben-Lev."

"That's more than enough," he said. "I don't want to hear anymore. Leave me alone. Don't call me again."

He disconnected. There was something in his voice I didn't recognize.

I called back. This time it rang at least ten times. I assumed he was filtering the call through a scrambler.

"Walk away from this, Dotan. Do me a favor and listen to someone else for once in your life. Let it go. It's a sinkhole you don't want to fall into."

"I can't do that. I'm already in it. I gave my word."

He let out a deep sigh.

"Jacob?"

"You don't know what you're getting yourself into." I sensed he was choosing his words carefully. As I said, Jacob is paranoid, but this was something different. I could picture him now: ensconced in a sealed room filled with screens in some isolated villa with an emergency exit tunnel to the beach, still looking over his shoulder. "What do I have to do, Dotan, to convince you to back off?"

Something in his tone persuaded me to listen more closely to what he had to say. I confess I'm not a good listener. I'm too used to relying on myself. "Okay, so give me something solid, some cold facts, and I promise I'll think about it."

"Sammy Ben-Lev was the owner of the Paradise Beach Resort until a few months ago. He got caught up in a venture that involved the purchase of the adjacent beach, and he lost his shirt. Millions of dollars down the drain. To avoid declaring bankruptcy, he sold the resort to a company that turned out to belong to the Russian-Israeli mafia. The head of the syndicate is a guy named Yuri Cezar. They call him 'Thainik'. When a guy has a name like that, you keep your distance. Rumor has it that running drugs and whores wasn't enough for Cezar, so he decided to make Koh Samui his own personal playground. There's a record of the sale of the property for an obscene amount to something called World Sea and Land Corporation, most likely a shell company. You won't believe how far its tentacles reach. They go at least as far as Moscow and Tel Aviv. Is any of this sinking in, bro?"

"Yeah, so?"

"Wake up, Dotan. You weren't born yesterday. The Russian mafia means trouble. Back off."

There was more to what Jacob was saying than he let on, but I couldn't put my finger on it. I was listening not only to the words, but also to the hidden message he was conveying, and it was obvious that he had a personal reason for not wanting me there.

"Is there something you're not telling me?" I asked.

There was static on the line.

"Don't hang up. I know you well enough to tell when you're bullshitting me."

After a long pause, he replied in a tone I'd never heard from him before, "Leave me alone. Go pedal your bike on the boardwalk in Tel Aviv and stare at the tits. There's nothing for you here." He didn't just disconnect. He did it as if a third party was listening in on the conversation. I've met quite a few paranoids in my time, but none can match up to Jacob.

There was nothing else to do but go back to the hole I call home. For the umpteenth time I wondered if I shouldn't find myself a better place. But what's the point? And mostly, for whose sake? In American action movies, there's a cat waiting for the hero when he gets home, and they share the last can of cat food. It always makes me laugh. Even an alley cat wouldn't stick around as soon as it realized that it couldn't count on someone being there to open a can of food for it.

The dream of "a place I can call home" invariably bumped up against reality. Maybe because I didn't really believe in it. I've never felt the need to own a home. A lot of my short-term girlfriends (and to be honest, that's all any of them have ever been) have told me that's the reason our relationship didn't last: my total lack of interest in settling down somewhere permanent. As far as I'm concerned, I can lay my head on a different pillow every night, and I don't really care if there's no pillow. Women have an innate antipathy for nomads. The chance of my devoting time to considering the purchase of a washing machine is pretty slim.

But I do have a computer. I turned it on and read up on the wonders of the real estate market in Koh Samui. It sounded like paradise. What disturbed me, however, was the statement that "property ownership in Thailand is as secure as anywhere else in the world." It sounded like hype to me.

I looked up World Sea and Land Corporation. The company site stated that their business focused on the buying and selling of property in up-and-coming tourist locations in Southeast Asia. There was a long list of places, starting with Pattaya in Thailand and Sihanoukville in Cambodia. Anyone familiar with those regions knows that many of the investments in the area have their source in money laundering. At the bottom of the home page was a link to a law office in Thailand that specialized in arranging the purchase of property by foreign citizens.

I checked them out, too. They seemed serious. I mean, it sounded like they were happy to roll out the red carpet if they could cover it in a thick layer of greenbacks. What caught my eye was the information that the owners of the law firm were prominent collectors of Buddhist art from Thailand, Cambodia, Laos, and Myanmar. "Great," I thought. "Another way to launder money."

I turned all this information over in my head. Jacob was a paranoid computer nerd, but he was no fool. Why had he disconnected my call and refused to speak to me anymore? There had to be reason.

Chapter Four

There was another person I had to call before I left. I rang Barnea at the International Crime Unit.

"You're in Israel? What's wrong? No more pussy for you in the East?"

Barnea is a character. I mean, for a cop. His mouth is as big as his fists, and his fists aren't big; they're enormous. In the Agency, we used to call him Mincemeat. That's what a suspect's face looked like when Barnea was through with him. He mellowed a little after going over to the police force and giving them the benefit not only of his brawn, but also of his equally prodigious brain and experience. Now that he was in the ICU, we'd rubbed up against each other more than once. The first time it happened, his fists were no match for my martial arts skills. There's no need to go into details. At the end of the day, it was the typical story of two supposedly grown men trying to prove whose was bigger. I wouldn't say we were friends, but he was someone I could call if it was necessary. But only if it was really necessary.

"I need information," I said.

"What's it worth to you?"

That's Barnea for you. The way he talks, you'd think he was in the shithole known as the civil service, one of the minions who are only looking out for themselves, the ones who don't want to be bothered as long as they're not too cold in winter or too hot in summer. But the opposite is true. Barnea is as straight as a spirit level. You could use him to hang a shelf.

"I'll bring Elijah an authentic judo suit from Japan," I offered.

He snorted. "You think that's all it takes to buy me?" he said, but I heard the pride in his voice. His son, Elijah, is already as big as his father and much faster, and he's only sixteen. I took him under my wing and taught him the Shaolin martial arts, the secret of proper posture, how to make his fingers like steel, and the thirty-six deadly pressure points on the human body. The boy has promise.

"The information I need might get you a promotion."

"Bullshit," Barnea said. "You're a real con artist. Okay, go ahead. I'm listening."

"What can you tell me about Sammy Ben-Lev?"

"How is it you're always in the middle of every Israeli shitstorm overseas?"

He coughed. It was the result of the Camels that were always stuck between his lips. You could hear the smoke coming out of his mouth when he talked. I almost moved the phone away from my ear so he didn't blow it in my face.

"Not on the phone," he said. "What I want to know is what you're doing in a café on Ben-Yehuda Street with the hottest divorcée in town?"

I didn't reply. I got that he was hinting at a connection.

"You're in shock, huh?"

"Yes, I'm in shock," I said, "Mainly at you. I didn't think your claws reached that far."

"You'd be amazed how far," he laughed. "I'll see you here Thursday morning."

"Let's make it sooner. I'm flying out on Thursday. Don't make me leave it to the last minute."

"Where to?"

"Bangkok."

He let out a whistle. "You got room in your suitcase for me?"

"You gotta be kidding. With your size? I'm not going with a traveling circus. I'll be there tomorrow, two-thirty," I said, disconnecting.

I took out the business card and called Iris Ben-Lev.

"We have to meet."

"Has something happened?"

"Maybe."

"You don't want to tell me now?"

"No. Tomorrow at eight p.m. at the Circle Café on Dizengoff."

"I'll be there," she promised.

Chapter Five

The next day, I showed up at ICU headquarters. I found Barnea sitting behind a wobbly desk in an ugly office that reeked of cigarettes. It was enough to lean your hands on it, and the desk would topple over. "Hey, pal," he said, getting up and coming around the desk to give me a bear hug.

That's what he was like: a bull with the heart of a lion. When we sat down, all I could see was the fire in his eyes. The man is one hundred and ten percent work.

"Let me explain what we do here," he said. "I'll quote from the mission statement. I learned it by heart when I got here. Like in the first grade. Trust me, whenever I feel I'm going to lose it, when someone advises me to take a detour around the target, I close my eyes, put my hands over my ears, and shut my mouth. Like that Buddhist statue of the three monkeys you brought me from Japan." He paused for a moment, smiled, leaned down, and took the statue in question out of a drawer. "Then I repeat to myself: 'The ICU will lead the nation's fight against international organized crime and its operations in Israel. The ICU will take decisive action against any attempt to undermine the foundations of the country and will work resolutely to preserve democracy and freedom in Israel'. Impressive, no?"

"Very nice," I agreed.

He looked pleased.

Then I added, "And not worth a rat's ass."

"You're right," he roared, slamming his fist onto the poor table. It bent under the pressure. "Every day, there's another motherfucker who thinks it doesn't matter."

"Sammy Ben-Lev," I said in an attempt to keep him on point.

"Sammy Ben-Lev is a clever bastard. He stinks like a rotten fish and thinks he can cover the smell with expensive eau-de-cologne. He's definitely one-of-a-kind."

Barnea turned to the grey file cabinet behind him and took a heavy brown file out of a drawer. He placed it on the desk in front of me. "Thick file, right? But if I had to sum it up, I'd say it all adds up to zilch." He opened the well-worn cover plastered with multicolored Post-its and took out a photo. "That's Sammy Ben-Lev."

A well-groomed man with curly black hair. Dark glasses. Designer suit and starched white shirt. Matching tie.

"What else?" I asked, reaching out for the file, but Barnea kept a tight grip on it.

"Easy," he said, throwing me a look and handing me a single sheet of paper.

Sammy Ben-Lev, aged 42, born in the prestigious north area of Tel Aviv. Graduated from the high school attended by the children of the city's elite. Achieved the rank of captain in the army, where he served as a company commander in a special forces unit. Fluent in English, Russian, and Arabic. First in his class at law school. Married Orna Kalzman, the daughter of a wealthy industrialist from South Africa. Got a master's degree in law in New York. Opened his own office in Tel Aviv, representing Israeli businesses operating overseas, particularly in developing markets in Southeast Asia.

The couple divorced after three years. No children. His ex-wife claimed he had cheated on her from the very beginning and throughout their short marriage. The divorce settlement cleaned him out because most of their money came from her family. A year later he married Iris Blumenthal, heiress to a bed and mattress empire.

"What a player," I said. "Sets his eye on the big prize."

Barnea selected a few more pictures and spread them out on the desk. Sammy and Iris on their way to an event at a fancy hotel. They looked like complete opposites, yin and yang. I wondered what had brought them together. His charisma or her money? Sammy, Iris, and Eden. Iris was

CHILD OF DUST

smiling while Sammy looked solemn, with a possessive hand on Eden's shoulder. She was standing between them in a dress fit for a Disney princess. Even in the picture, I could see the happy gleam in her eyes. She looked like a girl who knew she was loved and saw only good in the world.

"God knows what's happening to her now," Barnea said. "We don't usually get involved in missing persons cases overseas. That's the job of the Foreign Office and the insurance agencies, or private investigators like you who make their living at it." He lit a cigarette, inhaled, and blew the smoke into the air to keep it out of my face.

"So why this one?" I asked.

"Six months ago, we got a tip. The gray market was setting up real estate corporations in Thailand, targeting the tourist hot spots. It didn't take long to find out that one of the crime syndicates was buying properties on the beaches of Koh Samui as a way to launder money. Drugs, prostitution, that's not my department. There's a whole other unit that tackles drug running and human trafficking. But as soon as we're talking international organized crime, it becomes my business. We heard that Israelis and Russians were involved, and the alarm bells immediately started going off around here."

"How does Sammy Ben-Lev come into it?"

"His name has popped up a few times. Call it a hunch, but I'm convinced he's operating in the gray area between legal business and criminal activity. He's smart enough to make everything he does appear to be within the law."

"And you think his daughter's disappearance has something to do with his shady deals?"

Barnea drummed his thick fingers on the desk. It groaned under the weight. "I don't have anything concrete to go on, but if I were you, I'd follow the money and the real estate transactions."

I asked what I'd been dying to ask ever since I got there. It was the first time I'd met with him on his own turf. From what I'd seen so far, the ICU looked like a garbage pit.

"Tell me, Barnea," I said, "You're trying to bring down the fiercest sharks in the sea. These guys hide in the ether behind an infinite number of electronic disguises, and all you've got is a dog-eared cardboard file held together with

32

a fraying rubber band and handwritten notes from the fifties. Doesn't that seem ludicrous to you?"

He looked at me with the most offensive sneer I've ever seen.

"Follow me," he said.

He led me through an interrogation room to a flimsy wooden door painted in the beige color that used to be reserved for the toilets in public buildings. Behind it was a steel door. He pulled out an ID card and passed it through the reader. A screen appeared. He brought his eye to it, and a door opened, revealing a huge room filled with large screens and electronic equipment. It blew my mind.

"Welcome to Big Brother," Barnea declared, bursting out in laughter when he saw the shock on my face. "Come on. Forget Big Brother. I'll show you."

He pointed to the room we had just left. "That's just a front. It's for the perps we bring in for the first time. They see it and think the cops are jerks, that their lawyer can fuck us over with one hand tied behind his back."

The half-human, half-electronic hive was buzzing with activity. I was impressed. But I was also happy to leave and go back to his characterless office. We shook hands. I didn't expect our paths to cross again, but they did, and much sooner than I could have imagined.

Chapter Six

Caesaria

The salty smell of the sea was carried on the breeze. The halogen lamps on the boardwalk fell on the crests of the waves, making them visible in the dark. Hidden lights on the lawn of the beachfront estate in Caesaria cast a dim glow. The railing of the large porch was studded with ship lanterns her father had collected over the years. They were sitting in semi-darkness. Her father was in his old rocking chair, the one her mother had tried to throw out time and time again, but her father steadfastly refused to get rid of.

"Anyone for lemonade?"

Her mother got up and went into the kitchen. When she was far enough away, her father giggled and poured himself a small shot of whiskey from a bottle on the table. He sniffed the drink before taking a sip and emitting a sigh of pleasure.

"She doesn't let me drink anymore," he said.

"She's right," Iris replied. "You shouldn't."

"She's right, and you're right." He took another sip and replaced the glass on the table.

"What are you going to do?" her father asked.

"Search, and search, and search, until I find Eden."

Her father sighed. "Give me a kiss."

As she bent toward him, she smelled the Aqua Velva he had worn all his life. All his money hadn't convinced him to change his ways. It was only recently that she had begun to understand. Until then, she had brought him back another expensive cologne from every trip overseas. "Try this one," she'd insist. He'd just smile and put it away.

He grabbed her hand, taking her by surprise. "Do what your heart tells you. Nothing else matters. Not what anyone says and certainly not how much it costs."

She nodded.

"This man you found, the private investigator, Dotan Naor, right? Do you really think he can help?"

Iris thought for a moment before answering. "There's something about him. He's different."

This time it was her father who was silent. Finally, he said, "I checked into him."

"And?"

"Like you said, he is different. But I want you to know he has a history."

Staring out at the ocean, she said, "Who doesn't?"

"You're right again."

But she didn't see, or more accurately didn't sense, that he still had more to say.

"He screwed up in the past. Big time."

She covered her ears. "Please, Dad, I don't want to know."

"Iris," he said harshly. "You can't just ignore it. People who screw up like he did carry it with them for the rest of their lives. They can let you down again. Trust me. I know how the system works. And I know what happens with people who are forced out for good reason. It doesn't always mean they're bad people, but…"

Here it comes, she thought to herself.

She heard her father laugh in the darkness. "I know you, kid. You're thinking, now he's going to tell me his story for the thousandth time." He laughed again, picked up the whiskey glass, and sniffed it, breathing in the aroma. "Every father tells his story. That's how he makes sure he'll live on even after he's gone. That's the only reason. Not to preach. I got up and left before they told me to go. And that was the smartest move I ever made in my life. I call it growth." He took a sip of whiskey and put the glass back on the table. "This is the point when your mother tells me to stop talking nonsense. She's right, of course. I just want to know if you trust him."

"Come on, Dad. I only met him once."

"Once can be enough," he answered.

"He's so different. In the beginning, I thought he was intolerable. But the more I listened to him, the more I realized how determined and perceptive he is. It's like he could see what happened to Eden in his mind. I can't explain it. I felt he had the mental strength I need."

"Sorry, I don't understand that sort of thing. The question is if he can get the job done."

Iris burst out laughing.

"What's so funny?" her father asked.

"If you saw him, you'd know. He's a bull, physically speaking. But I also got the sense of an inner calm. I'm guessing it comes from the years he spent in the East."

"I can't say I understand what you're talking about. But at my age, I'm more accepting of the fact that some people think and act differently from me. He might be the kind of person you need. Maybe he'll be able to find Eden."

They sat in silence, staring at the waves.

"Can I say something else?" her father asked.

She couldn't remember him ever asking for her permission before.

"Go ahead."

"You realize you'll be alone with a strange man."

"Dad," she said angrily, "I'm not a little girl."

"I know," he said.

For the first time since Eden had disappeared, she saw a genuine smile on her father's face. His whole face lit up, like the light on the waves. She knew how much he loved Eden, how much he enjoyed being a kid with her again, going down to the beach with her in shorts and sending her into the water on the surfboard he'd bought her, both of them shrieking with joy.

"And I'm still a married woman."

Instantly, the smile vanished. The lines around his mouth became deeper, sharper, and a look of anguish appeared in his eyes.

"What's wrong, Daddy?" She hadn't called him that in a long time.

"There's something you should know. I didn't say anything about it before." He poured more whiskey into the glass. "Two weeks before Eden disappeared, Sammy called and asked me for a loan. A big one."

"How big?"

"He wanted a personal loan of five million dollars for an unlimited period and with no collateral to secure it."

Even in the dark, he could see the shock in her eyes. "Did you ask what he needed it for?"

He muttered something that might have been "uh-huh."

"What did he say?"

"That his investment in Koh Samui was in jeopardy."

"I don't like what I'm hearing," Iris said.

Her father went on in an apologetic tone. "Sammy was never a risk taker. I know him pretty well. I could hear he was under a lot of stress."

"It doesn't make any sense. As far as I know, the project is going well."

There was a long pause before he asked, "Are you sure?"

If there was anyone in the world she trusted unconditionally, it was her father. No one else. She knew how good his instincts were. Even though he was less involved now in the daily running of his huge mattress company, he still knew everything that was going on.

"It seemed to be, at least," she said quietly. "I could understand if he talked to you now, but not then, when I thought things were fine between us. Why hide it from me?"

"I don't know," he said. "At the time, I didn't think too much of it. But since Eden disappeared, it keeps coming back to me. I haven't told anyone. Not even your mother."

Iris remained silent.

"You know what I keep thinking?" her father asked.

She shook her head.

"That I should have given him the damn money. That's what I should have done."

Suddenly, she got it. Her father blamed himself for what happened to Eden. He felt guilty for embracing Sammy Ben-Lev, the brilliant young attorney, and welcoming him into the family, both at home and in the business. He had always been in total control of everything, and now his only granddaughter was missing, his son-in-law's integrity was in question, and he was letting his daughter go off with a stranger.

"It's not your fault, Dad."

"You say that, but it doesn't make me feel any less guilty."

"That won't help me find Eden. I need you to be strong."

Rising, she placed her hand on his shoulder. "You can't turn back time," she said. She kissed him on the cheek. "Say goodbye to Mom for me," she added, stepping onto the path that would take her away from her family home, away from her father. She knew things would never be the same. She couldn't ignore the tiny voice inside her. If only he'd given him the money, maybe then...

Chapter Seven

Herzliya Marina

Iris sat in the SUV in the dark driveway, her hands cradling her head as the tears fell from her eyes. There was a pressure in her temples she had never felt before. How was it possible? she thought. Three months ago, I had a daughter, a loving husband, a happy marriage, and now it's all gone.

She started the car and pulled out onto the road. A black BMW was sitting on the corner, its headlights off. Iris saw two large men leaning on the car, a bald man smoking and another whose face was hidden by a red cap. The bald one blew a cloud of smoke toward her. Their eyes met briefly. Suddenly she felt cold.

She passed them and glanced in the rearview mirror. She saw the cigarette flying off into the darkness. The BMW's lights came on, and it followed her onto the highway. They drove like that for a while, the BMW filling her mirror until it sped up and disappeared.

Getting off at the Herzliya exit, she turned into the street to the marina and the apartment complex overlooking the water. She pressed the button on the remote control, and the gate to the underground parking garage swung open. She parked the car and was about to open the door when it was opened for her. The two men from the BMW were standing in front of her. She struggled to pull the door closed, but it wouldn't budge. It might have been encased in concrete.

Iris got out and pulled down her skirt, making an effort not to appear frightened. The men, both a head taller than her, stood like a wall blocking her path. She tried to get by, but the one in the red cap grabbed her arm. The whole of his left arm was covered in a single tattoo: an enormous skull with three roses growing out of it. A long sword extended from the skull all the way to the man's wrist. A snake was curled around it, its head tattooed on the back of the hand with its mouth open and two fangs sticking out, ready to strike.

Iris twisted her body and hunched down in an attempt to get away from them. The bald man snickered. He may have been big, but he was still faster than her. He blocked her with his foot. The only way out was to crawl between his legs, but she had no intention of giving him that pleasure.

"What do you want?" she demanded.

She could smell the nicotine on their bodies and see the large pores around the broken nose of the man in the cap. In a heavy Russian accent, he answered, "You tell him, if he doesn't pay, you're next."

A scene flashed in her memory: Sammy saying, "I think we should get you a bodyguard," with her responding, "What do I need a bodyguard for? Am I in danger?" and his answer, "Of course not. But you never know. Just in case." The subject wasn't brought up again. It just faded into oblivion, as if the conversation had never taken place.

The hand with the tattoo pressed down on her shoulder. Iris felt as if her feet were being hammered into the floor. The man's other hand crawled up to the top button on her blouse, and his finger came down roughly, like the slashing of a knife, passing between her breasts and continuing downward until it stopped at the very last moment. She tried to scream, but nothing came out. She shut her eyes. The hand moved up to her face, the fingers drawing a line from her cheek to her upper lip, and then pressed hard on her mouth, forcing it open. He brought his fingers to his nose and breathed in deeply, waiting for her to open her eyes to look at him. "We'll crush you like bug," he threatened.

Finally, it was over. She didn't even know how long it had been, just that she felt humiliated and violated.

She heard tires squealing and loud Russian rock music fading into the distance. The words echoed in her ears: *Krasnaya, krasnaya krov*. She didn't know they meant "red, red blood," but even if she understood Russian, it's doubtful she could have been any more terrified than she already was. The fear was like a lump in her throat, paralyzing her from the inside out.

The elevator took her straight up to the penthouse. Two apartments had been knocked together, giving them the whole floor to themselves. One side used to be Sammy's office, but after the big blowup and the ensuing separation, they simply divided the apartment up, each keeping to their own half. She knew it was a temporary arrangement. They couldn't live like that for long. She wanted to leave, get as far away as possible, but that wasn't her first priority at the moment. All her energy was devoted to a single goal: finding Eden.

The door between the two sides of the massive penthouse was kept locked. She felt that constituted enough of a separation for the time being. In the beginning, Sammy used to knock on the door, but then he stopped and just kept calling her on the phone, trying to convince her to talk to him.

She took out her cellphone, pressing Sammy's number by force of habit, planning to tell him what had happened, about the threat and the humiliation. But she disconnected after a single ring. She stood by the large window that looked out on the marina filled with yachts and smaller boats and stared at the picture of her missing daughter. Eden smiled back at her from the photograph. Iris clutched it to her heart and whispered, "Eden, I promise you, I'll do whatever it takes to find you. I'll bring you home."

For the second time that night, her eyes welled up. She wept quietly, then dried her eyes and vowed: "That's enough. I swear, Eden, my darling little girl, I'm not going to shed another tear until I'm holding you in my arms."

Chapter Eight

My phone rang. This time, it didn't chirp; it played the tune of the mantra *om mani padme hum*. People tend to raise an eyebrow when they hear it coming from my phone. It's reserved for a single client at any given time. It was now assigned to Iris Ben-Lev.

"You're a freak," David once said to me. "Can you imagine anyone using the *Shema Yisrael* prayer as their ringtone?"

"Why not?" I said. "People choose whatever makes them feel good. Some people feel good when they hear the theme from 'The Good, the Bad, and the Ugly' or Bob Marley. For me, it's a Buddhist mantra."

"How can I tell if I'm being followed?" Iris asked. She sounded very upset.

"Do you see a car in your rearview mirror now? Either close behind you or keeping a steady distance back?"

"No."

"Where are you?"

"On the highway on my way to you."

"Speed up to 85 and then slow down. Worse comes to worst, you'll be pulled over. What kind of car was it?"

"A black BMW."

"Don't look for a parking space. Pull up on the sidewalk in front of the café. I'll be waiting outside."

She drove the car onto the sidewalk and switched off the ignition. I checked the cars passing in both directions. No sign of a black BMW.

Iris got out and came to stand beside me. "Do you see them?" she asked.

"No. Why do you think you were being followed?"

"Because they threatened me."

We went into the café, and she gave me a brief account of her confrontation with the two thugs.

"Did you notice anything unusual about them?"

"Two things. A heavy Russian accent and their tattoos. The one in the red cap had a huge tattoo all down his arm."

She described it to me. "Does it mean anything to you?"

"Yes. It's a Russian prison tat."

"The other one, the bald one, looked Mongolian. 'Mama' was tattooed down his arm in big letters."

I had to laugh. The Russians and their distorted sentimentality. Even killers are still tied to their mother's apron strings. I decided to keep some things to myself. Like the fact that a skull with three roses was the tag of a Russian gang, and a long sword signified a hitman. The addition of the snake about to strike meant that he relished his job. I'd never actually run into an ex-con who had done time in a Russian prison, but I knew they operated outside the native Israeli underworld. At least, I thought I knew that. Maybe I was wrong.

"What do people like that want from me?" Iris asked.

Good question, I thought. "If you don't have a taste for piroshki and vodka, you shouldn't be of any interest to them," I answered in a deliberate attempt to make light of the situation. But I saw she wasn't buying it. "Did you talk to them?"

"It was like talking to a brick wall." I could see the rage rising in her. Once again, she repeated every word they said.

"They came to deliver a message, to issue a threat," I said. "They did it by terrorizing and humiliating you. They wanted to show you who's the boss, that they had total control over you. That's their MO."

"So I should be grateful they didn't call me a slut?"

"They'd never do that. That's only for weak men. And these guys aren't weak. They're very frightening characters."

Iris was silent.

"You didn't tell anyone about them?" I asked.

43

"No." She hesitated a little before going on. "My first instinct was to call Sammy, but something stopped me." After another pause, she asked, "Was the message for him? Does he owe them money? Is that what this is about?"

"I think so."

That came as a blow to her. Women don't take a blow below the belt. They take it straight to the heart. When it happens, the heart is clinically dead. It takes a while to recover, but it will never beat the same way again. I've seen it more than once. And now I saw Iris dying right before my eyes. She didn't utter a word, but a shadow, a dark cloud, eclipsed her eyes. She was miles away, no longer with me. I presumed that images of Sammy and their life together were flashing through her mind at the speed of light, and then I saw a determined look come over her. She had decided not to draw the obvious conclusions. Not yet, anyway. Otherwise, how could she go on? How could she find her daughter?

My telephone chirped. I answered on the third chirp.

"I can't make it," David announced.

"Too bad."

"Hold on a second. Let me finish. Are you at the café already?"

"Yes."

"Any minute, a woman will walk in. Her name is Tamuz. You won't have any trouble recognizing her. Just picture a pretty young attorney, and you'll know her right away."

I raised my eyes. You couldn't miss her. She was gorgeous.

"She specializes in international law, transactions, and contracts."

I gestured to Tamuz and put the phone down. She came over to our table.

"This is Tamuz," I introduced her to Iris. "She's an attorney we work with. David thinks she should be part of the discussion."

We were alone in the café, save for the barista behind the counter. He presented himself at our table. Tall and muscular, he sported a three-day-old beard and nice tattoos on both arms. The guy had style.

"The waitress is out today. What can I get you?" he asked with a shy smile that contained a hint of I-know-what-a-fine-specimen-I-am.

Tamuz ordered a decaf cappuccino with just a touch of foam. "Soy milk," she stressed, eyeing him appreciatively. I ordered my usual espresso.

"Can you fix me a cocktail?" Iris asked.

"What kind of liquor?" There was a gleam in his eye, whether it was because of the cocktail he was conjuring up or the woman he was looking, at I couldn't say.

"Rum."

"I make one hell of a mojito." I saw his eyes jumping between Iris and Tamuz. It made me wonder if I was over the hill. The waiter left the table.

"Tell us about the hotel and the launch party the night before Eden disappeared," I instructed Iris, wanting to bring Tamuz up to speed.

"It's a beautiful resort. One of the finest on Koh Samui. The idea was to interest people who want to be pampered, to get special treatment." She sounded as if she were reciting from the brochure.

"Where is it located?" Tamuz asked.

"Near Chaweng Beach."

I let out a whistle. "Chaweng Beach is serious real estate," I said.

The real estate angle was starting to get interesting. It took real money to purchase a strip of land on the beach and erect a 5-star hotel. We could easily be talking tens of millions of dollars. Tamuz sent me a look that made it clear she also understood the ramifications. She asked the obvious question.

"You and Sammy own the resort?"

"Just Sammy, not me. He said it was better for him to be the sole owner because of all the papers that had to be signed and the negotiations with the bank. If I was a registered owner, I'd have to fly back and forth to Koh Samui all the time. But I don't want to talk about Sammy. Can't we just leave him out of this?"

My gut said he was a bad seed, but you don't always feel like offering your services as gardener. Especially not when you're face-to-face with the guy's wife.

"How did your husband get involved in the project?" Tamuz asked.

"He started out as the attorney responsible for dealing with the authorities in Thailand. Later, they made him a partner in lieu of the fee for his services."

"So, how did he become the sole owner?"

"The other partners wanted out. They got into financial difficulties and had to sell out."

"Can you give me names?" Tamuz asked.

"Ron Orel-Stein, he's the one who initiated the project. He's been living in Thailand for a few years with his Thai boyfriend. He invested a lot of money in it, but it all got eaten up. He took out huge loans he couldn't pay back. He was desperate. Someone introduced him to Sammy, and they signed a deal."

"Where is he now?"

"He lives in Koh Samui. He broke up with the local guy, and now he's got an Israeli boyfriend, some kind of computer nerd who sold his startup for millions."

I hadn't seen that coming. "Do you happen to know the boyfriend's name?" I asked.

"No. All I know is that he's paranoid. We invited them to dinner once. Ron said no way, his pal never leaves the house, on principle. The farthest he ever goes is their private beach."

There wasn't any doubt in my mind that she was talking about Jacob. How many paranoid Israeli computer nerds could there be on Koh Samui?

"Describe the launch party," I said.

"The PR company leased a jumbo jet to bring the guests straight from Israel to Koh Samui. The press went to town on it. The TV stations showed the fancy invitation with the ticket for the flight and an all-expenses-paid vacation. You can't imagine how many people pressured us for an invitation. Every big name in the country. They had no qualms about calling at any hour of the day or night and begging to be invited."

"We'll need a list of everyone who was there," Tamuz said.

The barista arrived with our drinks. He put the two coffees down in front of us and then, with a flourish, placed the mojito on a paper doily. He stood next to Iris, waiting for her to taste it.

She took a sip and broke into a big smile. "Outstanding," she declared. The barista went back behind the counter, grinning from ear to ear.

"Everyone was there," Iris went on. "The new minister of tourism, the director general of the ministry, company directors, media people, including the most popular newscasters, and models, of course. You know how it works as well as I do."

"Not really," Tamuz and I said at the same time.

"Sorry, I thought everyone did. We had a celebrity PR guy. He got everyone together for a group picture. The next day, it was in all the papers with the headline 'Opening of a Prestigious Israeli Boutique Resort in Koh Samui, Thailand Attended by Minister of Tourism and A-List Personalities.'"

"Who else was there?"

"You mean Israelis?"

"You can start there," I said.

"In addition to the ones we flew out, there were a few Israelis who live on the island permanently. Like the one they call the Judge. I told you about him yesterday. He had a whole herd of losers trailing after him. One of them, Mandelbaum, latched onto Sammy like a leech."

"Who else?"

"Now that I think of it, the Russians were also well-represented. I mean Russian Israelis, the ones that still act like Russians and still talk Russian. They didn't really mix with anyone else. They just stuck together, drinking champagne and vodka. Very well dressed, all of them. Custom-made suits, Italian shoes, expensive watches. They had Russian-speaking girls hanging on their arms. Real knock-outs, dripping with gold and diamonds." She paused for a moment and then added with a smile, "Even more than me. They all deferred to a man surrounded by a fleet of bodyguards, gorillas like the ones I met today. The only difference was they were wearing suits."

"Do you know his name?"

"Yuri Cezar."

Now, it was my turn to take a blow. I didn't like that Thainik's name had come up twice without my having the slightest idea who he was beyond what Jacob had told me. And why was Sammy Ben-Lev associating with a Russian-Israeli crime boss?

"Who else?"

"There were a few local people. I understood from Sammy that some of them were his business partners. The law in Thailand requires that fifty-one percent of any property held by a foreign company be in the hands of Thai citizens. One of them was an attorney I know Sammy worked with."

"What's his name? What else do you know about him?"

"His name is Somnook. They call him Khun Somnook as a sign of respect, but he looks like a kid."

"Do you know his full name?"

"You know Thai names. They're a mile long. No Westerner can pronounce them."

"Describe him," I said.

She played with the bits of ice still left in her glass as she tried to conjure a picture of him in her mind. "He looks like an innocent kid, but he's very slick. Custom-tailored Armani suits. Hands like jewelry stores. Speaks perfect English with a British accent."

"What happened after the event?"

"There was an atmosphere of anything goes, and a lot of people took advantage of it."

"What do you mean?" Tamuz asked, not getting the picture.

"It was like there were no boundaries. The waitresses were attractive Thai ladies. People acted as if they were available for anything. That wasn't part of the program, but everyone seemed to think they were included in the package."

"Explain."

"During the speeches, I saw Sammy whispering to the minister of tourism. A few minutes later, the minister walked off in the direction of his bungalow with one of the waitresses on his arm. It was like some kind of signal. The male guests began to disappear one by one, leaving behind the few women who had been invited."

I could see the repulsion on Tamuz's face. But I wasn't surprised by Iris's description of the event. Men who land in Thailand are happy to buy into the assumption that the country is a playground.

"What did you do? You and Sammy?"

"If you're asking if we organized an orgy, the answer is no."

Apologizing, I asked, "Where was Eden all this time?"

"She came and went," Iris said. "At first, she was excited by all the people at the reception, but she got bored very quickly and disappeared. I pretty much let her decide for herself what she wants to do. She doesn't have to be glued to us all the time."

"And then?"

Her voice became softer. "We went back to our room. We did a few lines of coke and were getting into bed when the phone rang. It wasn't a pleasant conversation," she added.

"Who was it?"

"I have no idea. I asked Sammy, but he just said, 'Forget it. Some people are idiots. You can't make everyone happy.' I knew he was hiding something, but I didn't want to press him, and maybe I couldn't in my condition."

"What did you hear?" I asked.

"I got the impression that someone was threatening him. Sammy's no pushover. He doesn't respond well if you try to back him into a corner."

"What do you mean?"

"I could see his rage. There was fire in his eyes and pure hatred in his voice. It frightened me."

"What did they talk about? Money?"

Tamuz threw me a look.

"I remember one thing he said. I think it stayed with me when I fell asleep, became part of a dream."

"What was it?"

"'You don't scare me'. The hair stood up on the back of my neck when I heard it. There was something menacing about the way he said it. But Sammy is a master at finding the right words to make things go away, to smooth them over. I'm just starting to realize how good he is at hiding things, no matter how serious they are."

Iris went back to playing with the ice in her mojito. Finally, she raised moist eyes and said, "Do you know how it feels to lose trust in someone you love?"

Tamuz fixed her eyes on Iris. "You feel betrayed," she said. "Vulnerable. You walk around with a block of concrete in your belly. Yes, I know how it feels."

Placing my hand on Iris's arm, I promised, "We'll find her."

Iris quickly wiped away the tears. "I swore I wouldn't cry," she said.

"One more thing," I said.

"What?"

"We have to talk to Sammy."

Fear flashed through her eyes. "Do what you have to. But I don't want to be a part of it. Here's his number."

"Drive safely," I said.

"I'm a good driver."

"That's not what I meant."

"I know. I'm not a fool."

"I don't think anyone wants to hurt you. They just want to threaten you, scare you."

"Why would anyone want to threaten me? I don't understand."

"We don't either."

We followed her with our eyes as she left.

"Want to talk about it?" Tamuz asked.

"No," I said. "Let's give it time to sink in. I'll meet you tomorrow at ten in the office."

When I got home, I did the one thing I had to do. Lighting a pair of incense sticks, I passed them around the walls to purify the house, paying particular attention to the corners. Then, I stuck them in the aluminum window frame so that the breeze blowing in would carry the perfume throughout the house. I sat down cross-legged on my thin yoga mat and lowered my head until my chin nearly touched my chest. I raised my hands in a *namaste* gesture in front of me, leaving a narrow space between them, and directed my thoughts about Eden into the small gap. It was like I was looking at a photo of her. She was a source of light, joy, and hope. I knew that finding the missing girl would take me on a long and perilous journey.

Chapter Nine

"Moron," said Boris Chiplonak, known as the Chipper. "Degenerate." The brown mastiff lying in front of the sofa didn't even raise its head.

"Why you talk to me like that?" said Sergey Korpichov, called Flathead because of the shape of his skull. He never went anywhere without his red cap. "We not buddies anymore?"

"We haven't been buddies in a long time." The Chipper was a small man, thin and high-strung, with chiseled features. The white bristle on his chin contrasted with his red face, flushed from vodka and agitation, and his long nose was crossed by a web of spider veins. His right ear was missing. As usual, he brought his hand up to the place where the ear should be. It didn't make him hear any better. Rather, it was meant to draw attention to the missing appendage. You don't lose an ear for no reason. It gets cut off as punishment for not listening.

Boris was a subcontractor who supplied thugs, villains, and scum for hire to anyone in need of their services, including the Russian mob and oligarchs. Every goon who spoke Russian, Ukrainian, or Latvian, or even a modicum of Yiddish or Odessan, belonged to him.

He picked up a sharp folding knife, preparing to use it to fit a cushion to the sofa he was working on in his cramped upholstery shop. Flathead flinched at the sight of the knife in the air. The mastiff raised its head and yawned.

"What's the matter?" The Chipper asked. "You got the jitters?"

"I don't know what you want from me," Flathead answered.

Boris went to the door and spat onto the sidewalk. Clearing his throat, he came back inside. "You and your pal are the two biggest fucking degenerates I've ever seen. You're lucky we're not in Moscow. You wouldn't even have one ear left. What? You didn't hear what I said? Follow her. That's all. But you had to act like a pair of motherfucking bullies. I must have been an idiot to let you take the BMW. I should have given you the bike." He pointed to a bicycle tethered to a lamppost outside.

"So what?"

"You're like a son to me, Sergey. But what am I supposed to tell Yuri Cezar if he calls?"

As if Boris had the gift of premonition, the phone rang. He burrowed into the heap of fabrics and foam until he found the phone at the bottom. "Da," he barked and then quickly launched into a series of apologies. Still listening, he waved a warning finger back and forth in front of Sergey. "Da, Yuri, da." Again, he listened. The finger now moved across his neck from side to side. Finally, he put down the phone. "Fuck you, Sergey. What am I going to do with you?"

"Boris."

"Stop with the 'Boris'." The Chipper was getting increasingly irritated. His irritation got worse when he saw he had cut the foam at the wrong angle. "You made me fuck up the order. I need a minute to think."

Flathead was silent.

"Yuri wants to know if I work with a bunch of imbeciles," Boris said, spitting on the floor. "I'm giving you one last chance, and that's it. Listen good. He wants to know what she's planning. And he especially wants to know who the faggot Dotan Naor is, the guy she's going to Thailand with tomorrow. I want you to pay him a visit. You screw up this time, and it'll cost you an ear or a finger. I'll let you choose. But I'm cutting something off."

Sergey didn't doubt him for a minute. He could see how skilled he was with the knife. His hand moved to his ear of its own accord. He got up, put on his red cap, and started out the door. Boris called after him, "Remember, degenerate. Ear or finger."

52

"Sergey," Boris called again.

"Da?" Flathead stuck his head back in the shop.

"You see that garbage pail outside?"

"Da."

"Throw your ugly hat in it," Boris ordered. "They'll see you coming from a mile away."

Boris passed his hand over the place where his right ear should be and picked up the phone.

"Yuri."

"Da."

"I can't rely on Sergey anymore."

"Why not?"

"I made him get rid of his cap. I humiliated him, and now he knows we don't trust him."

"So buy him a new hat."

"I can't."

"What's all this bullshit, Boris? Are we in kindergarten?"

"It wasn't just a cap with some stupid logo. There was nothing on the outside. It's what was inside that's important."

"Okay, so what was it?"

"To Sergey from Mama."

Yuri burst out laughing. He was laughing so hard Boris thought he was going to choke. But he didn't see the humor.

"You're not laughing, Boris."

"No. Because now he hates me. And Flathead is the type who nurtures his hatred. He'll do whatever he can to get back at us."

"Finish him off. Before he has a chance to do any damage. The last thing I need is for someone to open their mouth and fuck everything up. They're no good to us anyway. We put them on Sammy, and what did we get? Nada. They could fuck up all our business on Koh Samui. I've got a lot of money riding on that beach."

Boris disconnected and immediately dialed another number. "Mandelbaum," he said. "Listen up. I may be sending someone to you. I need him to keep an eye on things there. We've got a little problem here."

"What do you mean?"

"You'll see. Anyway, the problem is on its way there. I'm just giving you a heads-up."

"What about what's coming to us?"

"What are you talking about?" Boris said angrily. "I just sent you a nice bundle."

"All gone," Mandelbaum said. "Life here is expensive."

"We have a deal, Mandelbaum. Stop throwing all the money away on whores. Yuri wants to see a contract. You getting me? If that piece of sand isn't transferred to Yuri's name very soon, you'll be in deep shit. He wants to see a deed in his name. Got it?"

"Calm down," Mandelbaum answered. "We're working on it. But there're a lot of palms to grease."

"I don't want to hear any stories. I'll send another package with Sergey to cover expenses. We call him Flathead. He's a parasitic moron. After he finishes cleaning up the mess, throw him from a plane or something."

Boris listened and then said impatiently, "Of course, I don't mean a scheduled flight. Figure it out. Use him for whatever you want, but I don't want him back here. As far as I'm concerned, he can swim with the fish. No fish? What do you mean no fish? What about the fish sauce they splash on everything? What have you got there? Sharks? Okay, sharks. What? I can't hear you. What did you say?"

This time, he heard Mandelbaum loud and clear: "That's for the Judge to decide, not me."

"I don't give a fuck about you or the Judge. Don't expect anything more from me until I see a signed contract. You get the message?"

After disconnecting, Boris said to himself, "They're all degenerates. Every last one of them."

Chapter Ten

I heard rustling in the stairwell. It wasn't mice. There's nothing to eat in my apartment. It wasn't burglars either. They knew I had nothing worth stealing. I opened the door and said to the two thugs whispering on the stairs, *pozhaluysta voydite*. Just in case my Russian wasn't good enough, I added, "Come on in. I don't have any coffee."

I recognized them immediately: the two gorillas who had been following Iris the first time she came to see me in the café. They belonged to the worst category of goons exported by the FSU, ex-weightlifters whose brains were fucked up by all the steroids they took. They still had the muscles, but now they also had a swollen belly. That was a sure sign that they had dropped out of the league of serious Russian organized crime. So, they came to Israel. In our tiny country, a little Russian can be very intimidating.

The bald one with the Mongolian eyes moved forward, holding his fists out like a combine harvesting everything in its path. But the stairwell wasn't an open field. I saw the surprise on his face when I dropped him to the floor.

The other one, with a flat head and a white stripe across his forehead, looked like a trained wrestler. His left fist shot out, but I didn't wait to see if he was planning to land a punch or it was just a feint. I hit him in the biceps. He was stunned, but he immediately came back with a right hook. I was expecting that. I took a small step to the left and put my whole weight behind a punch to the ribs under his outstretched arm. The movements of wrestlers like him are pretty predictable. He responded with a left hook. I was ready for it and landed another punch to the ribs with my other fist. The air went out of him, and he sank to his knees like a sack of potatoes.

Now, it was time for the hard part: throwing them down the stairs. They each weighed at least 220 pounds, and when the body is limp, every pound counts. Like butcher meat. I actually felt a little sorry for them. New immigrants are often made to suffer beatings and humiliation, and here I was, adding another indignity.

The bald one was moaning. I picked his head up, but I had no intention of putting a pillow under it. "Who sent you?" I hissed.

"Boris," he muttered.

"Boris Chiplonak? The Chipper?"

He nodded. The nod was very faint, so I banged his head against the sharp edge of a step to improve his memory.

"Da, da," he said in his mother tongue. "Boris Chiplonak."

I made a mental note to pay a visit to the Chipper's upholstery shop in the southern part of the city. Flat Head managed to spit out, "You wait. It not over yet. You see us again." The neighbor's cat let out a quiet meow and continued on its way. I could swear I saw a smirk on its face before I closed the door.

Chapter Eleven

The drapes were drawn. She pulled them closed every night to shut herself off from the world. In the morning, a single ray of light would fall on Iris's face. The same moment was played out every day. She was in bed, and a smiling Eden, like a light beam, was standing by the window. Then she disappeared. She imagined Eden saying, "It'll be okay, Mommy," as if Iris was the child and Eden the adult. Nothing is okay, she thought. Her world had collapsed. How was it possible that everything good and stable in her life had shattered in the blink of an eye? Where was her darling Eden? That was the only question that still had any meaning.

She heard knocking on the door between the two halves of the penthouse.

"Are you awake?"

She was incapable of answering.

"Iris, we have to talk."

"Not now. I can't now."

"On the patio in half an hour?"

Agreeing, she forced herself to get out of bed, throw water on her face, and struggle to pull herself together. For Eden's sake. She found Sammy leaning on the railing, staring out at the marina. This is the man I lived with for fourteen years? This is Eden's father? she thought. His hair was as black as ever. Shouldn't he be getting grey? He looked too young and dynamic. He should be hunched over, distraught. He didn't look like a tormented father whose daughter was missing. He didn't look like a father at all. Who was this man?

Sammy didn't greet her or even give her a smile. She used to love his piercing black eyes. Now, all she saw was two expressionless beads.

"What are your plans?" he asked.

"Good morning, Sammy," she said. "Why do you want to know?"

"Isn't it time we went on with our life, Iris?"

"Our life? What do you mean? What life do we have?"

"Our life together. You and me."

"You and me?" She felt the rage rising like bile in her throat. "Without Eden? That makes sense to you?"

"You have to trust me, Iris. She's my daughter too. I'm doing everything I can to find her."

"So why don't I see a broken heart? Why is it that whenever we mention her name, you're as cold and uncaring as a fish?"

"That may be what you see, but it doesn't mean it's what I feel. You don't know what I feel because I don't talk about it. And it doesn't mean I'm not doing anything."

She wanted to believe him, but the iciness in his voice sent a chill down her spine. "I can't just sit around and wait."

"Leave it to me to do what needs to be done," he said harshly.

"I can't. I have to do something. I can't just stay at home and rely on you. Our world is dead. Gone. Nothing exists until we find Eden. Don't you understand that I don't have a life? I have no idea how you still do. I don't want to live anymore. Not like this. Not without Eden."

"You can't interfere. Let the professionals do their job. The police, Interpol."

Iris examined him. Was he warning her or trying to protect her? Why did she sense a threat in his words? Who was this man standing in front of her, the man she had married, the man whose name was their daughter's first word?

"I'm going to Thailand," she announced. She could feel herself standing straighter, growing taller and stronger. "I'm going to look for her. I'm leaving tomorrow."

She had finally managed to surprise him. She was returning to her own side of the apartment when she heard him call her.

"Iris."

His voice reminded her of how he used to speak to her. His eyes were softer, too.

"I want to see…You know. One more time."

It took her a moment to grasp his meaning. See what? Then the penny dropped. He wanted to see the tattoo beneath her navel, the two birds of heaven. She'd had it done on their honeymoon when Eden was conceived. There was a deadly look in her eyes. Now he has the hots for me? Now he wants to fuck me? How could he even consider the idea at a time like this? How could he think of pleasuring himself in any way? "Never," she spat.

She'd already learned one lesson. You can never take your words back.

She saw his eyes harden into dark beads again. "Don't get ideas in your head," he said, grabbing her arm. "And don't imagine for a moment that I'll let you go."

"You're hurting me."

"You belong to me, or you don't belong to anyone. Is that clear?"

"Say it again," she said icily.

"You heard me the first time," Sammy answered. "You better get it in your head. Nobody walks away from me. And that includes you."

Chapter Twelve

He answered on the fourth ring. "Hello?"

"My name is Dotan, Dotan Naor," I said.

"Do I know you?"

"I'm a private investigator."

"Kicked out of the Security Agency, I assume."

Start by insulting me, I thought. Nice. "You might say that."

Honesty is always the best policy. Especially because there was an element of truth in what he said. I went on calmly, not giving him a chance to attack again. "I've been hired by your wife, Iris."

"I wonder why she chose you," he said. "She's never been a good judge of character."

Just ignore him, I reminded myself. Don't respond. I continued as if we were simply exchanging pleasantries. "She hired me to look for your daughter, Eden. I understand she went missing in Thailand three months ago."

Silence on the other end. Total silence. I call it calculating assets, like a poker player trying to guess what cards the other players are holding.

"What do you want?" he asked finally.

"I'd like to meet with you," I said.

"That's not possible," Sammy said. "I'll be away for the next few days."

"If you could just give me a few minutes, it would be very helpful."

His voice became even colder. "I understand. But again, it's not possible under the present circumstances."

"What circumstances?"

When he didn't answer, I tried a different tack. "Can I ask you a few questions over the phone?"

"I don't think so. I'm sure my wife gave you all the information you need."

"Iris told me what she knows. I'd like to hear your version."

"Whatever she said, that's the only version there is. In some ways, she knows more than I do."

"What ways?"

"I was busy with the resort and the launch party, so naturally, my attention was focused elsewhere. You can consider her description of the events the full picture."

He disconnected.

Chapter Thirteen

The black BMW was standing in the shadow of a column in the parking garage. Sammy saw it when he emerged from the elevator. Without any hesitation, he got into the passenger seat and scrutinized the driver. A large man, he had a huge bald head, a deep furrow across his forehead, a cruel face, and tattoos all over his arms.

"My man filled you in?"

Sergey nodded.

"I need you in Thailand."

"You got it."

"I'll come later, and I'll want a full report."

"You'll know everything," Sergey said.

"Including what Yuri is planning."

"Yes."

Sammy paused for a moment, examining the driver's face. His eyes were cold. There wasn't a spark of life in them, only an icy murkiness. "Do you know what his plans are?"

"To eat you alive."

Sammy took a sealed envelope out of the inside pocket of his sports jacket and laid it on the console between them. Neither of them looked at it. "There'll be more where this came from." As he started to get out of the car, Sergey grabbed his arm.

"I was here yesterday," he said.

Sammy turned his head quickly. He saw the loathing in Sergey's eyes, but he could tell it wasn't directed at him. The huge man wasn't a threat to him, and he knew just how to use him.

"Boris sent me to frighten a broad. What's she to you?"

Sammy glared at the hand on his arm. Sergey let go. "What did she look like?" he asked.

"Blond, blue eyes, classy bitch."

Sammy opened the door and climbed out. Sergey opened the envelope. It held a tidy sum. He passed his middle finger along the edge of the bills and then stabbed it in the air. "Here's to you, Boris."

The BMW exited the garage and disappeared in the direction of Tel Aviv.

Chapter Fourteen

"How's it going, Eli?"

"Hey, Barnea, it's the middle of the night here."

"If you had a little pussy in your bed, you'd still be awake."

"What's eating you, Barnea? Don't I get enough of that from my wife? She's sure I'm partying here twenty-four hours a day."

"You're not?"

"No, Sir, I swear. One cold beer, and I'm out like a light." Eli Mazor sat up in bed. It wasn't every day you got a call from your boss at the ICU.

"I gotta give it to you, Eli. You put on one hell of an act. Whatever."

"I swear on my life, Barnea."

"Okay, okay. So what's going on?"

"I don't know what to tell you. Not a single lead. People here won't talk. They don't know, or they don't want to know."

"Where are you?"

"Koh Samui. I got here from Bangkok two days ago. I only came because you told me to. If you ask me, we ought to close the case. File it away as a missing girl. Gone. No trace."

"What makes you say that?"

"Three months is a long time. Even her pictures have been torn down by now. Here and there, you can still find a fading photo, but that's all."

Barnea listened in silence.

"You still there, Barnea?"

"Yes. I think something's going on."

"What?"

"Don't know. Something that's connected to the girl's disappearance. Who have you talked to there?"

"The local police, the tourist police. They're as cooperative as usual. No problem there. Covering their asses, of course. And my Thai isn't great."

"Because you don't fuck the local pussy."

Eli laughed. "No. Because I stopped going to classes. But listen. There's a bunch of Israelis here that are worth looking into."

"Why?"

"A gut feeling, mainly. Some are obviously crooks, and some are ex-cops or ex-army. From the generation before us. They all gravitate around Chabad House. There's something off about their behavior. Tell me, does the name 'the Judge' mean anything to you?"

"Should it?"

"Sixty-something. Everyone kowtows to him."

"Why are you telling me this?" Barnea asked.

"My gut tells me there's something nasty about them. They call themselves the F Brigade. When you ask them what it means, they laugh like a pack of screwy hyenas. All they care about, all they ever talk about, is whores and getting laid. You wouldn't believe the things I hear. It's disgusting."

"And...?"

Eli paused, struggling to phrase his answer. "Ask them a serious question, and nobody answers you. They're evasive, change the subject. Nobody wants to talk about their past. You always get the same answer: 'Forget it. We did more than our part for the country, the police force, the army, whatever. That's over and done with.' They try to screw with me. All the time. Look, I get it. They all have healthy pensions. You leave the army or the force at the age of forty, and you're set for the rest of your life. You can live the good life here. But it doesn't pay for the kind of life they live. They've got money to burn. You should see the jeeps they ride around in. The latest models. And each of them has a flock of local whores stuck to them like they were fly paper. The whole thing doesn't make sense. It stinks to high heaven."

"Keep an eye on them. See if you can find out what they're up to," Barnea instructed. "And look into the World Sea and Land Corporation and the Paradise Beach Resort they're involved in. Check the property records. Find out who the registered owner is. And keep on it. I'm not ready to close the case of the missing girl yet. It goes much deeper than we thought. Move your fucking ass. I don't want you sitting around on the beach all day staring at the local hookers with a beer in one hand and wanking off with the other."

"I swear, Barnea. I told you the truth."

"Okay, okay. Stop whining. What do I care who you fuck. Just make sure they don't fuck with you. You're in Thailand, pal. Maybe after two years of the good life, you've gotten a little soft."

"No way," Eli said. "I've been working out. I arranged a fight on Koh Samui. Trust me, it's not going to be a go-go dance."

"Put your energy to good use," Barnea said. "Don't waste it on nonsense."

"Don't worry, Barnea. I can eat the local guys for breakfast."

Barnea disconnected the call, but it continued to gnaw at him.

Chapter Fifteen

Boris Chiplonak, the Chipper, was at the entrance to his upholstery shop, sitting on a half-finished sofa with a bottle of Stolichnaya vodka and his open knife beside him. People who drink Stolichnaya don't give a damn about their taste buds. The brown mastiff was stretched out at his feet. It started to growl as I approached.

"I wonder why she doesn't like you," Boris said.

"The question is whether or not *you* like me," I responded.

"Like, love, amore. You know how we say it? Lyubov. The most beautiful word in the Russian language."

"So you're a linguist now?"

"What do you think I do here all day? Cut fabric? Here, I'll conjugate the verb 'bite' for you. Bite, bit, bitten. Lara, go."

The dog didn't even bark in response to the direct command. She simply grabbed my ankle.

She might be a mastiff, but a dog is a dog. I gave Lara a quick slap on the side of her head. She stared at me for a second and opened her jaws, gasping for air. Then she collapsed onto her side.

Boris watched in silence. He poured some vodka into his glass and passed it under the dog's nose. Lara came to, rose heavily, and went to hunker down by the sofa.

"What do you want?" Boris asked, picking up the knife.

"I want to know why your goons are harassing Iris Ben-Lev."

Gazing at the dog, he answered, "Capitalism is killing me. Did you know I used to play the saxophone in Lviv? I owned my own jazz club."

"This isn't the time for nostalgia. Why are you fucking with me? Back in Lviv, you wiped the asses of bigger motherfuckers than you. Just like you do here."

Boris played with his knife. You could tell there was a close bond between them. Between him and the knife.

"You Israelis, you're uncivilized bastards. You come here to my shop and talk to me like that? Let me tell you something in Russian. You know a little Russian, right? If you're nice, I'll translate it for you. In Russian we say, '*Yest chelovek yest problema, nyet chelovek nyet problemi.*' You know what that means? There's a human being, there's a problem, no human being, no problem."

"Not only a linguist, a poet too."

"I'm an upholsterer, but in my heart, I'm a flower. You know how much that Buddhist statue in her parents' house in Caesaria is worth? Millions! There are even more ancient ones in her place in the marina. I doubt if she even knows what she has."

"I didn't know you were an expert on Buddhist art," I said, taunting him.

"Money makes me an expert. Trust me, I can still tell a statue from the Gandhara period when I see one."

"There're a lot of fakes."

"Not in their house," he snickered.

"It was nice talking to you, Boris. If I see another of your gulag degenerates near the lady, I'll cut his ear off."

"That's just what I told them."

As I got up, the mastiff curled up even tighter.

"It's alright, Lara," Boris said, comforting her. "The bad man is leaving."

He threw the knife. It landed in the door frame. I didn't even turn my head. I didn't want to give him the pleasure. The Russians don't use their heads. Everything's emotional with them. We native Israelis grew up in a place where the only killing that takes place is in war. Period. Russians live in a place where it's killed or get killed. The knife was still quivering when I left.

Chapter Sixteen

I was meeting with David and Tamuz in the office for a final briefing before I boarded the plane.

"So what do we have?" David asked.

I let Tamuz put it all in order.

"Not much," she admitted.

"What do you mean?" asked David.

"Well, one thing is clear from what Iris told us. Sammy is mixed up in a big real estate transaction on Koh Samui. It started with the resort and grew into something we don't know the details of. What we do know is that he's in over his head. How much he owes and to whom we still have to find out."

"What do we know about this company, World Sea and Land Corporation?"

"There's a money trail that starts in Russia, passes through Tel Aviv, and reaches Koh Samui, where it disappears into real estate."

"Do you think Sammy took on partners from the Russian mob?"

"Even if he's at the far end of the Russian connection, there's no way out for him. Especially if he owes them money. Anything can happen."

"Where does the girl come in?" David asked.

"She's collateral for Sammy's debt, or they're holding her until they get something they want from him," I said. "That's one option, at least. Another is that they're punishing him. But it could also be a coincidence, and her disappearance could have nothing to do with his financial headaches. But you know how much we love coincidences."

"Does Iris know any of this? What do you think?" Tamuz asked me.

"I think she's starting to get the picture."

"So, how do we proceed?" David asked.

"We follow the money," Tamuz said. "But I can't see Dotan looking for the girl and at the same time wading through property records or bank transfers."

"Bottom line," David summed up. "Dotan goes to Koh Samui with Iris and concentrates on the fieldwork. You and I do the paperwork."

We didn't have anything more solid to go on. All we really had were gut feelings and bits of information with no indication of where they led. We had no idea they would take us to a stinking bog where men were at their worst, where they became monsters in a foreign land. I've seen quite a few ugly things in my life, but even I didn't know how far men can go, how they can strip themselves of all sense of morality, and how ruthless revenge can be. I hoped that Eden was still alive, that we would find her before they harmed her and be able to bring her home safe and sound. But I was very familiar with the twisted reality of Southeast Asia. Too familiar.

Chapter Seventeen

There was one more thing I had to do before I left. I went to see Valium at Hope House.

Every therapist who ever worked with him declared Valium a lost cause. I disagreed. He was a victim, not only an addict. He suffered from loss of memory as a result of years of hallucinogens. But it all started long before he began using. It's not easy to grow up gay in a religious home. It's even harder to volunteer for an elite army unit and hide the fact that you're gay. He turned to drugs after a traumatic event that occurred toward the end of his military service. I don't know all the details, but in a few rare moments of lucidity, he said things that gave me an inkling of the nightmare his life had become.

I came to know him one day when I got a phone call about some Israeli guy wandering naked in the streets of Varanasi, on the banks of the Ganges in India, shouting, "I am God. I am the power. Pray to me." I tied him to a chair in a local guest house and watched over him for two whole days until I was sure he wasn't going to harm himself. Then I put him on a plane with me and brought him to Hope House. And that's how I met Valium.

I was standing by the nurses' station when Johnny, Valium's long-time therapist, caught sight of me. A man in his late thirties, Johnny has a permanent smile on his face and infinite patience. "We're going to release him soon," he said. "A week or two at most. We haven't made a final decision, but that's more or less the time frame."

"Is he ready?" I asked, surprised.

Johnny gazed at me with his characteristic serene expression. "He'll never be ready," he said. "His pain runs so deep that he'll only be able to overcome it when he's capable of dealing with it. We've done all we can."

Johnny was one of the best therapists at Hope House. He had boundless empathy for the patients because he'd been down that road himself. He'd walked the Via Dolorosa trodden by so many Israelis, the downward spiral from an elite army unit to oblivion, from the first joint to never-ending darkness.

"Where will he go?" I asked. "As far as I know, he has no contact with his family."

"We tried to find him a foster family. No luck. In the army, they'd call him a lone soldier without any relatives in the country. But he's in a different world now, and it's one that frightens sane people."

I took a key off the ring in my pocket. "This is a key to my apartment. I'll text you the address. I'm leaving for Bangkok tomorrow. Take him to my place. It won't be a real home, but at least he'll have a roof over his head."

Valium was sitting in his spartan room, his eyes fixed on a fly on the window screen. The room smelled of floor cleaner. He was dressed in white cotton trousers and a black T-shirt. Several *malas*, the strings of prayer beads used by Tibetan monks, were wound around his right wrist. His long hair was pulled back in a ponytail. I could tell from his pale face and the black bags under his eyes that he hadn't slept in a long time.

He was rocking back and forth in his chair, periodically halting in an impossible balancing act on the two back legs. His body was frozen. Only his eyes moved, following the fly with the concentration of a hunter.

"Hey, Valium," I said.

He was in his own world, mumbling something. I moved closer in an effort to understand what he was saying. "Oh no, you won't get me!"

"Valium, it's Dotan," I said, trying to make eye contact with him. But his eyes wouldn't focus on me. He started rocking again. Finally, the chair landed with four legs on the floor, and he gave me a piercing look. Then he turned his head back to the window and began to sing at full volume. The muddled words had something to do with a fucked-up mind.

I was about to say something soothing, but just then my phone chirped. I debated whether to answer it or not, but in the end, I did. I kept my eyes on Valium, who was now rocking in silence.

"You all packed?" David asked.

"You know it only takes me five minutes to pack."

"Be careful."

"Who am I supposed to be worried about? Sammy Ben-Lev?" I answered contemptuously, although I knew he wasn't a person to be taken lightly.

Valium stopped rocking.

"This investigation is going to take us to much darker places than we thought. There are deeper layers we haven't even reached yet. You have to keep your eyes open all the time. And watch out for Iris. This case you took on, it's not going to be easy."

"It's never easy," I said, still watching Valium. "Let me know if Sammy boards a flight for Bangkok. I don't need any surprises on the macho front."

I could swear I saw a spark, a very brief flash in Valium's empty eyes.

"Valium, I'm going to Thailand," I said.

He didn't look at me, but he had his own way of looking. A sort of penetrating glance out of the corner of his eye. In those fleeting moments of lucidity, he was one of the most charming guys I'd ever met. Happy and suffused with inner peace. And he could come out with the most astonishing insights. His remarks had sent me in unexpected directions more than once.

Johnny was standing in the doorway. "Still sitting in front of the window, singing?"

I nodded.

"The father of one of the other patients saw how lonely he was and left him an iPod. You wouldn't believe how he responds to music."

"Does he respond to anything else?"

"Like what?"

"Like names," I said. "Maybe names from the past. Things that have been burned into his consciousness. Names he's repressed. The names of the people who fucked with his life, maybe?"

"Probably."

"Then I have a favor to ask."

He gave me a quizzical look. "What is it?"

"There's a copy of Valium's old army record in his medical file. I think I once saw a particular name there. I didn't pay much attention to it at the time."

He played with the key I had given him, deliberating. It was obvious to me that it wouldn't be easy for him to let me look at the file.

"I'll go get it."

He returned a few minutes later with a tattered file that documented the three years of Valium's life in the army. It was there: the record of a military police investigation of drug use in his unit. It contained witness statements, the results of the investigation, and a summary of the ensuing trials. I remembered correctly. One of the reports referred to a decorated soldier by the name of Hananel, known as "Valium." It was headed "Mental Breakdown." He was characterized as unstable, unreliable, and subject to mood swings, and judged unfit to carry a weapon of any sort. I knew from experience what that wording meant. He was branded for life. The report ended with the recommendation that he be transferred immediately to the charge of a mental health officer.

The report was signed by his company commander, Captain Sammy Ben-Lev.

If I could have, I would have grabbed Ben-Lev's miserable neck right then and there and squeezed hard. Lucky for him, the worthless motherfucker wasn't within reach. But that didn't concern me. I knew I'd eventually come face to face with him. It was just a matter of time.

Chapter Eighteen

We'd already checked in. Iris disappeared into the freezing expanses of the duty-free shops. I sat down on the carpeted floor at the gate, which was still closed, like one of those backpackers who can sleep anywhere.

Some people take a suspense novel with them to ease the boredom of waiting, but the friends that are with me wherever I go are a dog-eared copy of the *I Ching*, the Chinese Book of Changes, and a small carved teak box with three ancient Burmese silver coins used to interpret the text and divine the future. I rolled the coins around in my hands and tossed them onto the floor in front of me. Six times, I threw them, and was busy calculating the results when I heard Iris.

"I see you're keeping yourself occupied," she said, standing in front of me looking amused. She was holding a small bag that held what seemed to be perfume.

"Hi."

"It's like dice? A guessing game?"

"Something like that," I said.

"Can two play? I do pretty well at the casino." She crouched down and looked curiously at the lines I had drawn in my notebook. "What's that?"

"It's not a casino game."

"Then what is it?"

"It's a way of looking into the future."

"That sounds scary."

"It isn't, as long as you accept the principle that things change with time.

You throw the coins, check the combinations in the book, and get answers and advice. You can take it or not, your choice."

She picked up a coin and turned it over in her hand. "Can we ask anything we want?"

"Yes, but you might not get the answer you're looking for."

I handed her the other two coins.

"Do I have to tell you my question?"

"I already know," I said with a smile.

"I just throw them?"

"Yes. Six times."

She closed her eyes, took a deep breath, and threw the coins. Then she opened her eyes and repeated the same routine five more times. I marked down the combinations. When she was done, I looked at what I had drawn. Six short lines, one above the other. The fifth from the bottom was broken.

"Is that good?"

I laughed. "That's what everyone asks the first time they do it. We want things to be good; we want to be happy. Is that what life is really like?"

She stared at me. I was already learning to read her eyes. They gave everything away. There was no need for her to answer me. I saw the small cloud obscuring the golden ring around the pupil.

"Let's see what it says," I suggested.

I went on explaining as I paged through the book. "An unbroken line is a yang line, a broken one is a yin line. Yang is the masculine, the illuminated, the dragon. Yin is the feminine, the dark, the phoenix. The book has sixty-four chapters. Each one describes a state or a condition. See, this one is called *da you.*"

"What does that mean?"

"Progress," I said.

"That sounds good."

"Hold on a minute. Let me finish."

I read the text out slowly: "'Conform to Heaven and act in an opportune manner; hence from the beginning there will be no obstacle to progress.' When you practice I Ching, you have to follow the answer instinctively, but you also have to try to interpret it rationally."

"There's only one thing I want to know," Iris said. "Nothing else matters. Are we going to find Eden?"

Our flight was called for the third time. I answered her in the manner of I Ching, positive and ambiguous, clear and obscure, decisive and uncertain, pointing the way and enigmatic. "That's why we're going, isn't it?" I said.

II

Part II

Chapter Nineteen

Chaweng Beach

A green Toyota van drove slowly through the hot streets of Chaweng Beach, advertising a boxing tournament. On its side was a poster of two muscle-bound Thai boxers sparring with each other. Alternating between shrill Thai and broken English, the driver shouted through a megaphone, "Come see! Best fighters in the area! Tiger Thai fight Black Joe! Crazy Mike and Lompon Baby fight to death! Very best fights! Saturday Koh Samui Stadium. Come see. One time only. First-class fights."

Eli Mazor, the Israeli police liaison officer, was walking down the street when the van rode by. He listened for his name, but didn't hear it. He'd expected as much, but he was still disappointed. As the van got farther away and the voice issuing from the megaphone faded, he pushed away thoughts of his upcoming fight.

The shopping street on Chaweng Beach looked like any other shopping street on any beach in Thailand. Among the shops was a real estate agency with photos of villas for sale or rent taped to the window. A large sign in English declared, "Buy a Permanent Home in Paradise." Above it was the name of the agency in huge letters: World Sea and Land Corporation. Mazor pushed on the glass door and went into the air-conditioned office.

"*Sawadee kap,*" he said to the young man in a crisp yellow shirt seated behind a desk.

Raising his eyes, the agent replied courteously, "*Sawadee kap.* Can I help you?"

"I'm thinking of buying a piece of land, maybe building a small hotel or a residential building. Can you give me an idea of how to get started?"

The man hesitated for a moment before asking, "Do you have a local partner?"

"No. Do I need one?"

"The law requires it," the agent explained, thinking to himself how stupid the big *falang* was. But when a *falang* like him, a smelly, sweaty Westerner, comes in, he just might purchase a vacation home on impulse. Overcoming his repulsion, he maintained his polite tone. "There must be a partnership with a Thai citizen, and the Thai partner must own more than the foreign partner. At least fifty-one percent of the business."

"How do I find a partner?"

"We can do that for you. We can find you a partner we trust, someone honest and reliable."

"How can I be sure he won't con me?"

The agent forced himself to keep the smile on his face. "World Sea and Land Corporation is a reputable agency that has brokered hundreds of deals for satisfied Western customers. We work with one of the leading law firms. They go over the contracts and protect the interests of our customers."

"Can the partner be a local company?"

"That is also possible," said the young man. He was losing his patience and decided it was time to get rid of the big *falang*. "If you can find one."

"Can you recommend a company?"

"Yes, of course."

"So what do you say? Can I rely on you to start me out in business here?"

"Absolutely. We will be happy to get back to you. Leave your details with me."

Mazor was dying to grab him by the collar of his starched shirt and shake him until he got some info out of him. But he knew he couldn't do that. He wasn't in Israel anymore. Turning on his heels, he walked out.

The agent watched him leave, his expression inscrutable. Then he picked up the phone, pressed a number, and said quietly, "Khun Somnook, a *falang* was just here. Very big, very strong. Asked questions." He listened to the response. "Yes, *falang* from Israel. Cop. Most sure."

Mazor was at Shiloh's Place, the restaurant frequented by Israelis. A small bulletin board stood just outside the door. It held the usual notices, along with a fading picture bearing the caption: "Missing. Eden. 12-years-old. If you have information about her whereabouts, please notify the Israeli police or call…" The phone number was illegible, faded like the smiling face in the picture.

"What's up, dude?" Shiloh shouted. "Getting ready for the fight?" The customers all turned to look at the huge man coming in through the door.

Mazor sat down at a table and Shiloh came to take his order. "You coming to Friday night supper at Chabad House tomorrow?"

Mazor looked up at him. "My fight's on Saturday."

"Even better," Shiloh said. "Drop by, and you can get a blessing from the rabbi."

Simon and Aaron walked over and sat down at Mazor's table.

"C-c-c-come. The rabbi g-g-gives one hell of a b-b-b-blessing," Simon stuttered.

"How's it going?" Aaron asked.

"All good."

"G-g-great," Simon said, giving him a piercing look.

What Mazor saw in front of him was a tall awkward guy with thinning hair and bulging eyes. Because of his flaws, people tended to underestimate him. Around here he was known as Simple Simon. In the police data bank back home he was known as Bloody Simon, one of the top hitmen in the Bezalel Maslini crime syndicate in southern Israel.

"What brings you to Koh Samui," Aaron asked.

"The Thai boxing tournament on Saturday," Mazor answered. "It's a major event."

"So we heard." Aaron was the complete opposite of Simon, short and stout, with his tiny eyes constantly darting around restlessly.

"Should we p-p-put our m-m-money on you?"

Shiloh raised his eyes from the stove where he was frying an egg. "Yeah, give me a good tip. Who's a sure bet?"

Simon crushed a soda can and threw it toward Shiloh. It landed, dripping, on the counter. "Sh-sh-sh-ut up," he said angrily, before getting up and walking out.

Moving his chair closer to Aaron, Mazor leaned over and whispered, "Wouldn't you like to make the case go away?"

Aaron looked at him suspiciously. "What case?"

Mazor fixed him with his eyes. Then he took his badge out of his pocket and laid it on the table.

"Put that away," Aaron said nervously. "This isn't the place. That one," he gestured with his head toward Shiloh, "he's a ratfink snitch. He'd sell his mother down the river."

"I was in the Serious Crimes Unit."

"Was," Aaron stressed.

"I read your file. You went down hard."

"You're exaggerating. They exaggerated even more," Aaron said bitterly. "They were looking for a stooge. I'm not saying I didn't cross the line here and there, but I never fed no fucking lawyer false information to get a bad guy out of jail. There's much bigger fish than me out there. What do you want from me?"

"I can fix things."

"What do you mean?"

"You know what I mean. You tell me what I want to know, and I make the shit you left behind disappear."

Aaron didn't respond.

"What do you say?" Mazor said, pressing harder.

"Don't know. It's complicated."

"What's so complicated?"

"A month, two months ago, I would've jumped at the chance. But now," he glanced over at Shiloh, who was placing the egg on a table. But his ears were like antennae pointed in their direction. "Things have changed around here," Aaron went on. "It's too dangerous. It used to be paradise. Everyone, even the ex-cons, did their own thing, fucking, drinking, just having a good time. But that's over. The Russian-Israeli mafia moved in, and suddenly we're all like fucking big-time criminals."

"Do they have anything to do with the notice outside?"

Aaron looked toward the door and the white beach and blue sea beyond. "Stop leaning on me. I have to think."

"Give me something so I can start to see what I can do for you."

"I can't talk here. Come to Chabad House tomorrow. I'll only talk if the rabbi's present."

Throwing one last glance at Shiloh, Aaron got up and left.

Chapter Twenty

Chabad House, Koh Samui

Mazor made his way through the courtyard in front of Chabad House. Dozens of Israelis had come from all over the island for the Friday night prayers and the supper afterwards. They streamed in, greeting each other with happy smiles. Mazor watched as the whole of the self-named F Brigade arrived, dressed in white shirts and sandals with embroidered white yarmulkes on their heads. A man who looked to be about sixty-five led the pack. He had chiseled features, a small, well-groomed mustache, and cloudy eyes. As he walked toward the door, people gravitated to him, shaking his hand and greeting him with "Shabbat shalom, Judge." Mazor saw Aaron detach himself from the group and head for a side door, gesturing for him to follow.

He entered a space taken up almost entirely by a large wooden table filled with books and a row of prayer shawls in their embroidered bags. The rabbi was standing with his back to them, leaning his right hand on the table.

"Shabbat shalom, Rabbi," Aaron said.

The rabbi turned. He'd been a champion surfer before he became religious and went to study in a yeshiva. Over the years, his sun-bleached hair had gotten longer and grayer, curling into sidelocks beside his ears. He now sported a long beard as well. The only reminder of his former life was the mischievous glint in his blue eyes.

"Rabbi, this is the cop I told you about."

"Pleased to meet you, Rabbi," Mazor said, coming closer.

From behind the table, the Rabbi slowly passed his hand through his beard as he examined Mazor. "Aaron asked me to be a witness to your conversation."

"Before I say anything, I want to know exactly what's in it for me," Aaron said, looking nervously at the door.

"First, you tell me everything you know about the disappearance of the girl, Eden Ben-Lev," Mazor said evenly. "There's a lot of pressure on me to move the investigation forward. You give me something to go on, and you stay here until we prepare a soft landing for you back home, a full pension, and maybe even compensation for your pain and suffering."

"I want to see it in writing. I want it to say I'm an undercover agent, not some motherfucking informant, a worthless snitch."

"Give me twenty-four hours, and you'll get what you want."

"Swear to it, right here and now. Swear on the Bible."

Mazor shifted uneasily. Promises were one thing, but taking an oath on the Bible was another. The rabbi pushed a Bible toward him. Mazor placed his right hand on it. "I swear," he said.

"Not like that," the rabbi said. "Think about what you're saying. We are commanded not to take the Lord's name in vain. A man may turn to God to prove that he is speaking the truth. But if his heart is not pure, it can cause serious harm. To himself, as well as others. Do you understand that?"

The image of the fight awaiting him the next day flashed through Mazor's mind, and a cold shadow fell on his heart. "I do, Rabbi."

"Then repeat after me, 'I swear on the Bible.'"

Mazor quickly repeated the words, speaking barely above a whisper.

"Now you're my bro," Aaron said, throwing his arms around Mazor and hugging him to his chest. "Now I know you're not playing me."

The rabbi raised the Bible to his lips and kissed it tenderly. "Okay, that's it. Get out of here, you two. They're waiting for me to start."

Mazor and Aaron went back out to the courtyard. Neither of them saw the Judge go in through a small door, speak briefly with the rabbi, and then come back out. By the time they entered the main hall, everyone was already seated around a long table set for supper. The rabbi's wife was running back and forth from the kitchen to the hall, placing the first course in front of the diners: a finely chopped green salad and matbucha, a spicy tomato and pepper salad in which to dip the challah, still warm from the oven. Standing at the head of the table, the rabbi said a prayer and began praising the Lord, spicing each sentence with the provocative phrase "white or brown?" a nod to the two bottles in front of him. The "white" was a fine Israeli vodka; the "brown" a bottle of Jameson whiskey made by non-kosher hands.

"What would you like us to discuss this evening, Judge?" the rabbi asked, gesturing to his old friend who was sitting beside him.

Without a moment's hesitation, the Judge answered, "Exodus 21:18: 'And if men strive together, and one smite another with a stone, or with his fist, and he die not, but keepeth to his bed.'"

"An excellent choice, " the rabbi said, "especially seeing as there's a fight tomorrow. Two men will strike each other, one of them a Jew and the other a gentile."

"How do the bets stand?" the Judge asked.

"It's pretty even. The gentile has a slight advantage," answered Mandelbaum, known as the 'liaison officer'. "If anyone wants to place a bet, this is the time. I don't take bets on the Sabbath."

Everyone started pulling out money, purple five-hundred-baht notes, and beige thousand-baht notes. Mandelbaum collected them, counting the money and recording each bet. Finally, the Judge struck the table with his hand. "That's enough," he declared.

They all raised their glasses in a toast to Mazor, seated at the foot of the table. He was looking at his phone, texting Barnea: "I have a source who knows what happened to the girl. You'll have the whole story in twenty-four hours." Noticing the attention he was drawing, he put the phone away and raised his glass. "I hope you'll all come to cheer me on. It's not every day an Israeli takes part in an international Thai boxing tournament. *Lechaim.*" He held his glass in the air and then replaced it on the table without drinking from it.

The Judge stood up. "The F Brigade wishes you success in the tournament," he said. "Shabbat shalom."

"*Lechaim*," they roared in response, falling onto the food and downing multiple glasses of vodka in preparation for a night of pleasure in the holy land of Thailand, the land of milk, honey, sex, and drugs.

Mazor ate sparingly, said his goodbyes, and got up to leave. The rabbi leaned over to the Judge. "Should I bet on the gentile or the Jew?" he asked, nodding toward Mazor, who was already at the door. "What do you say?"

Contempt dripping from his voice, the Judge answered, "We'll let him go two rounds, and then we'll take him out. He'll get what's coming to a fucking Israeli cop, or anyone else who tries to shit on our paradise. As for that stinking rat," he said, gesturing toward Aaron, "we'll give him a makeover. By the time we're done with him, his face will look like a Picasso painting."

Spit was flying from the Judge's mouth. The rabbi placed his hand on his arm, "Amen, God willing," he said, thinking there might finally be some waves in Koh Samui the next day.

Chapter Twenty-One

Joe Mandelbaum, known as the 'liaison officer,' had indeed once been the liaison between the UN forces and the Israeli army on the Lebanese border. As he tells it, someone used his name to smuggle a large quantity of hashish into Israel. Naturally, he had nothing to do with it. But when the shipment was seized, he was court-martialed, demoted to private, and dishonorably discharged. His marriage fell apart, too. A friend suggested a vacation in Thailand to help him clear his head and recharge his batteries. It didn't take long for him to fall in love with the easy life in the country and decide to settle there.

Mandelbaum soon became the fixer for all the Israelis residing permanently on Koh Samui. No one was more suited for the role. Whenever a guy was feeling lazy and didn't want to get out of bed, or just felt like being pampered, he'd simply press 8, Mandelbaum's lucky number, on his speed dial, and whatever he asked for would show up on his doorstep. Two girls, three girls, a ladyboy, a bottle of Chivas, tabs to swallow, lines to inhale. Mandelbaum never said, "no can do." He'd take his ten percent, and everyone was happy. So what if, behind his back, they called him 'ten-percent Mandelbaum'? He'd been called worse.

It was Mandelbaum who made the initial contact with Sammy Ben-Lev. They met by chance, literally bumping into each other when Mandelbaum was leaving the foot massage parlor he owned ten percent of. They exchanged apologies, struck up a conversation, and continued it in the lobby of Sammy's new hotel. After an hour, during which the drinks kept coming, Sammy asked if he'd like to take a nap before dinner and handed him a key. Mandelbaum opened the door and found a beautiful local girl with a huge smile waiting for him under the soft silk sheet.

"I on the house," she said in broken English. "You want shower before?"

She rose from the bed dressed only in a minuscule thong. Stroking his dick gently, she said, "I like you baby. You got big baby. He want come?" Mandelbaum decided he didn't need a shower. He loved the Thai girls. They got straight to business, didn't fuck with your head. They made it all so simple. His former married life seemed like a distant memory, one worth forgetting.

Room service brought a sumptuous dinner for two accompanied by a chilled bottle of Chardonnay and a handwritten note from Sammy: "I hope she's taking good care of you. Make yourself at home. See you later."

The following day at noontime, he met up with the F Brigade at Shiloh's Place. They were furious. He'd hung them all out to dry, not answering his phone. They'd had to go out and get laid all on their own. They weren't used to being forced to put in the work.

"I'll make it up to you," Mandelbaum promised. "You have nothing to worry about. Just wait and see the treat I have in store for you. A first-class resort."

When they left, he stayed behind with the Judge and told him about Sammy Ben-Lev.

"I've heard of him," the Judge said with his cold smile. "Reel him in," he instructed. "Let him feel that whatever he wants, we're here for him. It'll pay off handsomely in the end. That's what I like about Thailand. Wherever you go, things fall into your lap. Paradise."

The whole of F Brigade lived off Sammy during the resort's trial run. He was uber-generous with them. They ordered drinks and told the barman to put them on their tab, which never arrived. They were first in line at the beachfront buffet, and if Sammy was around, they made sure to pat him on the back and declare, with their mouths full of his food, "You're a real bro, Sammy." Sammy would smile and say, "Enjoy yourselves. It's on me."

Sammy treated Mandelbaum like a member of family. Then one day he saw him eying Iris. "Mandelbaum," he told him firmly, "the wife and kid are off limits. To everyone. I just want it to be clear."

"You're like a brother, Sammy," Mandelbaum answered. "Any one of us would give our life for your kid."

Sammy suggested that F Brigade invest in the expansion of the resort, and, as a brother, Mandelbaum jumped at the idea. He examined the plans and let out a whistle when he saw the beachfront property Sammy had already purchased. He was even more impressed by the blueprints for the construction of private villas, each with its own garden and swimming pool.

"This is your future," Sammy assured him.

"How much do we have to kick in?" Mandelbaum asked.

"How many of you are there in F Brigade?"

"Ten core members," Mandelbaum answered. "Maybe another seven or eight who come and go."

Sammy did the calculations. "A hundred thousand each for the ten would do it," he said. "With the others, maybe two or three can come in together on a unit. They'll get their money back within five years. After that, it's all profit. And they can use the unit whenever it isn't occupied."

Mandelbaum considered the offer, calculated his ten percent, and convinced the members of F Brigade to invest one hundred and ten thousand dollars each in what would be a luxurious villa on the most beautiful beach in the world.

They all wanted in. They trusted Mandelbaum.

The future looked bright, until Mandelbaum got a call from Boris Chiplonak. He'd used his services in the past, mainly when he found himself holding a batch of checks stamped "insufficient funds." Boris would unleash one of his local hounds, who would return a few hours later with a big grin on his face and the full amount owed, minus Boris's twenty percent.

"Why are they always grinning?" Mandelbaum once asked. Seemingly surprised by the question, Boris replied, "That's how they get their kicks. And they even get paid for it. What? Don't you enjoy a chance to use your fists every now and then?"

"Listen, Mandelbaum," Boris said now. "I don't have to remind you that you owe me."

Mandelbaum's instant reaction was a sharp pain in the nerve endings at the back of his head, a sign his blood pressure had risen to over a hundred and sixty. He might as well have been eating salt by the spoonful or downing a whole bottle of Mekhong whiskey, which was more or less like drinking kerosene.

"Somebody wants you to keep an eye on what's happening on the beach over there."

"Who wants to know?" Mandelbaum asked.

"Someone big. It's better if you don't know. You won't sleep at night."

"I get it."

"No, you don't, but it doesn't matter. He's out of your league, you and those assholes you hang around with."

Mandelbaum was stunned. "How do you know about them?"

Boris laughed. Mandelbaum never liked the sound of his laugh, and he liked it even less now.

"Your friends, what do you they call themselves, the F Brigade? They stepped on a few toes. And they never shut their traps. My people tell me they ought to be wired shut, permanently. You want me to arrange it?"

Mandelbaum's temples were pounding. "No." He could already see their paradise fading away.

"The interested party is Yuri Cezar. He wants you to keep an eye on Sammy Ben-Lev and find out what the motherfucker is up to. Yuri put a lot of money into the pile of sand around the resort."

Yuri Cezar? Thainik? Mandelbaum's blood pressure soared to two hundred. The mere mention of the name of the boss of the Russian-Israeli mafia made a lot of people break out in a sweat. So much sweat was dripping off Mandelbaum now; he could have been in a Turkish bath.

"Why? Is there a problem with the resort?"

"There isn't any resort, and there never will be. That bastard Sammy took us for a ride. He cooked up some phony deal and played us for fools."

Mandelbaum's heart skipped a beat. "I'll take care of it," he promised.

"You better," Boris answered. "You don't, and I set my gulagers loose on you. Trust me, Mandelbaum. You don't want to see their grin up close."

Mandelbaum slumped back in his chair. He was screwed big time. And he wasn't the only one. It killed him to realize that Sammy had roped him into investing in a pile of sand. Even the Russian mafia had swallowed the bait. He took out his blood pressure pills and gulped down a triple dose to make the pounding in his head go away.

Chapter Twenty-Two

I have a simple routine for dealing with long flights: two whiskeys straight up before dinner service, a Campari and tonic when the flying waitress comes by with the drinks cart, and red wine to make the gunk they call airplane food palatable. Then I lie back in my seat, close my eyes, and put in earplugs to block out the chatter of my fellow passengers. This time, it didn't work. Whenever I opened my eyes for a second, I found a second head growing out of my shoulder. Our eyes were synchronized. As soon as mine opened, they did too, and then Iris straightened up as if nothing had happened.

"Are you asleep?" she asked.

"Absolutely," I answered, closing my eyes.

But she didn't take the hint. "What are we going to do?"

"What every tourist does when he lands," I said drily. "We land, go through passport control, and take a piss."

"Very good. Have you gotten the macho act out of your system? Now talk to me."

That made me smile.

The first sight of Koh Samui before the plane sets down fulfills the promise that every tourist is hoping to find there. The sparkling expanses of mirror-like water left after the monsoon rains, rice paddies in hues of green and gold, small houses clustered together under the shade of coconut trees, the wide sea, and the long white beaches. The island's airport is charmingly picturesque. Ladies and gentlemen, welcome to paradise.

The moment we exited the terminal, we were hit by the heat and humidity.

The flowers we'd been handed as we departed the plane drooped instantly, and our clothes stuck to our backs. Ladies and gentlemen, now welcome to reality.

"I booked us rooms in our hotel," Iris said, correcting herself immediately, "Sammy's hotel."

I was about to say, "bad move," but I didn't want to feed her anxiety. Instead, I said simply, "We're not going there."

The place we did go to was on the edge of the Lamai Beach area. A private bungalow with two rooms. It had a lovely garden that led down to the water beside a small sand bar. At low tide, you could walk across it to a tiny island occupied only by a hammock under a bamboo lean-to. I've spent a lot of hours lying in that hammock, sunk in thought.

The key was where it always was, in a potted plant by the door. A note was attached. I recognized the handwriting of Captain Sombersin, the retired local cop who owned the place. We'd collaborated on quite a few cases in the past. The message was short: "Be careful. Lots of bastards around. Powerful people are involved. Don't trust anyone, including your people. Especially your people. Take care."

If I were smarter, I would have taken Captain Sombersin's message to heart, smiled politely at the lady, and booked us both on the next flight home. The note was clearly telling me that sometimes, when the karma is bad, the best move is to beat a quick retreat. But I wasn't that smart.

Iris looked around the bungalow while I made a few calls. The first was to Eli Mazor. It went to voice mail. I didn't like that. After several failed attempts, I called Barnea back at the ICU and told him I couldn't get in touch with Mazor.

"He's on the island," Barnea said. "The idiot signed up for some infantile kickboxing tournament tonight. I haven't been able to get hold of him for a few hours, either. I got one serious text from him, but since then, he's gone silent."

I called Jacob.

This time, he picked up quickly.

"You here?" he asked.

"Where else would I be?"

"How should I know? I just hoped it wasn't here."

Laughing, I asked him if there was a boxing tournament that night in the new Chaweng stadium.

"Yeah. I hear some Israeli guy came from Bangkok to fight. They say he's built like a mountain, but not worth a shit. But someone's raising the bets."

"In whose favor?"

"Not some dumbass Israeli, you can be sure of that. You know Thai people. They're born scammers."

"When does it start?"

"Late. It's a marathon that goes on late into the night."

"Can you get there?"

"Two jackasses beating each other bloody isn't my thing. Even if one of them is an Israeli cop."

Even Jacob knows, I thought.

"Do you want me to come with you?" Iris asked when I filled her in.

"I wouldn't advise it. It's not the prettiest sight. I'll bring Mazor here after the fight, and we can talk."

She didn't say anything, but the expression on her face made it clear that she wasn't happy with the arrangement. I filled a large glass with ice from the freezer and then poured a generous shot of whiskey from the bottle of Johnny Walker Black Label on the table. It was hot out.

Chapter Twenty-Three

Long lines stretched from the stadium box office. A large crowd of Thais and Westerners was milling around outside the gate, waiting for it to open. I identified quite a few Israelis. I went to the locker room, where the boxers were in various stages of preparation for the tournament.

It wasn't hard to find Eli Mazor. He really was a mountain of a man. Almost a head taller than me, and I'm pretty tall. Broader in the shoulders, too, and I'm no wimp. His duffel bag was sitting on the bench in front of him. He was pulling on his shorts, moving slowly and deliberately. Most of all, he looked very much alone.

"Hi, I'm Dotan Naor," I introduced myself. "I've got quite a bit of experience in Thai boxing. I'd be happy to help you get ready. Oh, and by the way, Barnea says hello."

He threw me a piercing glance, but said nothing aside from, "Fine."

I looked at the clock. We had less than half an hour. "You ought to warm up a little; at least stretch your arms and shoulders."

His Thai competitors were staring at him in astonishment. Yes, he was big, but what really stunned them was how hairy he was. There wasn't an inch of his body that wasn't matted with hair. That had one major advantage: the body hair hid the size and rather poor shape of his muscles. They were big, but not well-toned. Too much weight-lifting, I thought. Short quads. Those legs wouldn't kick very high. And his swollen biceps weren't good for straight-arm punches. I pulled on a pair of training gloves I found in an open locker and told him to hit me. He was using too much power. After just a few punches, the sweat started pouring off him like a waterfall.

"Let's get ready," I said.

I got a large jar of tiger balm from his bag and spread the magic ointment all over him. Made from Bengali tiger bones and a lot of camphor, it's great for pain. It was beginning to sting, which is a good thing. The kicks and punches that were sure to come would hurt less. I wove the bindings around his hands and put his mouth guard in. "Close your mouth," I instructed. He bit down a few times. The guard was positioned properly. It would be a shame to lose a tooth or two simply because the guard didn't sit right. I smeared a ton of Vaseline on his face. It's one of the best defenses in a fight. It makes your opponent's hand slip, deflecting a punch.

"Do you know who you're up against?" I asked.

"Yes," he said, pointing to a tall, thin Thai guy a few benches away. His rival saw us looking at him and flipped us off.

"A loser. I can wipe him out with one hand tied around my back," Eli said confidently.

"Calm down," I said, but I was far from calm myself. I could see what Mazor probably couldn't. His opponent's legs were like concrete columns, and his long arms, with their well-developed muscles, were as flexible as snakes. As he moved his head left and right, I noted how freely it twisted, like the head of a cobra about to strike. And his eyes were cold. I knew Mazor was going to take a beating, and there was nothing I could do about it. I liked the look of the fight manager even less. His ugly yellow face was badly pockmarked, and there were fatty lumps around his mean little eyes.

"Listen, Eli," I said. "I came here to investigate the disappearance of Eden Ben-Lev. Barnea said you had a lead."

"Believe it or not, I found a snitch who'll tell all in exchange for empty promises. A real loser. I can't believe he used to be a cop. But let's talk about it over a beer after the fight. I'll let him go three rounds, and then we'll have the rest of the night to ourselves."

If there was any sense in my head, I would have pulled him out of the fight right there and then. But the adrenaline was already pumping through his body, and his ego was racing along with it.

"Just give me a little something to go on. What are we talking about here?"

"The asshole knows what happened to the girl. He said it's connected to a Russian-Israeli crime syndicate that's taking over Koh Samui. He was scared. That's why he's willing to talk in exchange for protection. Leave it alone for now. Ten minutes and a few good punches, and then we'll have all the time in the world to go into details. Come on. Let's go upstairs."

I pushed the gloves on Mazor and tied them tight. He checked them carefully to make sure they were comfortable and flexible enough. That's why he didn't notice the man who went up to the ugly fight manager, whispered something in his ear and shoved a thick package wrapped in newspaper into his hand. The fight manager looked from Mazor to me with a nasty smile on his face.

"Who's he talking about, Eli? What crime syndicate?"

Mazor didn't answer. We heard the announcer call the contestants into the arena for the introduction parade. I tied on Mazor's headpiece of colorful feathers and slipped a bracelet with tiny bells on his right wrist. "Come on," I said. "Let's put on a good show for them."

The fighters were lined up at the foot of the arena. Most of them were locals. They might look small and scrawny, but I knew they were deadly fighting machines. There were a few Westerners, including some young Russians, that didn't look too bad. The guy in front of us had tattoos all over his body. "Hey, mates," he greeted us. Obviously Australian. He wasn't young, but I got the impression he'd be able to remain on his feet for three rounds. Some men make their living boxing. They take the punches and survive from one fight to the next. Others come for the experience. I guessed the Australian belonged to the second category. But I still didn't understand why Mazor was there.

We were last in line. One by one, each contestant climbed through the ropes and put on a display for the audience, raising his gloves in front of his face and doing a little dance. When it was Mazor's turn, he was greeted by raucous laughter and booing. He straightened up, flexed his muscles, and showed off his huge body. The fighters filed out and went back to the locker room.

"When are we on?" Mazor asked.

I looked at the list on the wall. "Fourth match."

The first fight, between two young anonymous boxers, was meant to fire up the audience and get the betting going. The second was one of the headliners of the tournament, and the spectators were waiting with bated breath. When the two opponents, Tiger Boy and Black Joe, did their rooster dance in the arena, the betting went wild. Folded thousand-baht bills flew into the hands of the bookies. The announcer dragged out the introductions to allow more time to place bets. The fight was being broadcast live on the local sports channel. The whole of Thailand was in a frenzy.

There was a lot of blood. A lot of kicking and punching and lethal knee and elbow butts to the side. Each round lasted three long minutes. In Round 3, Tiger Boy, a talented young boxer and the crowd favorite thrust his elbow into the jaw of Black Joe, a large dark man from Southern Thailand. Black Joe's head flew back, and he fell to the mat, unconscious. The spectators were instantly on their feet, roaring, "Tiger Boy! Tiger Boy!" The paramedics climbed into the ring. It looked like Black Joe would be out of commission for a long time.

The next match was between the Australian, Crazy Mike, and Lompon Baby. "Wish me luck," Crazy Mike said as he passed me on his way to the ring.

I saw his opponent. He obviously got his nickname from his baby face, but he was no baby. "Hang tough, Crazy Mike," I said. "You're an elephant." He high-fived me with his gloved hand, a laid-back smile on his face. "Thanks, mate," he said.

He was going into the fight in the right frame of mind. But from the very start, it didn't go well for him. Lompon Baby was a killing machine, kicking and punching his opponent relentlessly. The Australian remained on his feet for the whole of the first round. In Round 2, Lompon Baby landed a sharp kick, and I heard the bones in Crazy Mike's right shin scream as they broke.

Mazor was up next. He was the first into the ring. I filled a bucket with ice cubes and went to stand in his corner behind the ropes. After he had pranced around a little—the most pathetic performance I had ever seen in a Thai boxing ring—I called him over. "Listen, Eli," I said. "I don't know what kind of karma you've got, but lean over."

He leaned over the ropes, and I put my hands on both sides of his head and sent him all the positive energy I was capable of summing up at that moment. We were in a world of our own. "Repeat after me," I instructed. "Hear O Israel, the Lord our God, the Lord is one."

Meanwhile, his rival was warming up in the opposite corner.

Mazor straightened up. He didn't doubt for a moment that he could trust me. I gave him his final instructions. "You've got long limbs. Don't let him keep you at a distance. Get in close and then give him all you've got. Ignore whatever he's doing to you. Just get in there and squash him. And put your heart and soul into it. Get it?"

He nodded. "Don't worry. The motherfucker is going down."

It was good advice, but in order to do what I told him, you had to be an experienced fighter. And Mazor wasn't. I was hoping there was the heart of a warrior under the muscle mass. That's what makes a good boxer. The ones who take the punches and look at the clock and the ref, counting the seconds or considering whether to take a fall—they have the heart of a bird. The Thais give it their all. That was my main concern.

The match didn't start well. Mazor's opponent was a dancer, skipping and hopping around as he rained fire and brimstone down on Mazor. The Israeli was a clumsy grizzly bear with worthless hammer-like hands. The Thai just toyed with him in the first round. Everyone could see it except for Mazor. When the bell signaled the end of the round, Eli was already unsteady on his feet, panting and sweaty as he made his way back to his corner.

"How'd I do?" he asked with a broad smile. "That guy's an asshole, right?"

"You can take him down easy," I lied. What else could I do? Tell him the truth? I handed him a cold sponge and pumped him up in preparation for the real beating I knew was coming. "Get in close," I reminded him, clenching my teeth.

In the second round, it was clear that Mazor didn't have a chance in hell. It began with a kick to his chest. There wasn't a question in anyone's mind that

began with a kick to his chest. There wasn't a question in anyone's mind that his scrawny opponent was about to crush his balls and hang them around his neck. First, his knees went to Mazor's kidneys, and then his elbows drummed his ribs. I could see Mazor struggling to catch his breath. The bell rang. He stumbled painfully back to the corner.

"Bastard," he muttered. It was beginning to sink in that he'd been set up.

"Put your heart in it," I said firmly. "Give it all you've got. Fight back." But what I was really thinking was that it would be better if he ceded the fight and got out of the ring. That's what I should have said, but I knew it wouldn't do any good. Adrenaline clogs the brain.

In Round 3, Mazor's opponent aimed for the face and kept up the bombardment. Mazor was already blind in one eye, but the Thai kept coming. He burst Mazor's eardrums and then broke his nose with a single blow. Large drops of blood flowed down his chin. He tried to wipe them away with his arm. At this point, the referee should have stopped the fight, but the crowd was roaring. They wanted more blood. That's what they'd paid for. The ref didn't interfere. The Thai struck Mazor in the jaw. The last blow was to his head. I could swear I saw bits of brain matter flying out, but they had nowhere to go except back onto Mazor's broken skull. He fell to the mat, unconscious. The fight was over.

There was nothing I could do but wait for the ambulance to take him to the emergency room. I went outside and called Barnea. "Your guy's been taken out."

"What's his condition?"

"By the looks of it, a total loss. I could get more out of a houseplant."

"Did he tell you anything?"

"Mostly, he got sweat on me. But yes, he did ferret something out. It seems the Russian-Israeli mafia is taking over. And they're playing hardball. People are scared. All the small fish are skittish. What happened to Mazor in the ring was bought and paid for. Someone didn't want him to talk."

"Find those motherfuckers and crush them. For me. You hear me, Dotan," Barnea said.

I didn't say, "I hear you," or "don't worry." I was beginning to think that the forces behind Eden's disappearance were much more powerful than I'd imagined.

There was a row of cheap restaurants across from the stadium with shaky, dirty plastic tables spotted with cigarette burns. They were filling up with people streaming out of the stadium, ordering beer, and analyzing the fights. I sat down at a table in one of the joints and scrutinized the crowd, looking for some sort of clue. In particular, my eyes sought out the man who had slipped the package to the fight manager. I finally caught sight of him leaving the stadium with a large group of Westerners. I could sniff out the Israelis even from a distance.

The one they called Aaron came over to me. He was a small, chubby guy with tiny, restless eyes. "Did you see the fight?"

"I saw it."

"He sure got his balls handed to him."

His friends laughed. I didn't.

"What's wrong? You can't take a joke?"

No one was laughing anymore.

"We saw you in Mazor's corner. What's he to you?" I remained silent. "What, you don't want to make nice?"

I still didn't respond.

"Okay. Don't talk. You don't want to know us. No problem. Just don't forget that the whole island of Koh Samui is no bigger than your mother's cunt. You can hide in the sand, but we'll dig you out like a crab."

They laughed again, like a herd of hyenas, and sat down a few tables away. One of them exchanged a look with me. He was an older man with gray hair, a small mustache, and a chilling expression.

Welcome to Koh Samui, I thought. A paradise swarming with vermin.

Chapter Twenty-Four

The cab let me off at the edge of the road. I made my way down to the bungalow. The path was dark. A single lamppost threw a ribbon of light onto the beach, and the waves quietly lapped the shore. I saw the glow of a cigarette. Iris was sitting on a lounge chair under a coconut tree, staring out to sea. The table beside her held a bottle of whiskey, a glass, an ice bucket, and a pack of cigarettes. There was just enough light to make out the shiny tracks her tears had left.

"What's up?" I asked.

She didn't reply, just pulled on her cigarette and blew the smoke out toward the water. I could see the tension in her face, in her clenched jaw.

"Talk to me, Iris."

Tears began flowing from her eyes, appearing as suddenly as a monsoon rain. She held out her left hand and uncurled her fingers. A small folded note lay on her palm. "Look," she said.

I took the note and opened it. The message consisted of a single word in English: Eden. I'd seen Iris's handwriting. She hadn't written it.

"I didn't know what to do with myself after you left. I couldn't stop the thoughts that kept running through my head. I tried, but nothing helped. So, I took a cab to Chaweng Beach. I thought I'd take a walk and do a little shopping and maybe it would calm my nerves. I was walking down the main street when I noticed a man walking beside me. He had a well-groomed beard, and he was dressed in a faded gray suit, funny pointed shoes, and a white turban.

"'Madam', he said to me. 'I can tell your future, your past, and your present.

I see things.' I kept walking, and then he took out a card and handed it to me. It said 'Mr. R. K. Singh, Indian astrologer'. I gave him back the card and told him I didn't believe in those things. Then he said, 'You don't pay me now. Only if you are satisfied, if you wish to pay. I must tell you I see a large black cloud over your head. It is not a happy sight'. That made me stop and really look at him for the first time. His eyes looked ancient. They seemed to swallow me up."

"Okay," I said cynically. "Then you sat down, and he took your right hand and stared at your face, right between your eyes."

"How do you know?" Iris asked, surprised.

"Fortune tellers like him are as common as house flies in the East. Indian Sikhs, Buddhist monks, astrologers, palm readers, Cambodian mediums, Chinese face readers. There's no end to the ancient wisdoms. They've turned into scams. Everyone believes in the occult. People don't make a single decision without consulting some kind of clairvoyant. Governments don't go to war, businessmen don't close a deal, families don't decide on a date for a wedding or a funeral without getting the approval of the stars and the constellations."

"So you're saying it's all a fraud."

"What did he tell you?"

"He took my right hand, but he didn't look at it. Just held it. His hand was hot. He examined my face and said I had the brow of a queen. I knew he was just playing mind games, but then he said I was a kind, compassionate person and that someone very close to me was taking advantage of it. It was like he stuck a knife in my heart." Iris paused, thinking about what she had said. Then she went on. "After that, he stopped talking and took out a little notepad and a pen."

"He wrote a single word, folded it, gave it to you, and told you to close your fingers around it, right?"

"How...," she started, but immediately remembered she'd already asked that question.

"I've seen them at work," I said in an effort to lower her expectations.

"I wanted to open my hand and see what he wrote, but he stopped me and said, 'There is a man who is far away. He is like an emperor controlling your life, but you do not know it. He is waiting. One phone call can put an end to the matter.' I didn't have the vaguest idea what he was talking about. I'm sure he could see the confusion on my face. He told me to open my hand. He'd written Eden's name. How did he know? Can you explain that?" Through her tears, she went on with her story. "He said, 'Madam, I do not take money from you. You need to help your daughter. It is urgent.' He started to walk away but I followed him and held out some money to him. He didn't want to take it. 'Just tell me one thing', I said. 'Is she alive? Is Eden alive? I have to know.' 'Madam,' he said, 'I am very sorry. I am only a simple face reader'. I saw that he was frightened. I didn't know why. He was frightened, I swear. I could see it in his eyes."

I remained silent. What could I say? I knew this parasite in a turban with the neat little beard on his chin. He was always at Chaweng Beach looking for his next victim. Who doesn't want to know their future? The Sikh saw a sad Western woman and thought he could make an easy buck. All he had to do was stare at her face and make a few general statements. But then he was suddenly struck by a bolt of lightning. For every hundred charlatans, there's one who can really see things. He saw the danger and blood surrounding the woman, the cloud of negative energy above her head waiting to envelop her. That's why he refused to take the money. If he took it, it would bind him to the evil rapidly approaching, like a monsoon on the horizon.

But I had no intention of saying that to her.

"They have very good intuition," I said. "And they've studied the ancient texts. So, a little something might be true."

"But how did he know Eden's name? Explain it to me."

"I haven't a clue," I said.

"And who's the faraway man like an emperor controlling my life?"

I shrugged.

The waves continued to lap at the shore as they have done from time immemorial. A fat black beetle fell from a tree onto the sand. Dazed by the light, they drop like stones.

All of a sudden, Iris said, "I was very hurt when you went off and left me here alone. Don't do that again."

I wanted to apologize, but what came out was, "Okay. It won't happen again."

"I want to know everything you do."

I took out the pack of Camels I save for precisely such moments and pulled one out. Straightening it carefully, I reached for her lighter.

"And most important, you have to tell me the truth, only the truth."

I lit the cigarette and lay down in a hammock, inhaling deeply. As I blew out the smoke, it rose toward the lamp and all the bugs buzzing around it and then disappeared into the sky, dotted with thousands of tiny lights.

"I have to be able to trust you completely," Iris said, pouring herself a generous shot of whiskey. She fished out a few remaining ice cubes, shook the cold water off her hand, swirled her drink around, and took a large swallow. "Want some?" she offered.

"Yes."

When I had downed the drink, she asked, "Did they hurt Eli Mazor because of us?"

"Yes."

"So wherever we go, people are going to get hurt?"

There was only one honest answer. "Yes."

The only sounds were the squeaking of the hammock and the thuds as the beetles fell on the hard sand.

I put down my glass and climbed out of the hammock. "Are you coming to bed?"

"No."

"Good night," I said, walking toward the dark bungalow. Before going inside, I saw her hand reaching for the whiskey bottle. This time, she raised it to her lips and drank straight from the bottle. Her hair glowed against the background of the water. Before I fell asleep, I saw a lonely gecko making its way along the thin thread of dim light that came in through a gap in the shutters.

Chapter Twenty-Five

The first rays of light stole into the room. I went out to the beach in my bare feet and spent an hour doing yoga, stretching, and breathing exercises. It was only when I sensed a pair of eyes staring at the tattoo on my back that I turned around.

She was standing in the doorway, barefoot, in a white dress, her golden hair loose on her shoulders. It was the most beautiful sight I had seen in a long time.

"I'm making coffee," she said, going back inside.

I sat down on the sand, cross-legged, before the rising sun. Bowing my head and closing my eyes, I brought my hands, palms facing, to my chest, leaving a tiny gap between them. Into it, I sent all my thoughts about Eden. I got to my feet and was rolling up the mat when I heard her call from inside, "The coffee's ready."

A big mug of coffee was waiting on the table. She had changed clothes and was now wearing a simple white T-shirt with a large picture of a smiling Eden. Above it were the words, "Looking for Eden." She stood there, charged by the goal she had set herself: to find her child. I knew the message would hit home. People would respond to a mother with a picture of her missing daughter on her chest. They'd be motivated to help, if only in a small way.

"Do you have the fliers?" I asked.

She nodded. I looked them over again. Beneath the picture of Eden were three lines of print: "Eden Ben-Lev, 12, disappeared from Koh Samui, Thailand in January. Generous reward for information leading to her discovery. Please contact..." Iris's cellphone number and email address followed.

Outside, I heard the sound of the truck bringing the motorcycle I'd rented, a Honda 150cc. I went out. The driver untied the motorcycle, set it up, and came toward me carrying two full-face helmets, one with a dark visor. Then he turned the truck around and drove away.

I started the engine and held out a helmet for Iris. She got on behind me, holding onto the bar around the saddle in order to keep as far away from me as possible. Once I was on the road, I turned into what the Thais call a "motosai," a cyclist who goes from zero to a hundred in seconds and weaves dangerously among the cars, hungrily gulping down their exhaust fumes.

In short, a hothead: not a bad persona if you want to blend in with the surroundings. I sped up and took the turns horizontally, passing the many open Suzuki jeeps on the road. Iris shifted her arms and clasped them around my waist, holding on tight and leaning forward. We must have looked like any other tourist couple. The motorcycle flew down the beach road, every turn offering the sight of another cove more beautiful than the last, if you ignore the fading billboards. Finally, up ahead was a huge, flashy sign that was impossible to miss: Paradise Beach Resort and Spa.

"This is it," Iris shouted in my ear.

"I can see that." Sammy must have a serious problem if his sign had to be the biggest on the block, I thought to myself.

The guard at the gate let us in. We made our way to the reception desk. The Thai staff greeted us with big smiles, the way they greet everyone. As soon as the head of reception caught sight of Iris, he hurried over.

"Any news?" she asked simply.

"No. Sorry."

We went down to the beach. The pictures we showed around aroused a modicum of interest, and Iris's shirt even aroused a modicum of empathy, but nothing more. The hotel guests are only there for a week or ten days. Besides, they're on vacation, and we were disturbing their paradise. Their eyes said it all: she's not my kid.

Next, we tried the vendors who were trudging wearily through the sand with cases of knock-off watches in their arms. Each one smiled warmly as we approached, but the smile disappeared as soon as we showed them Eden's picture, leaving only a blank expression. *"Mai ru,"* don't know, we heard over and over.

A young local man was leaning on the trunk of a palm tree, his buttocks resting on his ankles. As we drew closer, we could see his long dreadlocks, shaven temples, and the gold earring in his right ear. But it was his most outstanding feature that made Iris stop short: the tattoo of a swastika—the ancient Hindu-Buddhist symbol meaning "it is good"—in the center of his forehead.

Seeing the expression on Iris's face, he said, "I've got a few more like it." He pointed to the back of his neck, where another swastika was displayed. This one had four dots between the arms of the twisted cross. "Here too," he said, pointing to his bare foot, "like Buddha."

"What are you selling?" I asked.

He burst out laughing. "I make deliveries, joints, some tabs. Nothing heavy, no heroin or speed. Just what the Westerners need for a little high."

"Do you know this girl?" Iris asked, pointing to her shirt before handing him a flier.

Something flashed in his eyes, bloodshot from all the joints. "Your daughter?"

"Yes."

"Pretty girl."

"Yes, she's pretty. And she's a wonderful child,"

"I saw her. But it was a long time ago."

Iris nearly collapsed onto the sand.

"Where?" I asked.

"Here, in Koh Samui, naturally."

"When?"

"I can't say exactly. I see lots of pretty young Western girls. But she was only a kid. All I remember was that it was early in the morning. I was leaving a full moon party at the Green Mango. The alley was full of young partiers lurching toward the main street. They were making a lot of noise. I was on my own, which doesn't happen often. I was so stoned that I sat down on the curb. The cops come by in the morning to empty the pockets of all the kids too wasted to get home, but I was so far gone I didn't care. I was dozing off when a motorcycle woke me up. It was going slow. It slowed even more at the entrance to the alley. I think the rider looked into that Israeli restaurant, Shiloh's Place, but I can't be sure. Anyway, he didn't stop. A girl was sitting on the back, between the cyclist and a local chick. That girl," he said, pointing to the picture. "After that, I couldn't move even if I wanted to."

"Why not?" I asked.

He looked into the distance, his eyes clouding over. "Because they don't come back," he answered.

I knew he'd said something he hadn't meant to say.

"Who?"

"The Western girls. Isn't that who we're talking about?"

"What do you mean?"

"The girls who disappear. If you live rough like me, you see them all the time. They pass by and then vanish out there somewhere." He pointed to the calm sea that flowed from the beaches of Koh Samui to the other side of the Thai Bay and from there to the shores of Cambodia. A huge expanse of water, tiny islands, uninhabited beaches, and countless anonymous waterways. A huge expanse of disappearing girls.

"Who was the local girl? Did you recognize her?"

"One of the dozens who wear their feet raw on the sand trying to make a living. By the way, how much is it worth to you, what I told you?"

I pulled out a five hundred baht note. His eyes lit up.

"That's nice," he said with a crafty grin. "But you don't have to be so stingy. Her name is worth something, too. Right?"

"When you're right, you're right," I said, taking out two-thousand-baht notes.

"Five thousand. I'm taking a risk here."

"Why?"

"Why? Why does a dog lick its ass? Because tomorrow some rich player will pay another dog to kick my worthless brown ass, and I'll have to bend down and kiss his shoe. It'll be a while before I can show my face again, and I still have to eat."

"Right again," I said.

With a smile, he held out his hand with the practiced gesture of a beggar.

I took out the money, but I didn't hand it over immediately. "You were in a monastery?"

He nodded, not laughing this time. "I left the robe behind exactly one year ago."

"Why?"

He shrugged, and I got a clear vision of the Buddhist monk behind the outer shell. "Maybe it was my karma to be here when you came and tell you what I know. Who am I, a little worm, to decipher the great secrets?"

I gave him the money.

He folded the bills carefully and stuffed them in the pocket of his tight shorts. Then he put his palms together and bowed his head in the traditional gesture of gratitude. "They call her Nit Noi, little Nit. She weaves braids and dreadlocks. You can always find her on the beach."

To Western eyes, the vendors appear to be wandering the beach randomly. The truth is, however, that they divide it up among themselves like alley cats marking their territory. That way, they can all make a meager living. Noi undoubtedly had her own territory.

We walked toward the large statue of Buddha, the thousands of tiny multicolored glass tiles reflecting the blinding light. The aerial roots of the mangrove trees twisted their way into every damp corner. A branch was right above us. From it hung a long chain of Buddhist prayer beads; the reddish sandalwood rubbed smooth. Most of the *mala* was already hidden by young leaves and shoots, but the bottom edge was still exposed. I pulled it down. Attached to it was a small, embroidered bracelet.

The blood drained from Iris's face. "It's Eden's," she said. "I recognize it."

She turned it over and I saw the name "Eden" embroidered in fading letters. Cradling it in her hands. Iris bent her head. The light reflecting off the Buddha seemed softer. His smile was unchanging, eternal.

Chapter Twenty-Six

We found her on our way back. She was sitting on the last sunbed on the sand, braiding the hair of a little girl.

"That's her," Iris said without hesitation. "I remember her. Eden liked to follow her around the beach."

"Nit Noi," I said quietly. The young woman turned her head. She recognized Iris immediately and then saw the picture on her shirt and the string of beads in her hand. She stared at them, a look of panic on her face.

"We want to talk to you, Nit Noi."

The little tourist girl looked at us curiously.

"I finish here in minute," Nit Noi said.

Her fingers worked quickly, weaving the last of the girl's hair until her head was covered in thin braids dotted with multicolored plastic beads. She jumped up and ran to her parents, who were sitting in the sun nearby, watching over a naked toddler playing in the sand.

"We know, Nit Noi," I said.

She slid off the bed onto the sand and hunched up in a ball, weeping quietly. The tears flowed down her cheeks and collected in the sand.

"I solly, I solly," she said, unable to pronounce the "r" properly in her agitated state. She reached out for Iris's hand, but Iris pulled it away. Wiping her tears with the back of her hand, the petite Thai girl said, "I think about her every day. There is not one day I not think about her."

We stood above her, waiting. We didn't have the slightest empathy for the weeping young woman at our feet.

"Where is she?"

"I not know," she said, still crying. "We bring her to fishing boat harbor."

"What happened there?"

"They argue."

"Who?"

"The boat man and three *falangs*."

"What *falangs*?"

"The ones who pay us to get girl."

"What can you tell us about them?"

"They come in red Suzuki jeep. New. One stutter."

"What were they arguing about?"

"The boat man not want to take girl. He say they not tell him *falang* girl. He not agree to do that. He only take girls from Burma and Cambodia."

"What happened then?"

"They say nothing can happen to *falang* girl. They know Burma girl sometimes fall in water after boat man and helper play with her. If anything happen to *falang* girl they cut his wife in pieces with machete. Then his daughters and the daughters of his brothers and sisters are on next boat to Swamp Pak."

"Swamp Pak?" I asked.

She nodded.

"Where is that?"

"I think Cambodia. It is where they take girls."

I knew Cambodia was becoming a hotbed of prostitution and pedophilia, but none of my investigations had ever taken me there.

"What else did you hear?"

"The boat man say he not want to take girl because he scared of harbor police. They look for drugs and girls. He talk about risk. The white girl stand out and he can not hide her in barrel or octopus net. They must pay him not to tell police. He say when money talk, people not talk."

"What happened next?"

"When boat man say he need more money, one *falang* put shocker to neck of helper until he fall. Then he say to boat man, that is your payment. He say the girl not go on this boat, she go on next one. Until then, they keep her in butterfly garden."

"In the butterfly garden?" I asked, surprised.

There are butterfly gardens all over Thailand, gardens enclosed in nets where tourists can go in and see hundreds of different species of butterflies flitting among the flowers and plants in a breathtaking display of their short-lived beauty. I knew there was one on Koh Samui. Was that what she meant?

"Yes, I sure. They say it few times."

"So they didn't put the girl on the boat?" asked Iris in a cracked, halting voice, intervening for the first time.

Nit Noi looked up at her and shook her head. "They put her in car and go away," she said.

"Did they hurt her?" Iris asked.

"No, ma'am. She not understand what happening. We make her sleepy, give her water with little *ya ba* powder."

Ya ba, the crazy pills. Chemical trash. What else did they give the poor girl, I wondered.

"I very solly," Nit Noi said to Iris. "I not know why Buddha let me do this. I dead after this. I think about her every day. I light incense sticks for her. I know what I do will stick to me all my life, even after."

We left her on the beach. What else could we do? Turn her in to the local police, who wouldn't do anything anyway? When the most profitable industry in the region is the sex trade, women and little girls are abducted every day.

Chapter Twenty-Seven

"I want to go to the harbor," Iris said.

"We won't find anything there."

"I don't care. I have to see it with my own eyes."

I steered the motorcycle through the narrow, winding streets of Koh Samui to the fishing harbor and parked it on the dock. A ferry had just tied up. Tourists and backpackers were exiting from the upper deck while a line of motorcycles, followed by cars and light trucks, emerged from the deck below. The passengers and vehicles scattered. Within minutes, the ferry had emptied out.

We stood there gazing at the expanse of blue water. It was as flat and lifeless as a broken mirror. We made the way back in silence, oblivious to the enchanting landscape of Koh Samui around us.

Iris didn't say a word until we were back in the garden of our bungalow. "Why did they take Eden?"

I remained silent.

Iris stared at me, scrutinizing my face, looking for an answer. "Do you think it was just bad luck?"

"I don't believe in bad luck. Malicious intentions and criminal elements are always at work behind the scenes."

"What are you saying?"

"For the time being, we have to assume they didn't choose her at random. And we have to keep looking."

"If...," she started.

I knew she couldn't finish the sentence, so I finished it for her. "If she's still alive."

"Yes. If she's still alive, where will we find her?"

What could I say? What I was really thinking? That we'd find her in some filthy whorehouse waiting for someone to buy her virginity? I hoped it hadn't happened yet. But three months is a long time in a place where flowers wither too quickly, where the life of a young girl is no more than one day in spring. The next time you see her, the flower is already drooping.

"I'm worried that she's in Cambodia. I think Nit Noi pointed us in the right direction."

"Cambodia?" Iris asked, wide-eyed. "What's in Cambodia?"

"A torrent of tears. A monsoon. The flesh market, the exploitation of children—a whole array of atrocities alongside unimaginable beauty."

She didn't cry. In an admirable display of restraint, she said as matter-of-factly as possible, "Let's go."

"Not yet. We're not finished here. A lot of elements have to be in play for a Western girl to disappear. It's not so simple. First of all, we have to find out who the three Westerners in the red jeep were and who they were working for. We have to start scratching at the skin of the monsters. And there are plenty of them here."

"I don't care about that. I didn't come here to settle a score. If there's any chance she's alive, we have to hurry. We have to go to Cambodia and find her."

"Cambodia is an impoverished country. It's dangerous and corrupt. Anything we find out here will shorten our search there."

"I don't like it, but I'll accept that you're the expert. You make the decisions." Without waiting for an answer, she got up and went inside.

The light went on in her room, attracting hundreds of night creatures. They banged into the screen, breaking a wing or a leg, and tried in vain to save themselves. All because they were drawn to the light.

The light went out. I heard Iris weeping and appealed to Guan Yin, the goddess of compassion and mercy who hears the sobbing of every living creature, to send her a ray of comfort. I turned out the lights. Large fruit bats circled above the trees in search of ripe fruit and tasty insects. Little geckos roared like lions. The mosquitoes began biting, out for blood. What a world.

Chapter Twenty-Eight

I t was early in the morning. We made the effort to smile at each other.
"There are a couple of people we have to talk to today," I said.
She raised her eyebrows questioningly.
"A guy I know. His name is Jacob. Then, that attorney, Somnook. How well do you know him?"

Her smile vanished. "I don't like him. All I know is that a lot of people here seem to use him. When are we meeting with him?"

"Twelve."

"I have to look good," she said, sighing. "I'm in no mood to make an impression on anyone, but the man's obsessed with appearances, his and everyone else's."

She disappeared into the bungalow. When she came back out, she was like a beautiful lotus flower. I was definitely impressed. Then I kicked myself for being an idiot. The woman was living a nightmare, and I was checking her out.

"Do I look okay?" she asked.

"Absolutely," I said as coolly as I could manage.

She didn't respond. Her eyes softened as I started up the motorcycle, and she climbed on behind me. It took a while to locate the path to the isolated house surrounded by large rocks that hid it from every direction except the sea. It was Jacob's hideaway, as remote and unseen as he could make it. I switched off the ignition and dialed his number from the burner phone.

"We have to talk."

"I'll meet you in Chaweng at noon," he suggested.

"No. Now."

"It's not really convenient for me now."

"Now," I repeated.

"Where are you?"

"Outside your window."

I heard him catch his breath in surprise. Above us, an electric blind was raised. "I don't believe you're doing this to me," he said before disconnecting.

The door opened. Jacob was standing there in a tracksuit and bare feet. He'd lost a little hair since I'd last seen him, but he was as ghostly pale as ever. Obviously, he didn't expose himself to the bright Thai sun. He let us in.

"Coffee?" he offered.

We nodded.

"Aren't you going to introduce me to the pretty lady?"

"The lady can introduce herself. I'm Iris. Iris Ben-Lev."

He was wise enough to turn his attention to the espresso machine to hide his surprise. The gasp I heard came from Iris, not Jacob.

"Ron, what are you doing here?"

The young man who had appeared seemed equally taken aback. He was wearing a kimono and embroidered slippers. Stammering slightly, he said, jutting out his chin, "Jacob and I are together." He looked uneasily at Jacob, who was holding a glass of espresso in one hand and scratching his head with the other.

I burst out laughing, helping to break the tension and putting everyone more at ease.

"He's your source?"

Jacob nodded. Iris gestured to Ron. "He's the man Sammy bought the hotel from."

It was my turn to be surprised. "Why don't we sit down, have some coffee, and try to make sense of this."

Ron disappeared, returning a few minutes later dressed in cotton pants, a thin button-down shirt, and flip-flops. Jacob raised the large blind, revealing one of Koh Samui's most picturesque sights, a beautifully symmetric horseshoe bay. We drank our coffee in silence, gazing out at the landscape and hoping to absorb some of its beauty before jumping into the shit we knew was coming.

I told Jacob about the boxing match and what they did to Mazor. "I need you to help me get a line on the Israelis here," I said. "Let's start with the short, stocky guy with gray hair and a thin moustache."

"The Judge," Jacob said. "He's the don, the leader of the pack, the brains. But he's also the executioner. Very scary man."

"The tall, slim one is Mandelbaum, right? What's his role?"

"They call him the liaison officer. He's the fixer, the advisor, the middleman. He handles most of the finances, tells them what to invest in, what to declare so it doesn't interfere with their pension rights, their social security benefits. They haven't a clue, so they trust him with their money. He's a snake."

"What about the others?"

"They call themselves the F Brigade. Trash, every one of them. Half of them were forced to take early retirement from the army or the police force. The other half are petty criminals. They get along very well together."

Jacob fell silent.

"What are you thinking?"

"That we're screwed. We made a perfect life for ourselves here, but that's it. It's over."

"Stop whining. There are plenty of nice places in Southeast Asia."

"You don't get it. There's no place like Koh Samui. It's paradise. But when assholes like the F Brigade start setting the tone, they fuck it all up. They don't operate in a vacuum. They're just the tip of the filthy iceberg. Someone saw the potential to make easy money under the table. Ron can tell you exactly how it works."

Ron was holding his coffee. I saw his handshake. "And you think these people are connected to the disappearance of your daughter?" he asked Iris.

She stared at him for a long time before answering. "Yes."

"I want you to know how sorry I was to hear about it," Ron said. "What I'm going to tell you is only meant to help. If there's anything I can do, I'm...," he glanced at Jacob, "we're ready to do it."

All the emotion was making me sick to my stomach.

"There hasn't been any ransom demand," I explained, "so we're looking in other directions. One is a possible connection between Eden's disappearance and the resort project."

"That doesn't make any sense," Ron said decisively.

"Maybe, but we're looking into every possibility. I understand you're still a partner in the project."

"No, not anymore."

I threw a look at Iris.

"I was told you were," she said apologetically.

"We sold our share," Ron said. "We don't have anything to do with it anymore, except for the fact that my ex, Phan, is listed as one of the seven Thai partners the law requires."

"Explain, please."

"Sure, but I have to go back to the beginning. I knew Phan from Silicon Valley. We were partners in a very successful startup. We sold out at just the right time. Each of us ended up with a tidy sum. Very tidy. We were together by then. After a few dream vacations in Thailand, we started to fantasize about a place for people like us. You know, gays. Super refined and relaxing. We thought it would be a wise investment, and it would give us a steady income for our future life together in Thailand."

There was a lot I could say about this annoying little newborn millionaire and his dreams, but I kept it to myself.

"To make a long story short, Phan had a few connections on Koh Samui through a local attorney who's a distant relative of his. You know what Thai families are like, right?"

"You mean Somnook?" I asked.

"How did you know?" Ron asked in surprise.

"I've heard of him."

"Yes, that's him. He's Phan's second cousin. I think their mothers are cousins, or something like that. Anyway, Somnook told us about a great six rai beachfront property south of Chaweng Beach that was up for sale."

"How much is a rai?"

"A little over a third of an acre," Jacob chimed in. "It was a nice chunk of property. Look, there's no chance of getting anything in Chaweng Beach itself these days. The prices are sky-high. One rai goes for three or four million dollars."

"The property he offered us," Ron went on, "was situated in a good spot. Quiet, and not far from Chaweng. So we bought it. We took out a hefty bank loan. The banks here will match your investment dollar for dollar. We invested everything we had. The whole lot."

"How much?" I asked.

"Does it matter?" Ron said, rearranging himself uneasily in his chair.

"It matters very much."

"Four million dollars."

"So it was eight million together with the loan?" Iris asked.

"Yes. But even before construction began, Phan and I realized we'd bitten off more than we could chew. Everything cost an arm and a leg, much more than we anticipated. Our money was being eaten up very quickly. And the minute you show the slightest sign of trouble, the bank is on your back, ready to suck your blood. In a word, we knew we had to sell out. But the prices we were offered here were ridiculously low."

"So that's where Sammy Ben-Lev comes in?"

Ron looked over at Jacob. "Tell him the whole story," Jacob said.

"Look, in Israel, people like to fantasize about easy money. They're sure they're smarter than everyone else. I met Sammy at a party. He jumped at the idea. He said he had the backing of a group of serious investors. In no time, the deal was signed. When he purchased the property from us, the hotel was almost completed. We took a big loss. Easy come, easy go, they say. Anyway, our dream went up in smoke like the money the Chinese burn at funerals. Except that ours was real."

"How much did he pay for it?" Iris asked, breaking into the conversation for the first time.

"I don't know if I ought to reveal the figures," Ron said hesitantly.

"It's important," I said.

"He gave us two million in cash and agreed to give us another two million within a year. We haven't seen the rest of the money," he said, looking at Iris. She was getting whiter by the minute. "Unfortunately, I don't think we ever will."

"Why not?" I asked.

"Rumors say he got in over his head. After we closed the deal, he showed up one day and asked what we thought about the adjacent property. He said he had an opportunity to purchase it for a steal, that the owner was a simple fisherman. I think he said he was a little backward."

"What did you tell him?"

"We gave him our opinion. We thought a small boutique hotel could do very well, but it wouldn't make the millions Sammy wanted. The only way to make that kind of money was to increase the risk, enlarge the resort, and attract A-list tourists. To do that you need beach. The beach in Koh Samui is worth its weight in gold. Every grain of sand weighs a carat. On the face of it, it sounded like a good deal."

"What do you mean, on the face of it?"

"There were rumors. Actually, Phan heard them."

"What rumors?"

"The kind you hear in Thailand," Ron said, trying to get out of the knot he had tied himself in.

"Tell me." This time, it wasn't a question. I'd stopped being nice.

"They said the fisherman wasn't the fool Sammy thought he was, that he was the cousin of the head of the Koh Samui civil engineering department."

"What are you trying to say?"

"I'm not trying to say anything," Ron sputtered. His face went red and then white. "I'm sorry, Iris. This conversation is making me very uncomfortable. I feel very bad about the whole situation."

"Can I say something?" Jacob chimed in. "I'm going to be blunt. The minute Sammy arrived on Koh Samui he acted like a coconut. Ever see a coconut washed up on shore? That's what he was. He saw the hotel, and realized he was onto a good deal and planted roots. But that's not enough. You have to grow. And you can't grow alone, or you'll shrivel up and die."

I was hoping he was done with the botanical metaphors, but when Jacob gets going, nothing will stop him. "When Sammy bought the adjacent property," he went on, "they pulled a fast one on him. And when he realized he'd fallen like ripe fruit into their hands, he did the same thing to the next in line. Whether he did it on purpose or he was forced to, I can't say."

"Explain," I said again, although I was starting to get the picture.

"After he bought the hotel from Ron and Phan, he decided to go big, add more rooms, turn it into a fancy resort. He was offered the adjacent beachfront and he got all excited. He thought he could eat the simple fisherman for breakfast. Then he found out that the fisherman had a distant cousin who was the head of the island's civil engineering department, and another one who happened to be the deputy governor. That was all news to him. And he didn't know the island was run by five families. If he understood how things work here, finding out about the guy's family connections would have been his first warning bell. But he thought he had God by the balls. He negotiated with the owner of the property, and they came to an agreement. He gave them a large initial payment and went to Bangkok Bank to get a matching loan. The bank holds the lien on a lot of properties in Thailand, properties bought by a lot of Sammys. They checked the papers, and it turned out the plot he purchased is classified as agricultural land. He wouldn't get planning permission for anything more than a lean-to. That's when he realized he'd been taken for a ride. But he didn't give up. He decided to fight back."

"Meaning?"

"He figured he could get the land reclassified."

"Is that possible?"

"It's the same in Thailand as in Israel. Anything's possible," Jacob said with a smile. "The only question is how much it's going to cost you and how many palms you're willing to grease. The list is pretty long, practically as long as a list of wedding guests. It starts with the public servants who have to sign off on it and ends with the senior officials who want a piece of the pie. And there's no guarantee you'll get what you want in the end."

"Give me figures."

"Look," Jacob said, "I can only give you estimates. We're talking about two and a half acres of beachfront property. I'd say he probably paid around two million dollars for the adjacent beach, and he'd need another three or four million to build the resort. That doesn't include what he'd already paid Ron and what he promised to pay him later."

I let out a whistle. It was a lot of money. Sammy must be carrying a debt of close to ten million.

Jacob seemed to have read my mind. "That's where Israelis take a beating. They have big plans, but they don't want to pay."

"I thought you said Sammy understood what he had to do," I said.

"Maybe he did, and maybe he didn't. Even if he did, I don't think he liked it. Nobody likes to feel they've been played for a fool. It was a big slap in the face. He'd poured millions into worthless sand. My source tells me that even at this early stage, he laid out around a quarter of a million and promised at least a million more. All under the table." He turned to Iris, who'd been listening quietly. "I'm sorry, but that's the truth."

She didn't respond. Her face seemed frozen.

"The question is, how much capital did he have, and where did he go to get the rest?" I said.

"The gray market," Jacob replied.

"The gray market is just a euphemism for organized crime," I said. "I need a name."

"According to the rumors I picked up on, he rolled the deal over to the Russian-Israeli mafia, sold them the same worthless sand he was sold. The name that keeps coming up is Yuri Cezar. He's the godfather. They call him Thainik. If that's true, then Sammy must have the balls of an elephant. Or else he's a dumb ass who has no idea who he's dealing with. But I find that hard to believe."

"You don't watch enough National Geographic," I said. "You can't see an elephant's balls because they're inside. And they're about the same size as a rabbit's."

Jacob laughed. Iris didn't. Ron fidgeted uneasily.

"Look," Ron said with a sigh, "if you think the Thais are morons, I can tell you they're not. You just don't see it because they hide their feelings. Keeping a cold heart, they call it. Showing emotions is a sign of weakness. But Israelis interpret their blank faces as a sign they're feeble-minded. And the Thais use that to their advantage."

"What are you trying to say?" Iris asked. Her voice was as sharp as a knife.

"That they sold Sammy sand for the price of gold, and when Sammy sold it on, he stirred up a hornet's nest in the form of the Russian-Israeli mob."

The ensuing silence was not only long, but heavy. It felt like we were in an abandoned building waiting for the wrecking ball to land, leaving us standing in a pile of rubble. I saw the look on Iris's face. The picture Jacob had painted of her husband was less than rosy. In fact, it was very dark. I wondered if she had lived with him without any sense of who he really was. She didn't seem to be the naïve type.

"That still doesn't explain what happened to Eden," I said.

"That's your job," Jacob said.

I pictured the little girl with the big smile and green eyes. I didn't want to think of her as collateral for an unpaid debt. I saw the fear in Iris's eyes, but she wasn't crying. I imagined she didn't have any tears left.

"I didn't know anything about it. I should have known," she said. I didn't know who she was apologizing to. Certainly not me. Maybe Eden.

Chapter Twenty-Nine

S omnook's law firm was located in a modern office building. The doorman, in a white shirt and cap, raised his head from a bowl of noodles. "Khun Somnook, third floor," he said before going back to inhaling noodles, working his chopsticks rapidly. The sound of clinking and sucking followed us all the way to the elevator.

The elevator opened straight into Somnook's office. In the lobby was a stunning collection of display cases in which butterflies in glorious gem-like colors were pinned. Every species of moth and butterfly in Thailand seemed to be represented, including some that were larger than songbirds. The collection immediately brought to mind the butterfly garden, and I imagined Iris was thinking the same thing. When we entered his office, Somnook was standing by a table with a small aquarium on it. Inside were pale sand, two plants, and a black tarantula of the type the Thais call "evil" or "vicious." The lid was open. Somnook was holding a forked stick with a butterfly at the tip. The tarantula waited, motionless. The butterfly struggled to escape, but it was wasted effort. Without warning, the spider was on the stick, nearly as high as Somnook's hand. The attorney quickly dropped the stick. By the time it hit the bottom of the aquarium, the butterfly was already in the tarantula's mouth.

Somnook straightened up, caught sight of us, and gave us a big smile that revealed a perfect set of pearly white teeth. He looked very polished in an Armani suit, as fresh as if it had just come off the hanger, a matching tie, Italian shoes, and a diamond pin in his lapel. His thickly gelled hair stood up in carefully arranged spikes. He was clearly the product of some elite boarding school far from the heat and humidity of Thailand, a man who would never use public transportation and would certainly never go on foot under the broiling sun.

"It's a nasty creature, your tarantula," I said.

"Yes. Fast and furious," he said in a flawless Oxford accent. "The alter ego of the typical slow, diffident Thai."

He didn't shake my hand, maybe because of the showcase of gold rings on his fingers, each one studded with a whole mine of precious gems. Everything in the office looked expensive and refined. We took our seats in elegant mahogany chairs at either side of a matching desk ornately carved with hundreds of figures, trees, and flowers. Somnook clapped his hands, and his secretary rolled in a drinks cart, giving me time to review his outstandingly successful life history displayed in photographs on the wall: coming on stage to accept his law degree at Oxford, bowing his head to receive a blessing from a chubby bald monk in an orange robe; shaking hands with any number of Thai dignitaries, all of them, including him, in custom-tailored suits and all with the identical contortion on their faces they like to call a smile.

The secretary poured green tea into tiny cups and cold water into tall, ice-filled glasses. As she quietly closed the door behind her, Somnook asked, "So, how can I help you?"

I was taken aback by his directness, so atypical of the Thais. "My name is Dotan Naor. I'm a private investigator. I was hired by the lady," I said, nodding toward Iris, "to find her daughter, Eden Ben-Lev. I'm sure you've heard of her. She went missing a little over three months ago."

"A very sad story," he said. "Madam, I have indeed heard of your tragedy. It broke my heart."

When your enemies start dripping honey, that's the time to beware. "Khun Somnook," I said, using the term of respect in an attempt to soften the question, "Do you have any idea who abducted Eden?"

"It is so out of keeping with Buddhist values that I find it hard to imagine any Thai could be responsible," he replied.

I exchanged a glance with Iris. I knew what she was thinking.

"Have you ever heard of the butterfly garden?" I asked.

"As you can see, I have a fondness for butterflies, especially in display cases. There are a lot of butterfly gardens in Thailand. The one on Koh Samui is particularly interesting. It supplies me with whatever specimens I ask for. There are beautiful butterflies on the island, some of the rarest species in all of Thailand. As you know, the life of a butterfly is very short. It emerges from the chrysalis, spreads its wings, makes its first flight, releases pheromones, mates, and dies. A single day in spring. Very sad, and thoroughly inevitable."

Another poet, I thought. A whole generation of slippery eels that doesn't give a damn about traditional Buddhist values has grown up here, crooks who invoke the name of Buddha as easily as putting on an Armani suit. No, not eels. They're *nagas*, the seven-headed serpents more deadly than venom-spitting cobras.

"Thank you," I said. "We're grateful to you for the lesson on butterflies."

"I'm not finished," Somnook responded. "Do you know how many enemies butterflies have? Birds, lizards, frogs, spiders as you saw, and the most dangerous of all—collectors. There are many butterfly collectors who are willing to pay large sums of money for them."

I was dying to put my hand on the edge of his neck, where it meets the shoulder, and press down a little. Just enough to stop the flow of venom. I despised the way he spoke in riddles. He must think we're idiots. I could see Iris had the same reaction. Her hands were clenched into tight fists.

"What's the price of a butterfly?"

"The cheapest ones, like the common tiger moth, can cost twenty or thirty dollars. But a rare species of papilionidae can go for thousands. Now imagine a rare butterfly is discovered, one with unusual colors or shape. Then things become even more interesting. If a serious collector wants it, nothing will stand in his way."

He looked directly at Iris, who didn't bat an eyelash.

I was losing patience with his innuendos. "What can you tell us about her husband's hotel? How was Sammy Ben-Lev financing it?"

Somnook's smile vanished instantly. His face turned cold and expressionless. "I can tell you that Sammy cheated me and disappeared."

Iris was stunned. "What do you mean disappeared? He's in Israel, taking care of other business."

"Really?" The question was dripping with sarcasm. "Did you know he owes five million to the bank? They want their money, with interest, so they come to me. Khun Somnook, they say, where's the money from your *falang*? The beach administration wants their fee of two hundred thousand dollars, and the engineering department wants another hundred thousand for the permits. And then Russian mobsters show up in my office, and they also demand money. Are you sure you want me to go on? There's a long list."

"Why do they come to you?" I asked.

"Why?" He was losing patience. "Because I'm his registered local partner, as the law requires. Sammy must come back. He must take care of his affairs here and pay what he owes."

"As his partner, you're not responsible for any of it?

"No. My share in the partnership is just on paper, to satisfy the legal requirements. But I'm getting all the pressure. Everyone wants their money, but there's no Sammy and no money."

"What do you want?" Iris asked evenly, as if her only interest was the business side of Sammy's fuckup.

"What do I want?" Somnook began twisting the gold ring on his finger. It was studded with a ruby that could easily have adorned the crown of the queen of England. When a Thai loses control, things start getting interesting. "What do I want?" he repeated, spitting the words out like a snake spitting venom. "I want my money and all the money he owes. Do you know what will happen if I don't get it?"

He didn't wait for an answer.

"If he doesn't pay up, you won't get your daughter back. That much I know."

That brought me to my feet.

"Don't even think of reaching your claws out in my direction," he said.

I had no intention of getting down and dirty with this piece of shit. With lightning speed, I reached into the aquarium. The tarantula was drowsy after sucking the life out of the butterfly. I picked the woozy bug up with two fingers and threw it into Somnook's lap. It quickly came to life, and started climbing up his elegant Armani suit toward the exposed skin of his neck. Tarantula bites are no fun. I say "bites" because it bites its victim more than once. The question was if Somnook was allergic to the spider's venom or not. It was an interesting question, but we didn't wait to find out the answer. I grabbed Iris's hand, and we walked out the door, leaving a screaming Somnook behind us and almost bumping into the secretary, who was rushing into her boss's office.

Chapter Thirty

Iris took my arm and looked me straight in the eye. "Sammy asked my father for a loan. If only he'd given it to him."

"Don't start blaming yourself."

"What were you thinking, throwing that spider on him?" she said sharply. "We could be arrested. You gave him an excellent way to get rid of us."

I pointed toward the mountains of Koh Samui, a primordial rain forest and a good place to hide. "Let's go find the butterfly garden," I said.

We got on the motorcycle and headed toward the interior of the island. The Khao Pom mountain towered above us. It had rained, and the snaking road was still wet and slippery. The mountain peak was covered in thick fog from the mist that rose after the rain.

Finally, we saw it, a large old sign pointing the way to the butterfly garden. We went another half mile at a slow pace, until we caught sight of a hidden valley between the cliffs. We saw a bare concrete building in front of a few crumbling mud huts. The straw roofs were covered in blue tarps to keep out the rain. A sign on the building read "Butterfly Valley Hotel."

The dilapidated structure might once have been a nice hotel, but now the concrete was cracked, the iron railings were rusted, the roots of ficus and cotton trees were taking over the entrance, and bougainvillea that had grown to enormous proportions were climbing up the few utility poles still standing.

A young woman was standing by the bushes where clothes were drying. When she saw us, she rapidly gathered up the laundry and hurried toward the building, glancing anxiously behind her. Iris called out to her, but she just quickened her pace and disappeared inside.

We followed her in. Wooden doors were hanging off rusty hinges, and mildewed mattresses were piled up in the corners. A snake curled up in the sun was frightened by the shadow we cast and crawled into an old mattress. Huge cockroaches strolled leisurely across the floor. We heard the sound of bats on the high ceiling above us.

"What's going on here?" Iris asked.

I gave her an encouraging smile as we continued to follow the young woman until we lost sight of her. A circle of light appeared in the dark corridor and we heard a loud bark followed by the sharp command, "Adolph!"

A large wolfhound was standing in the light. It didn't growl, simply stood there, blocking our path. "Stay close to me," I said to Iris. The dog was intimidating, but it was still a dog. Again, we heard the command "Adolph" and a sharp whistle. The dog turned around and disappeared.

We went out to the back. At first glance, we seemed to be in an ordinary Thai village. But there were no farmers leading wooden plows drawn by water buffalo, no women sifting rice or weaving palm leaves for a new roof. There were no flooded rice paddies, no fruit trees, no pigs or chickens. Just a few decaying huts that looked utterly neglected. Young girls were sitting in front of them. Some were Thai, but I could also identify faces with the characteristic features of the Khmer from Cambodia, the Mon from Myanmar, and the Hmong and Miao minorities from China.

As soon as they saw us, they scattered into the huts, and their young faces began appearing in the cracks, staring out at us. A lot of dark eyes, round or almond-shaped, in yellow or brown faces with broad flat cheekbones. The eyes were curious, frightened, and astonished at one and the same time. A white man and woman had appeared out of nowhere.

We were no less astonished than they were. Iris hung on tightly to my hand. There was a heavy odor of organic compost in the air, as if we had entered a sealed, humid greenhouse that had been neglected for a long time, leaving the plants to rot.

In front of the largest hut, a fire was burning in a circle of sooty stones. A man in a wheelchair was leaning over it, roasting meat on a long fork.

"What the hell are you doing here?" he demanded in a heavy German accent.

He rose from the wheelchair, still holding the fork. The dog salivated at the sight of the fat dripping from the meat. The man looked at us with dull black eyes. Any spark of life that had once been in them had gone out long ago. His tall, thin body was wrapped in a faded red bathrobe, a small ratty rug was draped over his shoulders, and his bare veiny feet rested on the rusty foot pads of the wheelchair. He was almost entirely bald, the remaining hair hanging in dirty clumps at the back of his head.

"Adolph," he commanded, "come!"

The dog took up a position beside the wheelchair, still staring hungrily at the dripping meat.

"Iris, come out here," he shouted in the direction of one of the huts.

The Iris beside me shuddered and held on to me even tighter. She tried to catch the eyes of the girls, but they were focused only on the man.

A scrawny elderly Thai woman emerged from the hut. She was dressed like a bride on her wedding day, in a purple sarong and drooping orchids in her graying black hair. There was a hint of madness in her eyes, along with opium-induced serenity. She was holding a long thin pipe stained brown from years of use.

"Ja, Heinrich *mein liebling?*" she asked, addressing him as her lover.

The man twisted around in his chair, waving the fork in the air. The dog hungrily followed the movement of the fork. "What are these people doing here?" he asked in English. His voice cracked from the effort and irritation, making his German accent even heavier.

"Maybe they want girl, nice little girl," the old woman said, giggling. "Heinrich, *mein liebling*, you like the fat?"

"Are you here for a girl?" the man asked us. The woman tottered toward him, her bare feet moving in the small steps of a Thai dancer as she puffed on her opium pipe. "Choose nice little girl. We have many girls. Choose any one you want and we give you good price," the woman said, giggling again. "Iris," the German roared, shaking in his chair. His black eyes had come alive. He tried to move forward, but he didn't have the strength in his arms to propel the wheelchair.

The old woman sat down outside a hut. The girls came out hesitantly and gathered around her. She pulled a brush from her sarong and began passing it through her hair. The girls started weaving it into a thick braid. She was still giggling.

My Iris went over to her and showed her the picture of Eden.

"Do you recognize this girl?"

The old woman didn't stop giggling. The man squealed with rage, attempting to spit in my direction.

"*Jude*," he thundered in disgust. "You're *Jude*, Jews. I can tell. Go away."

I showed him another picture of Eden and he again tried to spit on me. The slap I landed on his cheek made the whole wheelchair rock, throwing his head to the side. The fork fell to the ground. The dog bolted down the meat and then sat down next to the fork, pinning its eyes on it and licking its black face with its pink tongue.

"Where is she?" I demanded, holding the picture up in front of him.

The German straightened up in his chair and whispered venomously, "She warmed my bed. She sat here." His chubby fingers with filthy black nails gestured to the space between his legs. "She sat here and licked my dick." He laughed spasmodically, his body jerking uncontrollably in the chair. "You ever see a girl who gets it for the first time?" he asked, still laughing. I knew the contemptible old man was lying, but I couldn't stop shaking. Iris looked at him with eyes sunken in misery.

"First, she opens her eyes wide from the pain, and then she says the most wonderful word in the world: mommy, mommy. Oh, *Jude*, you don't know how good that feels. If you only knew."

I couldn't listen anymore. I shoved the wheelchair into the sun. He tried to shield his eyes from the bright light, but I grabbed a clump of hair and pulled his head back so that his eyes were pointing directly at the sky. "Take a good look," I said, "because you're not going to see sunlight much longer."

In a strange wail that was meant to be a laugh, the German said, "I know. I'm dying. A girl gave me her smut. So young, and already diseased. They give you pleasure, grant you life, but they also give you the kiss of death. Gonorrhea, syphilis, AIDS, whatever. I'm eaten up inside. I'll be dead soon. But you, *Jude*, you're not going to find your little girl."

He knew I could easily break his neck, but he also knew I wasn't going to do it.

"She's not here. You know where she is? I'll tell you. It's no secret. She's in the best place for little girls. Cambodia." He aimed for another laugh, but immediately started coughing, nearly choking. We walked away from the decaying old German and his doped-up bride who traded in the flesh of young girls. They were both dead. It was just a matter of time.

Chapter Thirty-One

Tel Aviv

The phone was ringing. Boris Chiplonak looked for it in vain under a pile of fabric. By the time he found it, he was so aggravated that he spat into it, "If I knew you stuttered, I never would have let you work for me."

He listened and then asked, "What about the girl? Where is she now? She better get there in time, or you'll pay the price."

He listened again. "Okay, I got it."

He pulled out a Pall Mall, tore off the filter, and flung it out onto the sidewalk. Then he lit the cigarette and pressed a number on the phone.

"Cezar," he said.

He heard the hoarse sound of coughing. "Yeah, what?"

"The girl's on the way. Everything's fine. It's been taken care of."

"Really?"

The blood in Boris's veins began to freeze.

"You're fucking with me, Boris. I poured two million dollars into worthless sand in Thailand, and you're telling me it's been taken care of? I try to put my hands on a little girl to get my money back and look what a mess you make of it. That fucking asshole Dotan Naor is on Koh Samui, and you say everything's fine? You leave tracks any imbecile could follow, and you tell me everything's fine? What's wrong with you?! Now I hear that Sammy Ben-Lev is following his bitch to Koh Samui. The girl is already old news and

139

now they're raising a fuss again and you still think everything's fine? What is it? I don't pay you enough? Lately, whenever you tell me everything's fine, it isn't long before I find out it isn't. You trying to fuck with me? If you are, just say so. Don't hold back. I want to know."

Boris was in shock. Yuri Cezar was a man of few words. At most, he barked or growled. And now? He'd never heard him talk so much. "Yuri, I swear, everything will be fine."

"Listen up, Boris. I gave you one little thing to take care of, one little girl. And you made a *pizdets* of it, a total fuckup. You know what that does to my reputation? I hear the word 'fine' one more time, and you don't want to know what I'll do to you."

Cezar disconnected. Boris stood there, feeling as if his limbs were being torn off. If Yuri's right, he thought, then someone is screwing with me big time, and I don't even know it. To get his mind working again, he did the only thing he knew. He got a bottle of vodka from the refrigerator and took a piece of herring left over from the day before out of its newspaper wrapping. A bite of fish and a sip of vodka was enough to start calming his nerves. Fish are weird, he thought. Every fish eats a smaller fish, and then a shark shows up and eats the biggest one. But the shark can still choke on it, or its stomach can explode. Laughing to himself, he knew just what he was going to do. He was nobody's patsy.

He pressed a number, but it went to voice mail. "Sergey," he said into the machine, "why don't you answer your phone? Listen up, because I'm not going to call again. Take him out. You understand? Finish him off."

There was only one more call he had to make.

"Mandelbaum," he said into the phone, "Sammy Ben-Lev is arriving on Koh Samui today."

"What am I supposed to do about it?" Mandelbaum asked.

"Keep an eye on him, that's all."

A bunch of morons, every last one of them, Boris thought after ending the call. He picked up the near-empty vodka bottle and poured the last drops down his dry throat.

Chapter Thirty-Two

Koh Samui

T he biker stopped in front of Shiloh's Place and switched off the ignition. Taking off his helmet with the dark visor, he hung it on the handlebar. Without the helmet, his bald head gleamed in the sunlight. Sammy Ben-Lev was sitting at a corner table where he couldn't be seen from the door. His back was to the wall. He was dressed in a white shirt with rolled-up sleeves and perfectly pressed black trousers, looking totally unbothered by the heat and humidity. His black suit jacket was hanging over the back of the chair. On the table in front of him were a cup of espresso and an ashtray holding a lit Marlboro Gold.

The hefty biker looked around and then strode straight to Sammy. Without a word, he sat down at his table. "I've been following them," he said. "They found the German. Before that, they talked to that slick lawyer. What's his name?"

"Somnook," Sammy replied. He picked up the cigarette, inhaled, and blew two streams of smoke out of his nose. "We'll have to take care of him too at some point. He's been dogging me. The piece of shit screwed me good. He could've warned me, could've told me Yuri thinks I sold him worthless sand. I thought I had it all under control, but the motherfucker didn't say anything. All he wanted was his money. That's all he cared about, his fucking percentage."

Raising an eyebrow, the biker leaned closer to Sammy. He could see the bags under his eyes. "Are you okay?"

"Why?"

He pulled a cellphone out of his jacket pocket and played the recording of his last conversation with Boris Chiplonak: "Take him out. You understand? Finish him off."

"He means me?"

The biker let out something like an "uh-huh."

"So?"

"You recognize the voice?"

Sammy shook his head.

"His name is Boris Chiplonak. But he's not the only one. Mandelbaum called me. The F Brigade is looking for a hitman."

That name was very familiar to Sammy. "Why?"

"To take you out." Sergey Korpichov, Flathead, burst out laughing, causing the tattoos on his neck to convulse. "They figured out you conned them."

Now, it was Sammy's turn to laugh. He pulled on his cigarette.

"What do you want me to do?" Flathead asked.

"I think it's time to get rid of that Dotan my wife is trailing around after."

"Think about it and let me know. I promise you there's a solution to every problem."

"What do you mean?"

"There are lots of ways to go about it," Sergey answered. Without taking even a second to consider, he went on. "That bike they're riding around on, a Honda Africa Twin, it's got a powerful engine. But it's not worth much if a Toyota Landcruiser happens to swerve into it. Both the rider and anyone sitting behind him are going to suffer a serious head injury for sure. Whether or not they're wearing a helmet. Capisce?"

"That's my wife you're talking about," Sammy said angrily.

"I thought that's what you wanted, no?"

Sammy remained silent.

"Look," Sergey said, "if it's just him you want to take out of the game, it's no problem. I can send a gang of local bullies to break a few limbs. Or I can do it myself."

"I hear it's not so easy."

The big man laughed. Surprisingly, his laughter was genuine. Sammy realized the muscle he'd hired was getting a big kick out of the whole thing. "Bullshit. My granny In Odessa called a person like him a *kleine menshechele*, a little man."

"That's not what I hear."

"What do you hear?" Sergey asked, amused.

"I hear he's a master of martial arts, that he practiced kung-fu for years in China, and that something bad always happens to anyone who comes up against him, either mentally or physically."

"Bullshit," Sergey repeated, choosing not to mention what had transpired in the stairwell. "People brag. What can an unarmed man do if you point a gun at him and you know how to use it?"

"All I want is for him to give up the search. Without him around, my wife will simmer down and come home."

Sergey nodded his big head. Satisfied, Sammy went on to the next subject.

"What about the information I asked you to get? What did you find out?"

Sergey remained silent.

Sammy puffed on his cigarette impatiently.

"Say something."

"After what I did for you, I want to see some hard cash first."

"Why? What did you do?"

"I gave the filthy German what's coming to him. Motherfucking scumbag."

"What?" Sammy exploded. "How are we going to get anything out of him now?"

"Don't worry. I did what we used to do to the Taliban in Afghanistan. He was grilling himself a nice little meal of sausages and bacon, so I just joined in the fun. I added his feet to the grill. That was before I strangled the motherfucker and broke his neck." Sergey burst out laughing.

"What's so funny?"

"It's a private joke," the big man said. "I let the girls out. They flew off, disappeared in a second."

That took Sammy by surprise. "Did he talk first?"

"Talk? He sang like a nightingale. They don't even sing like that in Chabad House on Friday night."

Sammy waited for him to go on.

"She was there. Your kid. I showed him the picture you gave me. He recognized her immediately. The dates matched, too."

The blood drained from Sammy's face. He was usually as cold as ice, but when it came to his own daughter, the ice broke. He made an effort to keep his voice steady. "Where is she now? Did he say?"

"Cambodia. He sent her on a boat with some other girls like they told him. They have plans for her. The asshole thought it was funny. Said he'd be glad if they brought him a few more gifts like her."

"Gifts, huh?" Sammy repeated with disgust, "Did he say who?"

"Yup," Sergey answered. "He even took pleasure in telling me. You wouldn't believe how much pleasure a man can get from singing when you hold his feet in coals. He gave me the names, each and every one of them. Israelis. He said they were good clients. They come, pick up some merchandise, use it a little, and then bring it back and exchange it for something new. And they pay extra without even haggling. He said he did good business with them, especially because they had strange taste. He had no problem selling them the ones the Chinese and Japanese won't touch."

"I really don't want to hear the details," Sammy said. "Just give me the names. All of them." He lit another cigarette from the butt of the last one and chugged down the last of the strong bitter coffee, holding the cup so tight that his knuckles turned white.

"The F Brigade," Sergey said. Enjoying himself immensely. "The core members. They're all in on it, every single one of them."

"The F Brigade? Who?" Sammy was shaking with rage. "I want the names."

"You know them very well," Sergey answered. "The liaison officer Mandelbaum, the one they call Simple Simon, some guy called Aaron from Hadera, and of course, the Judge."

"But who were they working for? Who ordered her abduction?"

"Do I have to tell you? You know the answer," Sergey said.

"Yuri Cezar?" Sammy asked, whispering the name.

CHAPTER THIRTY-TWO

Sergey nodded.

"Why Cambodia?"

"I told you, he has plans for her if you don't pay up."

Sammy didn't reply. Flathead gazed at him in silence. Then he took a cigarette from Sammy's pack, lit it, and called to the man behind the bar, "Coffee."

Shiloh examined Sammy Ben-Lev and the big man with him. He could feel in his bones that trouble was brewing. Letting out a sigh, he thought to himself, that's it, the good times for Israelis on Koh Samui are over. He knew that as soon as there was trouble in paradise, it was just a matter of time before he'd have to pack his bags and start over somewhere else. He brought Sergey his coffee.

"You're going to have a lot of work," Sammy said. Sergey could see the flashes of rage and hatred in his eyes. "There'll be nothing but scorched earth left by the time I'm through here."

Sergey wasn't stupid. An overgrown thug with a Russian accent and prison tats isn't necessarily a moron. He sat there thinking. His relationship with Boris Chiplonak was a thing of the past. Boris had dishonored him, and from that moment on, he owed him nothing. He was a free man.

"You want to make a deal?" he asked. He kept his voice neutral, but inside, he was thinking, come on already, gimme a chance to make some money here, asshole. Gimme something, fancy man, you stinking idiot.

"What do you want?" Sammy asked, leaning toward him and looking around to make sure no one was listening.

"A hundred thousand for the whole job."

"A hundred thousand what?" Sammy asked.

"U.S."

"Are you out of your mind?" Sammy exclaimed, raising his voice and nearly jumping out of his chair. Remembering where he was, he lowered his voice. "For a thousand, two at most, I can get rid of anyone I want on this island."

"Chill, Sammy. It's a small price to pay to clean up all the shit you stirred up. Fifty thousand sound better? Ten thousand a head. You're getting a bargain."

Sammy lit another cigarette. "Okay," he said. "We're talking about everyone who had a hand in taking my daughter. Specifically, the three bastards and the slimy judge who likes little girls. And make them suffer. I want their souls to hurt even after they're gone. Got it?"

"What about Dotan?"

"As far as I'm concerned, you can cut off his balls before you take him out."

"Why? You think he's doing your wife?"

Sammy's face went bright red from fury. Swallowing, he spat, "That's none of your business."

Flathead laughed. "Whatever you say, boss." He knew he'd have Sammy in his pocket for a long time to come. "I need ten up front."

"It'll take me a few days to get it together," Sammy replied. "But you'll get it. You can get started."

"I wasn't born yesterday, Sammy. But you know what? I'll do it for you as a gesture of good faith."

Shiloh called out, "You guys want something to eat?"

He came over, took their order, and returned to his place behind the bar. But his ears were tuned to their conversation like antennae, picking up every word.

"You're a lawyer, right?" Sergey asked after their business had been concluded.

"Yeah. So what?"

"It doesn't bother you what you're doing? I heard you used to be a top gun in your profession, and what're you doing now? Setting scores with losers? What does that say about you?"

"Yeah, I used to be a real hotshot," Sammy said bitterly. "Until I realized that everyone was cheating everyone else just to get rich. They all want to be close to the sources of power and money, whoever they are. Prosecutors don't have any problem setting up a chump who has to look up to see the poverty line or a nobody who deals drugs on the corner, but they don't mess with the big fish. Why risk it? Trust me, it finally sank in."

"Nice speech," Sergey said, "but what's your point?"

"There's no such thing as truth or justice, just predator and prey. It's very simple."

"You had to waste time at university to find that out? I learned it the first time I set foot on the street in Odessa. I could have taught you for free."

"Nothing's free," Sammy said.

"So what does that say about us?"

"What us? You and me?"

"No," Flathead said, "all of us."

"That you don't get anything you don't take by force."

Shiloh put a grilled cheese sandwich down in front of Sergey, the melted cheese and tomato seeping out of the edges of the crusty bread. The big man let out something between a hum and a grunt and started bolting it down. Sammy watched in silence.

When Sergey was done, he wiped his mouth daintily with a napkin, scooped up the crumbs from the table with his huge hand, and shook them out on the plate.

"Okay, so when do I see the money?" he asked.

"Two days, three at most," Sammy answered.

"I hope you're not fucking with me," Sergey warned. "Cause I'm going to start on the job, and once I get started, I don't stop."

He stood up and walked out. A young Thai girl was leaning on his bike. He pinched her ass, and she straightened up, startled. "Hey, big man," she said, "You want take me for ride?"

Flathead picked her up and placed her on the saddle, laughing as he bent down to retrieve the flip-flop that had fallen from her foot. "Let's go," he said. "I'll give you a little something in advance."

Chapter Thirty-Three

Sammy entered the Chaweng Beach branch of the Bank of Bangkok, walked past the row of tellers, who didn't even raise their eyes, and went straight to the manager's office. A Thai of Chinese extraction, the manager was a slick, polished gentleman in thick-framed glasses. Long hairs were growing from a mole on his chin. Sammy knew from previous visits that he had a habit of stroking those hairs when he was pleased. At that moment, his hand was gliding over them again and again.

Sammy took a seat opposite the manager, who smiled, took out a sheaf of documents, and spread them out on his desk. They were all statements of the savings accounts of foreign residents. The bank put on a welcoming face to such people. Like others who retired to Thailand, each member of the F Brigade had opened an account in the bank, deposited his savings in it, and had his pension and social security benefits transferred there every month. What they didn't realize was that the document they signed when they opened the account contained a sub-clause no one ever bothered to read. Clause 7b, to be precise. Actually, they couldn't have read it even if they wanted to since the document was in Thai, and most of the bank clerks didn't know enough English to translate it for them. Even those who did know English would find it hard to explain the meaning of the clause in simple terms. In short, it stipulated that in the case of the death of the account owner for any reason, the funds would revert to the bank, and any heirs would have to prove their legal right to the money. The parties agreed that the Court of Thailand would have exclusive jurisdiction over any such proceedings.

The first statement Sammy looked at belonged to Aaron Algabari, Aaron from Hadera, who had forty-two thousand dollars in his account. The next three statements bore the name of Joseph Mandelbaum, whose accounts totaled two hundred and seventy-two thousand dollars. Sammy raised his eyes. "Nice, huh?" he said with a smile.

The manager kept silent, his expression as inscrutable as ever. Only his hand moved more quickly over the mole hairs. Sammy quickly reviewed the remaining statements. Simon Ben-Shetach, Simple Simon, fifty-four thousand; Joseph Ben-Dosa, the Judge, a hefty two hundred and fifty thousand. There were other names, most of which Sammy had never heard before. What difference did it make? All the names would be erased soon enough.

Sammy straightened the pile of documents. "The accounts will disappear?" he asked.

Stroking the hairs on his chin, the manager answered, "As if they never existed."

"Your regular commission?"

"No. It's twenty percent this time. And that's a bargain."

Sammy was taken aback. The slick Chinaman is trying to squeeze me, he thought. "Not going to happen," he said. "I'm bearing most of the risk. Fifteen percent, and that's a lot more than I intended."

The manager took a sip of the tepid tea in front of him. "No," he said. He was still a cold-hearted Chinese-Thai bank manager. Emotions didn't matter. All that mattered was how much he got out of the deal. "I've got extra expenses. The district manager's daughter is getting married this month, and I have to bring a worthy gift. I might even have to pay part of the cost. The IT manager is waiting for me to invite him to dinner at a Chinese restaurant, and I have to pay for the food, the drinks, and the hostesses," he said calmly.

"Let me do the math," Sammy said.

"I already did," the manager answered. "The accounts come to one million seven thousand dollars. I get my twenty percent total of two hundred and one thousand. No less. And you come out ahead. Far far ahead."

"Done," Sammy said. "How much time do you need after death is pronounced?"

The manager took off his glasses and polished them with a small chamois cloth. "How soon do you need the money?"

"Twenty-four hours," Sammy answered. "After that, I'm taking off for Cambodia."

"That's not out of the question," the manager said, replacing his glasses. "But you'll have to add five thousand dollars for my IT man so he'll make it look like the sums have been withdrawn over the past two or three months."

They didn't shake hands. You don't shake in the East. At most, you go to a restaurant, eat a fancy dinner, and get drunk. Then you smile and know you've closed the deal. Sammy simply nodded and walked out.

The manager watched him leave through the glass door. Stroking his mole hairs gently, he did the calculations in his head. How much he would pay for the twenty-four carat gold bracelet for his wife, in the hopes that that would be enough for her. Add the price of an imperial jade necklace for mistress number one so she didn't nag him all the time and an electric bike for his Russian doll with the amazing bosom he dreamed about every night. All very wise investments, he thought, smiling to himself.

When Sammy's phone rang, he wasn't surprised by the timing. He knew there was no such thing as coincidence.

"What's up, Sammy?"

"Everything's going great," he said truthfully.

"When can we get together?" Mandelbaum asked. "There are a few things we have to iron out. The guys have been restless lately. They're worried. They want to see some collateral."

"No problem," Sammy answered. "Give me a day or two to get everything in order. I don't see why they need collateral, but if that's what they want, no problem."

"Is our investment safe, Sammy?"

"What do you mean? Of course it is."

"I don't want them to think I've been suckered. They trust me one hundred percent."

"What's gotten into you all of a sudden, Mandelbaum? You know you're like a brother to me."

"Okay. I'll take your word for it."

Sammy turned off his phone and tossed it into a pond. The koi went wild, pouncing on it. But the taste of the metal wasn't to their liking. The phone sank to the bottom and became entangled in a thicket of reeds. His face lit up in a grin. He hadn't smiled like that in a long time.

Chapter Thirty-Four

Joe Mandelbaum was sitting in the small Hana's restaurant near Chabad House. He'd been moody ever since they got mixed up in the abduction of Sammy's daughter. They didn't need that kind of headache. Why did they ever join forces with the Russians? The assholes were poking their nose into everybody's business on the island. And why did they let themselves believe their investment would buy each of them their own villa? What were they, pinheads?

His phone rang. He stared at it for a long time, not answering.

"Are you going to answer that phone or not?" Hana called from the kitchen when it kept ringing.

"Mandelbaum speaking." For the next few minutes, he just listened, struggling to process what Shiloh was telling him. Finally, he said, "And you heard all that with your own ears?"

"I can't quote what they said word for word. I'm not a court reporter. But yes, that's the gist of what I heard."

"Do you understand what you're saying?"

"Mandelbaum, I don't want to understand it. I'm sorry I ever heard it."

"Alright, Shiloh. You know I don't forget my friends."

"This time, I'd rather you did," Shiloh answered. "My gut is telling me to pack my bags and get out before the tsunami comes."

Mandelbaum's gut was telling him the same thing. But he had a long history of packing up and leaving. Things were good here. He had a great life in this Shangri-La, this paradise. If he could just hold back the tsunami. But how?

He called the Judge, Simple Simon, and Aaron from Hadera and told them all to get themselves down to Hana's right away. She was making chicken schnitzel, he said, and besides, he had something important to tell them.

As soon as they got there, they started in on the mountain of schnitzels Hana placed on the table, using her homemade pita breads to soak up her special tahini. Between one bite and the next, they tried to get something out of Mandelbaum, but he just sat there, as unresponsive as a brick wall. Finally, when the plates were empty, he told them that there was a contract out on all of them.

Aaron from Hadera felt nauseous. Simple Simon tried to say something, but nothing came out. The Judge remained silent, merely turning his chair around and gazing out at the water.

"What are we going to do?" Mandelbaum asked.

"Take preventive measures," the Judge said. "We fire the first shot."

"I d-d-don't get it," Simple Simon stuttered.

"You still got your pieces?" Mandelbaum asked.

"Wanna see?" Aaron asked, reaching behind his back and pulling out his police service weapon. He didn't turn it in when he left the force. Instead, he waited until an old friend was on duty at the airport and was ushered through security like a VIP, the gun concealed under his jacket.

"Not here, asshole," Mandelbaum reprimanded him.

Leaning in closer, they devised a plan that would take down not just one, but two, and maybe three of the threats. Simple Simon, pedantic by nature, spelled them out: "Sammy, Flathead, Dotan Naor."

"You got them all out," Aaron laughed, slapping him on the shoulder. He liked to tease Simon, but he knew that when it came to wasting someone, no one could get the job done faster or cleaner than his stuttering friend. He stood up. "Gentlemen, my boat is waiting," he said.

"Are you sure this is a good time to go water skiing?" Mandelbaum asked, concerned.

"I've been waiting for calm water for weeks. The monsoon is killing the season. Finally, the sea is as flat as a mirror today, and I have no intention of wasting it. Give me half an hour. You can watch me from here."

"I'm going to see where the action is," Simon said, following him out.

Chapter Thirty-Five

Aaron drove his red Suzuki Jeep to the beach, where Skip was waiting to take him out. The young Thai was standing in water up to his knees, working the winch to lower the boat into the sea. A red Maxum 3000 SCR speedboat with a sunroof, she was Aaron's baby, a twin sister to his jeep. The name "Daisy" was painted in cursive letters on the bow. He stroked the boat he had named for the first local girl he met. She was everything he had imagined when he dreamt of the East.

Daisy was a damsel in distress, and he was her knight in shining armor. She told him about the son she had left in a village in the north, bringing tears to his eyes, and he gave her money to send back home. She told him about her abusive husband. And he felt like strangling the bastard. She was a true friend, if only for two weeks. As soon as her namesake was in the water, Aaron took her out into the calm bay. A huge motorboat with two giant Rolls Royce engines was rocking on the water, and he wondered why anyone needed such a monster. As they passed it, he caught sight of a large Western man in red trunks and a red baseball cap standing at the wheel and looking back toward the stern, where a thin column of white smoke was rising from the engines. Aaron was delighted to be out on the water again. He waved, but the man in the red cap didn't wave back.

He slipped his feet into the skis. Skip threw him a life jacket, but he waved it off. "I don't need it," he said.

"Whatever you say, boss," Skip said, shrugging his shoulders.

Aaron slid into the water. They began with a straight run and then started doing wide turns. As the minutes passed, Aaron stood up straighter, his chest widening from the fresh air filling his lungs. He hadn't felt so good in a long time. He was enjoying himself so much that he didn't hear the sound of the huge engines approaching. It was only when he pulled himself up even straighter that he saw Skip waving his arms wildly. He didn't have time to figure out what he was trying to tell him. Something dark and heavy descended on him, and suddenly, he was in the water. There was a sharp pain above his knee. He tried kicking, but something was wrong. Only one leg worked. He couldn't feel the other one. When he finally managed to get his head above water, he saw the missing leg, still in its ski, twirling in the wake the motorboat had left behind. In shock, he struggled to grab hold of the cable and pull himself back onto his beloved Daisy, but the cable was no longer attached to the boat. Turning his head, he saw the motorboat speeding toward him and the ice-cold expression on the face of the man in the red cap at the wheel. This time, he raised his hand and waved—goodbye. The boat ran over him, slicing off his remaining leg. With the last of his strength, Aaron flailed ineffectually at the water. Soon, he was sinking to the bottom. Within seconds, the predators had gathered. A frenzy of giant crayfish, eels, and exotic fish fed on his dead body, jockeying for room in the whirling cloud of flesh, skin, and blood.

The motorboat disappeared into the distance.

Chapter Thirty-Six

Mandelbaum was standing, wide-eyed, in front of the large window of Hana's restaurant. Everyone on the beach, the leaf rakers, the boat and jet ski renters, the few tourists outside in the noonday heat, were all staring out to sea. Now that the bone-chilling screaming had stopped, the scene was again calm and pastoral. A single small red speedboat with a sunroof idled in the bay, the local lad onboard frozen in place. People shouted to him from the beach. Coming to his senses, he began sailing to shore. Everybody rushed toward him. Skip leapt off the boat into the water, holding a rope. He lay the rope on the sand and sat down, clasping his head in his hands. He didn't budge from that position until the police arrived.

Mandelbaum turned around. The Judge was still sitting at the table. He'd seen it all from there. "I'm going to pack my bags," Mandelbaum said. "I hope we can get the motherfucker on that boat before I leave."

The Judge turned to him, fixing him with his eyes. "Where do you think you're going, Mandelbaum?" he asked coldly.

The F Brigade's liaison officer stared back at him. "As far away as possible, Your Honor."

"You're going to abandon this piece of paradise we built with our own two hands?"

"Paradise?" Mandelbaum answered. "Paradise is closed for business. It's over. We've been kicked out. And we all know why."

He walked toward the door, stopping to breathe in the odor of fried schnitzels and roasted eggplant wafting from the kitchen. "I suggest you do the same. It's time to get lost."

"And you really think that's possible?"

Mandelbaum didn't reply. He rushed out to his Vitara jeep, so new the rear seats were still covered in plastic and sped toward the apartment hotel on Lamai Beach, where he'd been staying for the past few months. He parked, left the key in the ignition, and made his way down the white corridor. The windows looked out on the calm sea, but all he saw in his head was the thick, blood-red eddy of human remains. He looked away.

The door to his unit was open, but he saw no cause for alarm. The chambermaid's cart was standing in the doorway. He pushed it aside and called out in English, "Come back la—" He never finished the sentence. An iron crowbar crashed into his right shoulder, crushing his bones. Before he could get his breath back, his left shoulder received the same punishment. Mandelbaum was a big man, but he had to look up to see the ugly grinning face of Sergey Korpichov. Bending over with surprising agility for a gorilla like him, Flathead landed another blow, this time to Mandelbaum's knee. His victim collapsed to the floor, terrified.

"That's for the girl," Flathead said. Mandelbaum didn't get it right away. There were so many girls. He tried to raise his hands to shield his head, but he couldn't get them to respond. He tried curling up, but one leg refused to budge. He raised his head slightly from the floor, just in time to see Flathead swing the crowbar in preparation for the blow that would crush his skull.

Sergey gazed fondly at the curved end of the bar. With his left hand, covered in a black glove, he picked up a towel and wiped off the blood, hair, and skin sticking to it.

He had a few more things to take care of, but he was in no hurry. All this physical activity in the salty air in the heat of the day had made him hungry. He decided he could take the time to enjoy a good steak.

He wasn't worried. He knew he'd find Simple Simon in the vipers' nest. Gambling opened in the afternoon. He'd leave the Judge for later, before supper. Meanwhile, he'd start at the salad bar. A man had to look out for his health, after all. The waiter placed a few thick slices of rib-eye in front of him, perfectly charred on the outside and just the right shade of pink on the inside. It reminded him of Aaron from Hadera's leg circling in the blue water. That brought a grin to his face. He chewed the meat slowly, savoring every bite as he considered options for Simple Simon and the Judge and made his decision. All he had left to think about was Dotan. But that could wait. There was no rush. He had plenty of ideas for him, too.

Chapter Thirty-Seven

Simple Simon was indulging his passion. No one loved Thailand as much as he did. He felt as if it were made for him. Wherever he went on Koh Samui, there was always a bet to be laid. The Thais were compulsive gamblers. What a paradise!

He started at the cock fights. The crowd was excited, the adrenalin rush reaching its height when one of the cocks slashed the other with the sharp metal spur attached to its leg. The blood flowed. Actually flew. Who wouldn't get excited? You place your bet and see the results immediately. Win or lose, it doesn't take more than two minutes. And it always ends in death.

When he tired of the cock fights, he got into a pick-up cab, a share taxi fashioned from a pick-up truck, that was taking passengers to the cobra fight. The cab was almost full, mostly with Thais, but a fat, sweaty German with red cheeks squeezed in beside him. "Is this the car to the cobras?" he asked.

Simon nodded. The driver collected fifty bahts from each passenger. They drove along the coast south of Lamai and then turned onto a side road that passed through a papaya grove. The pick-up bounced along the muddy track until it reached its destination. Dozens of men were already there, Thais and Westerners alike. Each of them had a small bottle of Mekhong whiskey or a cold Carlsberg in one hand. Simon saw that the arena was ready. He paid a thousand bahts for a seat in the front row and made his way down the steps. From where he was sitting, he'd be able to see the critical moment when the cobra bit the young man in the arm or leg. As soon as he was struck, they'd drag him out of the ring and give him a shot of the antidote. Then he'd be ready for the next round. There weren't a lot of volunteers for the job, despite the good money it paid. Simon had once seen a snake leap into the air and bite a small dark man in the neck. They didn't even bother with the shot. An Englishman called out, "Never mind. He was a Muslim from the south. Just one less snake." The crowd roared with laughter.

The spectators in the noisy arena were at fever pitch. Several fat Thais in shiny silk suits came in and took seats beside Simon in the front row. He felt privileged to be sitting with such obviously distinguished gentlemen. All eyes were on them as they placed their heavy bets.

Three cobras were brought in. Round one was just meant to warm up the crowd. The snakes were milked daily, leaving them with little venom, and the young men sent in to do battle with them were already immune. You could tell the boy who walked into the arena knew the snakes. Maybe not by name, but he knew them. He put on an acrobatic act, spun around them, made faces at them, and even stuck his tongue out at one just to provoke it. In response, the cobra puffed itself up and rose up in front of him. The audience was delighted. But they knew the main course was coming soon.

The real action started in the second round. Simon felt himself panting in anticipation. He was clenching his fists so tight that the knuckles went white. Sweat was pouring down his back. Two cobras were in the arena when an innocent-looking youngster walked in. You could tell the boy had come straight from a village where he'd probably herded buffalo and had headed for the city to try his luck doing what he was well-practiced at in the fields, catching snakes. He wasn't the first misguided country boy, and he wouldn't be the last. A Burmese python, or even a boa constrictor, would present no problem for him, but a cobra wasn't child's play. And these were two angry king cobras filled with deadly venom. He'd have to catch both of them by the head, one in each hand. Those were the rules of the game. The Thais were betting on the snakes. Simon wasn't sure. The boy moved around the arena deftly. He decided to put his money on him.

The man beside him leaned over. "You like young boys, yes?" he said, sticking his pockmarked yellow face right up against Simon's. Simon was about to respond angrily, but the man picked up the bottle of whiskey between his feet and poured them both a hearty drink. They clinked glasses, shouting "*chon gaew*," crash glass, Thai for "bottoms up."

The boy grabbed the two snakes, and the crowd went wild. Simon's neighbor shoved his face up against him again, nearly choking him with the reek of alcohol and shrimp sauce. Then he refilled their glasses. "We see what happens in next round," he said.

The bookmaker was moving among the spectators, paying out the winnings. He handed Simon a thick wad of thousand-baht notes. Simon grinned. His neighbor grinned at him. Simon peeled off a bill and tossed it to the bookie, who brought his palms together in front of his forehead and thanked him, *khap khun khrap*.

In the next round, a herculean young man faced off against two large and no less herculean cobras, each about six feet long. The crowd fell silent. You could cut the tension with a machete. The man grabbed one of the snakes by the head, but it twisted so powerfully in his hand that he lost his balance and fell on his back. The other cobra slithered closer and bit him in the ankle.

Once again, the bookmaker paid out to the winners, including Simon, who had bet against the man. His neighbor had lost. "You lucky man," the Thai said, "Number one." He poured more whiskey into their glasses, tossing in a few ice cubes from a bowl under his seat. Again, they clinked glasses. When the Thai laughed, Simon was shocked to see sharp, slightly curving fangs, just like the cobras. As if he could read his mind, his neighbor pointed to one of the fangs in his mouth. "I cobra-man," he said, laughing again.

The crowd was in an uproar. Simon didn't notice the tall Westerner in the red baseball cap standing behind him. Nor did he notice the Thais in the front row exchanging glances, or his friendly neighbor winking at the white man. What he did see, however, was that the partition separating the arena from the audience had been lowered, giving the cobras easy access to the spectators. That's what they were there for, after all, blood and more blood.

The snake bags were opened, and the cobras crawled out. The crowd counted in unison: one, two, three, four. There was no question the organizer knew his audience. Two of the snakes had a history of biting, one was medium-sized and rather clumsy, and the last was a dynamic young specimen that was saved for special occasions. All four curled up in the arena. Snakes only move when they have to, when there's a good reason. They didn't have long to wait. The bookmaker started his rounds. Simon realized that he was saying something different this time. He heard the word *falang* repeated several times, each time eliciting an enthusiastic roar from the crowd. Simon knew *falang* meant foreigner, but he couldn't figure out what it had to do with the betting. He saw that people were risking much more than they had before. The Thais beside him were no exception. Each one took out a thick wad of dollars. The bookmaker stopped in front of them, and they carried on a lively exchange that seemed about to escalate into an argument. Apparently, the bookie didn't want to take their bets. The man next to Simon touched his pocket, hinting at the presence of a blade. With his own neck on the line, the bookmaker took the money.

The audience fell silent. All of a sudden, someone grabbed Simon by the shoulders, and he felt himself flying through the air straight into the arena. One second, he was thinking, what's going on here, and the next second, he wasn't thinking at all. The only things he was aware of were his temples throbbing in fear and his heart doing its best to break out of his chest. The sound of his crash landing in the arena brought the cobras out of their stupor. One of the larger ones rose up. Simon caught sight of his former front-row neighbor grinning and baring his fangs. The snake threw its head forward, but Simon managed to get out of the way in time. He couldn't imagine how he'd done it. His arms and legs were shaking in the effort to decide between fight and flight. He could hear the crowd roaring and clapping. He heard the fat German from the cab shouting, "Make them fight for it." Petrified, he made a fatal mistake. Without thinking, he inched backward, trying to get farther away from the huge cobra. It was his survival instinct that did him in.

The edgy young cobra was waiting for him. There was no more than a yard between them. It's incredible what those snakes can do. It simply flew through the air, a coil of muscle released with astonishing aerodynamic efficiency, and bit him in the neck, sending its venom straight into his artery.

Simon stood there in shock, the poison racing through his body at the speed of one hundred and eighty beats per minute. It reached his nervous system, paralyzing him. He didn't even feel it when an older snake slithered over to him and bit him above the ankle with lazy indifference. He collapsed to the ground. The last thing he registered before his eyes glazed over and his treacherous heart stopped pumping was his smiling neighbor shouting that he had lost the final bet and the large man in the red cap beside him, his thumb pointing downward.

Chapter Thirty-Eight

The phone didn't stop ringing. It wouldn't have made any sense for me to take my phone with me when I went to stare out to sea and think. We were sitting at a small table under a palm tree, a large pitcher of lemonade in front of us. The ice had melted. Even a glacier from the Himalayas wouldn't last long in this heat.

Finally, Iris broke. "Your phone's ringing," she said.

"Who could be calling me?" I wondered.

"Go answer it, and you'll find out."

It's amazing how much impatience an electronic device can convey. Almost as much as a human being. Reluctantly, I got up, but I can't say I rushed to the phone. I picked up the little monster and said sharply, "What?"

"Do you live on another planet?" Jacob said. "Are you totally out of it?"

"What are you talking about?"

"What do you think phones are for?" By now, he was screaming. "I've been calling for ten minutes. You know what that means? You know what it does for my anxiety? You're giving me a nervous breakdown. By this time my signal is being picked up by all the antennae in Koh Samui, Bangkok, and Tel Aviv. Now everyone knows where I am. Just wait till I tell you what's going on. It's going to start a fire under more people than you can imagine. Do you have any idea of the position you put me in?"

"Calm down, Jacob." I wasn't in the mood for his nonsense.

"What, calm down!" he shrieked.

"What's wrong? You're making me nervous. I can't remember when you ever talked on the phone for more than two minutes straight."

I heard him take a few deep breaths in an effort to steady his nerves. Then he told me what he'd picked up from the phone lines buzzing on Koh Samui. He described in detail what had happened to Aaron from Hadera. "At first, they thought it was an accident, but then they saw the man at the wheel of the big boat turn it around and steer straight for him. There was no question what his intentions were. Hang on a minute," he said, breaking off the call. My phone went dead. I kept it in my hand until it began chirping again. "I was about to tell you what happened to Mandelbaum, but you won't believe what I just heard. They threw Simple Simon into the cobra arena. Everyone's waiting to see who's next. They've started a pool."

"What are they betting on? What are you talking about?"

Jacob paused. "Wait a second. I'm getting more. They say the Judge is the next target. The whole island is in chaos. No one wants to lose out on a chance to make easy money. The odds are ten to one, and they're just getting higher. People are going wild. Everyone on the island wants a piece of the action. It's out of control."

"Jacob, stop fucking with me and start talking sense."

"Listen up. I'm going to try to put the bits and pieces I picked up in some kind of order. Boris Chiplonak hired a hitman from the Russian mafia, a gorilla called Sergey, to take Sammy out. Around the same time, the F Brigade realized that all they'd ever see from Sammy Ben-Lev is sand. No villas, no money. So Mandelbaum put a contract out, and who did he find to ice Sammy? The same Sergey who came to Koh Samui to do the job for Boris. But that's not all. By now, Sergey is going rogue. He also made a deal with Sammy. Sammy found out the F Brigade was involved in the abduction of his daughter. He hired Sergey to make them pay. Do you get what's going on here? It's a slaughterhouse. And by the way, they say you've also got a target on your back."

I didn't answer immediately. I'd been expecting that at some point. It made sense. "Who's after me?"

I heard Jacob crack his knuckles. I had to laugh.

"You're as mad as a hatter. What did I say that's so funny?"

"You didn't answer my question."

"Look, Dotan. I'm really sorry."

"Hey, I'm not dead yet."

"It's Sammy," he said.

I looked out to the beach. She was sitting there as if she'd always been part of the landscape, gazing out to sea and seeing what was without knowing what would be. She was an amazing woman, but she didn't know that her husband was in shit up to his eyeballs and had sent a Russian thug to take out a bunch of degenerates. He was also trying to get rid of me. And maybe her as well.

"Shiloh told me," Jacob went on. "He thought Sammy had hired a Russian bodyguard because the bank was pressuring him to pay back the loan. They say he conned the Russian mob, and that's why they took his kid, and they're holding her until they get their money back. It took a while for Shiloh to realize that the thug hanging around with Sammy was a hitman he hired to polish off the F Brigade."

"Who's next?"

"The Judge and you. That's the whole list. You can put 'late' before the names of all the others."

"Where can I find the Judge?"

Jacob gave me general directions and then asked a question I knew was very hard for him: "Do you need help?"

I was well aware that the last thing he wanted to do was to come out of the rat hole he was hiding in.

"No. Just give me the full name of the hitman."

"Sergey Korpichov. They call him Flathead. He graduated from Russia's special education system. A demolitions expert. He's always got a red baseball cap on his head, and he rides a huge motorcycle."

That was enough. I knew who he was talking about.

"Promise me, Dotan, when the action starts, you press my number, preferably with the phone in video mode."

"Why?"

"What do you mean why? So I'll know what's happening to you. So I'll know if someone finally managed to break that hard shell you call your skull."

I went back outside and gave Iris a smile. "More lemonade?" I asked, picking up the pitcher.

"Why not?" she said, raising the most beautiful blue eyes in the world. Again, I saw the golden haloes around the pupils. I wondered if it was the last time I'd ever see them.

"I'm going out for an hour or two. If I'm not back by lunchtime, there's something I want you to do for me."

"What?" I saw a cloud pass through the blue sky of her eyes.

There was a yellow legal pad on the table. She'd written out a list of thoughts and questions that had occurred to her during her search for Eden. I wrote down a telephone number and a city.

She turned the pad around and read it out. "Anan Ben-Or, Phnom Penh, Cambodia. Who's he?"

"If I'm not back by lunchtime, you pack up immediately and take the first flight to Bangkok. From there, you go to Phnom Penh. Anan Ben-Or may be the only person who knows where you can find Eden."

Iris stared at me, not saying anything. She understood.

I felt her eyes on my back as I walked away, but I didn't turn around. There was no need. Even with my eyes closed, all I could see were her blue eyes with the golden haloes, and behind them, always Eden's face. I swore to myself that I'd find her daughter and release her from the hell she was living in. It wasn't the first time I'd taken such an oath. I knew that what had to be done would be done, and whatever happens, is meant to happen.

Chapter Thirty-Nine

The motorcycle engine was already roaring when a large Toyota Landcruiser drove slowly down the path and blocked my exit. The door of the jeep opened and Barnea, from the ICU, stepped out. I always knew the guy was big, but standing there in my way he looked like a rock that I would need a bulldozer to move.

"What's wrong? You couldn't wait to get Elijah's karate suit?" I asked.

The last time I saw him was in his office in Tel Aviv. This time, the surroundings were very different. "I wasn't expecting to see you here," I said. "In fact, you could say you're the last person I expected to see here."

"I hope I'm not the last person you ever see," he answered. He placed his huge hands on his hips. "I can't let you leave. Not now. Not today."

"What do you mean?"

"Listen, we don't give a damn about the Judge. But we're going to get Sergey Korpichov and put him behind bars for a long time. He's not just some neighborhood bully. He's a psychopathic killer."

"All I know is that he's already begun his killing spree, and he won't stop until he eliminates his last target. And as far as I know, that's me."

Barnea examined me closely.

"We want to take him alive, Dotan. We've been on the tail of the Russian-Israeli syndicate for months. We've traced the movement of millions of dollars from Russia and Israel to Thailand and Cambodia. They specialize in little girls. They've made a business of it, conducting public auctions. They're holding another one soon. We have to find out where and when. Get it through your head, Dotan. Agents from police forces around the world, as well as Interpol, are all descending on Thailand and Cambodia. They're reopening all the missing persons cases involving young girls. Sergey is our only lead at the moment. If we can put our hands on him, we'll get in ahead of everyone else."

"Not interested," I said.

"What do you mean, 'not interested'?"

"You want me to repeat myself? Okay. Not interested."

Barnea fell silent. The tension drained from his body. But not from his brain. I could almost see the wheels turning.

"Why not?" he asked finally.

"You're here in the name of society, law and order. But I'm only obligated to my own cause. The society and the law and order you represent impose conditions. My obligation doesn't. You waste your time and energy on people who don't deserve an ounce of consideration. I don't. The man you're after isn't a member of my family, he's not a friend of mine, we didn't share a cell in prison, we don't belong to the same gang. There's only one thing I know for sure. If I get the chance, I'll wipe him off the face of the earth. That's my obligation."

"Because of Iris? Because of the missing girl?"

"No. There's no question he's a bad man. He's a criminal, and he should be behind bars. But essentially, it's much simpler than that. I'm here, and he's coming for me."

Barnea still didn't move aside. "In my world, there's a police force, laws, and courts. Those are the only things I understand. And I know you. You understand them just as well as I do. So you can stop with the philosophy and the Eastern mantras."

We stood there facing each other on either side of the inevitable chasm between the social order that was barely surviving and the knowledge that personal duty was a higher cause. How could I explain that fulfilling my duty even imperfectly was better than discharging social demands to the letter? It would even be okay if I had to die doing it. That's something you have to accept. You come to terms with it. I knew Barnea got me. There was no way he could stop me.

I don't know what he was thinking at that moment. I can't read his mind, so I have no idea why he suddenly decided to get out of my way. Barnea's public duty brought him to me in order to try to persuade me not to carry out the most extreme action: killing another human being. But he had enough life experience to understand as well as I did: whatever happens is meant to happen. He moved aside.

I got on my bike and turned the key in the ignition again. Nothing had changed, except for the two words Barnea uttered just before I rode away, "Good luck."

I nodded. The motorcycle leapt forward, and the wind from the sea whipped my face. I knew I was heading toward a moment in time that was meaningless in and of itself, but contained the whole of the meaning of life within it. I was going to kill.

Chapter Forty

The Judge knew there was no point in running. He had lived life to the fullest. In retrospect, his life looked like a cheap soap opera, entertaining at best. It was now time for the final episode.

In the first episode, we meet a child born in Persia whose family moved to Israel in the 1950s. Like other new immigrants at that time, they started out in a tent, advanced to a tin-roofed shack, and from there to a three-and-a-half room apartment, a little over 600 square feet, that housed all seven members of the family, including his grandmother.

In Episode Two, the father, who had been a prosperous textile merchant in Persia and worked as a tailor in the Holy Land, saved up enough to open a fabric store in Tel Aviv. The youngest son, he worked side by side with his father after school, unrolling one bolt of fabric after another and despising the wide-hipped women who came to the shop from the market and fingered the clean cloth with their rough hands, staining the soft cotton, smooth satin, and delicate silk.

The only bright moment in his day was when one of the women brought her young daughter with her, the girl clinging to her skirt. A thrill would pass through his body, and he would become the most amiable of salesmen. While the mother examined the finest fabrics he had to offer, he would pass by the girl, rubbing up against her, touching, feeling, and pinching gently. Just hard enough for him to see the look of surprise and pain on her face but not enough to frighten her or make her cry out for her mommy. If a girl seemed about to open her mouth, he would give her an intimidating look that shut her up immediately.

In Episode Three, he went to study law. "I don't want you to be a simple merchant like me," his father said. "Become a judge, distinguished." He was a brilliant student, talented, articulate, and with an excellent memory. He loved the written word and the power it wielded. In his third year of law school, he was introduced to Part 5 of the penal code, sex crimes, and Section 345, rape. Sub-section 3a referred to sexual intercourse with a minor female below the age of fourteen, even if it is consensual. He found himself loitering around schools, holding a law book and pretending to study it while his eyes wandered. They saw everything he did, and more importantly, they saw what he was going to do. Illegal consensual intercourse (Amendments from 1988, 1990, 2004), sub-section 1a read: "Sexual intercourse with a minor female over fourteen years of age and under sixteen years of age who is not his wife or sexual intercourse with a minor female over sixteen years of age and under eighteen years of age by exploiting relations of dependency, authority, or guardianship, or by false promises of marriage will incur a penalty of five years in prison." He laughed.

In Episodes four and five he started a family and advanced rapidly from prosecutor until his appointment to the bench. He was known as a strict judge who put the fear of God in felons. In secret, he worshipped the devil, but who knew? Who could imagine that he, the distinguished upholder of the law with a model family and his own seat in the synagogue was a child molester who raped little girls while exploiting his authority over them? When the accused appeared before him, he would bang his gavel and declare, "three months in prison" or "four years in prison." They all went to jail in his court. No one was ever acquitted. Everyone was a criminal. And nobody knew that better than he did.

Now, the soap opera was drawing to an end. Shiloh was standing in the doorway. He saw the Judge bent over the table. In his whole time on Koh Samui, he'd never seen him like that. And all alone, too. He hesitated a moment before addressing him. "Your Honor?"

The Judge straightened up and looked at Shiloh with the most lifeless eyes the restaurant owner had ever seen in his life. "Your Honor," he repeated. "Simon is also gone. They took him out. It was a terrible death."

"Okay, so what?"

"Your…"

"What are you trying to say? That I'm next? You think I don't know that?"

The Judge burst out laughing. Shiloh was stunned. He'd never heard him laugh before, either.

"They're all gone," the Judge said. "There's nobody left to take me home. Do you want to give me a lift?"

Shiloh cursed the moment he'd opened his mouth. What did he need this shit for?

"I know you don't," the Judge said. "You're nothing but a coward and a loser. Don't worry; he's not gunning for you. You can go back to frying your miserable omelets and grilling sandwiches with cheap cheese. Wherever you go, all you'll ever do is wipe up crumbs. You don't have to worry about the pathetic thing you call your life."

Shiloh didn't respond. It's better just to take the shit he's throwing at me and keep my mouth shut, he thought.

He walked toward the door, the Judge following closely behind.

They drove the whole length of Chaweng Beach in silence, passing the hotels, dress shops, flip-flop stands, restaurants, and foot massage parlors. The street was crowded with tourists. "When it comes right down to it, this is one great place," the Judge said.

Shiloh nodded in agreement.

"It's a shame to leave."

"It's not easy to start over somewhere new," Shiloh said offhandedly.

The Judge threw him a glance, not responding. Shiloh let him out at the top of a path that led to a picturesque traditional wooden Thai house in the middle of a coconut grove. The branches were heavy with bunches of the yellowish fruit. The season had just begun, and piles of king coconuts were waiting on the ground to be gathered up and carted away by truck.

The Judge walked slowly toward the house. It had served him well ever since he first rented it, and he had grown more and more attached to it as time went by. There were no windows, only wooden blinds and a huge four-poster bed with mosquito netting. Lying in that bed he felt more powerful than he ever had on the bench of the county court.

Instead of going inside, he sat down on the large wooden chair out front, gazing into the distance. He knew it wouldn't be long, but he wasn't expecting it to happen so soon.

Something heavy hit him on the head. He couldn't tell what it was. The next time he opened his eyes, he found his feet tied to the chair. He couldn't move. Lying on the ground in front of him, as if it had fallen from a tree, was a large coconut. He guessed that was what had hit him. Then, he noticed dozens of ants rushing about among dark stains in the sand. He didn't understand what he was looking at until he saw another drop fall and watched as the ants hurried to reach it before it was soaked up in the soft, warm sand. That's when he realized it was his blood.

Finally, he looked up and saw a large man, his bare chest matted with curly hair like fur. There was a red baseball cap on his head and a gigantic tattoo across his chest: big skulls with white lilies growing from the eye holes. The tattoo of a long sword extended the whole length of his arm. A snake was twisted around it, baring its fangs.

"Murderer," hissed the Judge. "I've seen my fair share of scum like you."

He spat on the ground. In utter concentration, Flathead took up the pose of a traditional Greek discus thrower. But instead of a discus, he was holding a medium-sized king coconut in his enormous hand. Having lived in the coconut grove for several years, the Judge estimated its weight at around a pound and a half.

"You're nothing but a worthless motherfucking Russian thug," the Judge swore at him.

Flathead didn't respond. The Judge's eyes moved between the coconut and the man holding it in two hands, swaying back and forth as he focused on his target. His arms moved forward as he took up his stance with practiced precision. The Judge saw his muscles tense, his body rise, and lean backwards, and then spin, the left hand releasing the coconut and the right hand hurling it toward him. He raised his arms in an attempt to shield himself, but the coconut was coming at him at sixty or seventy yards a second. There was no way he could stop it. The hard-shelled fruit struck him in the chest like a cannonball, shattering three ribs. He let out a harrowing scream that sent a chill down the spine of every field worker in the grove. They fled. Even the monkeys in the trees, cracking the coconuts with their teeth, ran after their owners, dragging behind them the long ropes tied around their necks.

The grove emptied out. The Judge, still bound to the chair, couldn't go anywhere. The blood and cold sweat dripping off him was joined by a puddle of piss when his bladder gave way, all coming together to create a huge stain beneath him. The ants went wild. They kept coming, including a whole row of termites emerging from their hill. The Judge had always believed the anthill was empty. He liked to pee on it.

With a huge grin on his face, the Russian giant picked up another coconut and again assumed the pose of a discus thrower. As a young man, before fate landed him behind bars, he was good enough to just miss out on making the Olympic team. He sent coconuts flying toward the Judge one after the other, deliberately missing his head. He was saving that for the end. The Judge, semiconscious, already looked like hamburger meat, pulverized and bloody. Before picking up the last coconut, Flathead spit into his hands and rubbed them together. The Judge's head cracked like an egg, dropping lifeless to his chest.

The ants were busily walking back and forth between their hill and the stains under the chair. Blood continued to drip from the dead man, providing nourishing food for the ants to take back to their hidden colony among the king coconut palms.

Chapter Forty-One

I saw him as soon as I rode my motorcycle onto the sand in front of the house. He was tied to a chair, dead. The hairy Russian gorilla in the red baseball cap was standing nearby, wiping the sweat off his chest. He had impressive muscles, but I knew that if he was sweating like a pig after—how many?—I counted six coconuts on the ground, he didn't have the right constitution for a tropical climate. Before it was over, I would have tired him out, drained him, and brought him to boiling point. When Sergey Korpichov caught sight of me, he rubbed his hands together in anticipation. He had two powerful giant fists, each the size of a small coconut itself.

"So we meet again," he said.

I nodded.

"What do they say? Not every day's a holiday. Just so you know."

"Too bad you didn't learn your lesson last time," I said. "Now I'm done teaching."

Flathead didn't reply. As I expected, he advanced toward me, his fists thrust out to protect the vulnerable areas, his face and upper chest. I saw his mouth turn up in a grin and his eyes narrow as he prepared to crush me. I held my ground, my arms sticking straight out like duck beaks, one higher than the other. I didn't feel the slightest fear. I was totally centered.

Flathead sent a fist flying toward me, but my right hand deflected it. I took a step back. He tried the other fist, but my lower left little beak pushed it aside. He came closer. I barely moved. You don't have to move much. All you have to do is deflect the force of your opponent's exaggerated movement. My hands flitted in front of me as if they had a life of their own. Flathead aimed his right fist at my chin in an attempt to take me down quickly. My right hand deflected it again. The look in his eyes conveyed his confusion. The question was written on his face: Why didn't my fist hit the target? It should have landed on the left side of his jaw.

It was my turn to attack. With my right leg, I aimed a high kick at his neck. He teetered, stunned. I gave him a second to regain his balance and mainly to sweat. With the back of his right hand, he wiped away the perspiration that was dripping into his eyes.

Again, I stood directly in front of him, my hands sticking out like two hovering ducks. The constant movement was driving him crazy. He attacked again and again, and each time I deflected the blow, took a step back, crouched down and rose up with another punishing kick, the mandarin duck leg, a technique learned from many years of practice. Rivers of sweat were pouring down Flathead's hairy chest and face. I decided to start by breaking those arms he was so proud of. I landed a sharp blow with my palm below the elbow and heard the radius break, in turn damaging the ulna underneath. He could no longer move his muscles or control the movement of his forearm. His fist was hanging in the air, stiff and lifeless. Preoccupied by the attempt to get at me with his left arm, he didn't feel the pain right away. I came at him from the other side, breaking his other arm. Both were now useless appendages.

I didn't give him time to think. Precisely aimed kicks shattered his kneecaps. He crashed, confounded, to the sand. Registering the condition of his worthless limbs, he looked up at me, exclaiming, *blyat*, fuck.

"Who sent you?" I asked.

"You know the answer. Sammy."

"It doesn't matter that I'm looking for his daughter?"

"Doesn't matter. He'll find her himself. The only thing that matters is that you're fucking his wife."

There was a certain logic to that.

"You took out the F Brigade?"

The trace of a smile appeared on his face. He spat blood. "One by one. And I enjoyed every minute."

"You don't have any problem with it?"

Again, he spat. "They died like scumbags. Same way they lived. The Judge was the only real man among them, but the pervert liked little girls."

"This can end right here and now. There's no reason for Sammy to concern himself with me. All he has to do is pay the Russian mob what he owes them, and he'll get his daughter back."

"That's what you think? You don't know Yuri Cezar. Sammy will never get his daughter back. Not even if he gives back every dime. Yuri doesn't think like normal people. There's only one thing he wants—revenge. The girl? She's better off dead. But me, I have one more thing to do."

"What's that?"

"Kill you."

"I don't think that's going to happen."

"You're probably right. Too bad," Flathead said.

I listened to the rustle of the palm branches in the breeze blowing from the sea. Gently, I pressed my right hand against the top of Sergey's thick neck, one of the thirty-six fatal pressure points on the human body. My fingers closed in a technique known as "black dragon extends its claws." They locked around his Adam's apple. The life went out of Sergey Korpichov, Flathead, and he fell forward heavily. "Go in peace," I said, although I doubted his soul would ever be in peace.

There was a large seashell on the sand. I picked it up and blew into it. It made a loud trumpeting sound, a victory blast that cleansed all sins. The parrots ceased squawking, the monkeys stopped chattering in the treetops, and for a brief moment, even the cicadas were silent.

III

Part III

Chapter Forty-Two

I t was early morning. They were on a train chugging slowly to the Thai-Cambodian border, passing through the rural landscape of rice paddies, farmers guiding buffalo-pulled plows, and arid forests waiting for a fire to generate new growth. Vendors walked back and forth among the cars selling food and drinks: rice and fish in banana leaves, bamboo stuffed with sweet sticky rice, fried fish, hard-boiled eggs in soy sauce, fried beetles, and tarantulas. Iris was glued to the window, obsessively folding and unfolding a picture of Eden sitting cross-legged on the sand with an enigmatic smile on her face. She looked at my hands and finally asked the question that had been on the tip of her tongue all morning, "Were you hurt?"

"No," I answered. "I just sent someone back to the state of innocence they were in when they came into this world."

She examined me with her beautiful eyes.

"I put them out of their misery," I explained.

"You look like you're proud of it."

I hated to kill, but I had to admit that I gained a certain satisfaction from killing Sergey Korpichov. I thought of all the bodies left behind on Koh Samui. Barnea would have a lot of work cleaning up after the Israelis. The island was a paradise. Sea, sand, forests, butterflies—they'd always been there, pristine and untouched by evil. Human beings brought the evil with them. The F Brigade was the embodiment of evil, and now it was gone, wiped out. Maybe now things could return to their former untarnished state.

"What's the plan?" Iris asked.

"Hopefully, we'll get to Phnom Penh by tonight."

"Why are we going there?"

"I have a friend who's lived there for a few years. He may be able to help us."

"You mean Anan Ben-Or? The man you told me to contact in case…"

I nodded.

The train slowed even more. Children ran alongside it, shouting "bon-bon" and "pen." Dressed in their school uniforms with their shiny hair carefully combed, they all had big smiles on their faces. Iris scrutinized them closely as if Eden might be among them. They waved, and she waved back. It was an optimistic moment. I wasn't sure how long that feeling would last.

The train pulled into a station and came to a stop. The passengers, mostly backpackers, gathered up their belongings and headed for the door. Iris and I became the target of every porter and driver struggling to make it through another grueling day in the world of Buddha.

"You need rickshaw to border?"

"Tuk-tuk, sir? Only forty bahts."

A young boy pushed through the crowd, handing out fliers for Angkor Wat, the magnificent complex of temples in Cambodia. "I have minivan air condition," he chanted, "I have fine guest house in Siem Reap, only ten dollar for night. You come with me. Buses come late. Take you to bad guest house."

"No, thank you."

"You want guide for Angkor Wat? My uncle good guide."

"No."

"I get whatever you want. You want Cambodian girl for ménage à trois?"

Iris stopped dead in her tracks, appalled.

The boy wasn't put off by her expression. On the contrary, he smiled and said, "Welcome to Cambodia, Madam." Then he turned his attention to a bus that had arrived from Bangkok filled with more backpackers.

At passport control, the Cambodian immigration officer only had eyes for the bowl of noodle soup with fish balls a boy from the cafeteria had brought him. With undisguised reluctance, he looked up at us. "You have yellow vaccination book? No? You go other counter." Picking up his chopsticks, he used them to point to an unoccupied counter. "Pay ten dollar and get vaccination book. No book, no visa," he said, picking up a fish ball.

"Okay." I turned to leave.

"We don't have vaccination books," Iris said, worried.

"And we won't get any either," I explained. "It's a common scam at the border."

Surprised, Iris looked back at the immigration officer, who was gobbling up his food hungrily, totally ignoring the long line of tired, sweaty back-packers stretching out in front of him. We watched as he leaned back and lit a cigarette, still oblivious to the people waiting.

"Shouldn't we ask the officials here if they know anything? Show them a picture of Eden?"

"Not a good idea. Borders are dangerous places. You can't tell who's straight and who's crooked, who's taking money to look the other way when it comes to drug running or the sale of little girls. You have to assume they all are. So you don't ask questions."

"We could have asked that boy," she said.

"Yes, we could have. And within ten minutes, every immigration officer would know why we're here. Even worse, they'd know we were liable to make waves and jeopardize their income."

We passed under the sign that declared "Welcome to Cambodia."

Chapter Forty-Three

The journey to Phnom Penh passed in silence, both of us dozing off. Anan Ben-Or lived on the outskirts of the city, near the Bassac River, one of the tributaries of the Mekong. It was a lovely wooden Cambodian house painted over in pale lacquer. Flowering window boxes hung from the windows, and there was a small kitchen garden at the front. Chickens and pheasants wandered freely through the yard while pigeons sat on the edge of their coop, cooing gently. Everywhere, the touch of a loving hand was apparent. The sound of monks chanting sounded from the Buddhist temple next door. As we approached, the prayers drew to a close. A cluster of child monks in their orange robes and plastic sandals burst noisily from the temple.

Ben-Or was sitting in the backyard, his bare back to us. On it was a tattoo of a Mayan calendar that seemed to glitter in the sun. The most striking Asian-Israeli child I'd ever seen, a boy of about four or five, was playing at his feet. He had the exquisite beauty of the East, a broad face and black slanted eyes, but the hair that bounced on his neck was golden blond. With every movement he made, his hair came to life in a dance of brilliant flames.

"Oh, it's you," Ben-Or said, looking up. Seeing Iris beside me, he rose from his chair.

Iris was mesmerized by the child. "Sorry," she said, pulling her eyes away, "I'm Iris."

"This is Eden, my son."

Iris's jaw dropped.

Anan Ben-Or had hardly changed in the years since I'd last seen him. Just a touch of gray had appeared in his shoulder-length hair.

"Come, I'll get you something to drink," he said. We followed him to the wide covered porch at the front of the house. Pointing to the young monks heading back to their classroom, he said, "They're war orphans. We brought them here." The chanting resumed, first individual voices and then a choir singing in unison. Anan Ben-Or handed us cold lemonade in chilled glasses. "Margarit will be here later," he explained, "and then we'll have supper. Unless you're hungry now."

Iris sent me an irritated look for having scared her off street food. "I see you are," Anan laughed. He disappeared into the house and returned with a tray filled with local fruit, tart green mango, red guava, and tiny bananas no bigger than a finger. Going back inside, he brought out a pot of coffee and porcelain cups painted with dainty flowers. Iris picked up a cup and examined it curiously before holding it out for Anan to fill.

"Everything here is so beautiful, so calm," she said with a sigh.

"It's not always this peaceful."

A dark cloud seemed to pass over his face, but was gone instantly. He sat down in a deep chair, rolled a cigarette, lit it, and inhaled deeply. "If you want to talk, I'm listening."

Iris told him about her daughter Eden. Anan Ben-Or glanced at his son, playing in the yard. "It's amazing how they have the same name," she said.

"Yes," Anan replied.

I told him what we had found out and why we thought Eden was in Cambodia. He listened closely, periodically asking me to repeat a certain detail. I knew he was looking for the holes in my story, for the bits of information we might have overlooked. He was looking inward, to the Cambodia I didn't know, the one where he had chosen to make his home.

When I told him about the butterfly garden, he became very agitated. "Bastards," he spat.

I asked him why he was so upset.

"For a while now, there's been talk of a network of human traffickers who abduct young girls. They say it's run by organized crime working with corrupt officials. It seems to be getting worse every year. There's a lot of money involved. As a side operation, they started snatching Western girls from tourist sites, especially in Thailand. They don't only use them to satisfy the appetites of Western perverts in Cambodia. They also supply them to harems in the Persian Gulf and Saudi Arabia. Apparently, there's a growing demand for them lately in the Arab world."

Quietly, Iris asked why, why now. She was keeping such tight control of herself that I was afraid something had happened to the gutsy woman I had come to know. The continued absence of her daughter seemed to be snuffing the fire out in her. Without Eden, she was slowly dying.

"The harems are kept by wealthy perverts. They're under closer scrutiny these days because of pressure from the Americans and Europeans, so they're afraid to come to the East to feed their hunger for little girls. They prefer to get the merchandise—pardon the expression—delivered to their doorstep."

Iris kept silent, horrified.

"It's rumored the girls are forced to convert to Islam, and then they're kept hidden away under the guise of the third or fourth wife. They have almost no chance of escaping or of anyone finding out who they really are and coming to their rescue."

Iris was fading before my eyes, as if her worst fears had been confirmed. She looked over at me, her eyes gaping.

Anan poured out the last of the coffee. "I'm going to get Margarit," he said, getting up. "I'll be back in less than an hour. Keep an eye on Eden for me, will you?" The request, directed specifically to Iris, appeared to reignite a tiny spark in her. The roar of Ben-Or's motorcycle faded into the distance. We sat there in silence.

Finally, Iris asked, "How can he help us?"

"I don't know yet. We'll have to wait and see." Actually, Anan Ben-Or was the only person who could help us look for Eden in Cambodia. I didn't trust anyone else in the country, except for a few aid workers doing God's work saving souls from misery, hunger, and war. Everybody else had a vested interest. In impoverished countries, vested interests are the system, and the system is corrupt.

Chapter Forty-Four

I ris got up and went to stand at the edge of the porch. The landscape was breathtaking. The murky river flowed lethargically, carrying with it floating chains of hyacinths. An occasional rowboat steered by a woman with a single oar, or a small motorboat with a sunshade made of woven palm branches navigated the water. I knew Iris was blind to the picturesque beauty. I didn't have to tell her that the serenity was deceiving. Cambodia is deceiving. Anguish seethes under the cover of tranquility. It is a downtrodden, unsmiling nation. A world of torment. Unlike an earthquake or a volcanic eruption, torment cannot be measured. Nor can it be compared to other torment. Can Cambodia be compared to Biafra? To the Holocaust? Can Eden Ben-Lev be compared to the tens of thousands of girls in Southeast Asia who are sold into prostitution every year by their poverty-stricken families? I was reminded of the proverb one hears so often here: If the sky could cry, there would never be drought in Cambodia.

"Is that his real name," Iris asked abruptly. "Anan Ben-Or, cloud son-of-light?"

"Yes," I said, relieved she was talking again.

"What kind of name is that? He was born with it?"

"He was," I laughed.

"Have you known him a long time?"

"Yes."

"Where do you know him from?"

"It's a long story."

That was the easiest way to say nothing. I didn't want to tell her that whole periods in Ben-Or's life were covered in fog and that I myself had been part of those shadowy times. I wondered what and how much I should tell her, if anything. What could I say? There once was an Israeli who lived on the edge until he fell in love with a beautiful Eurasian whore who left the brothels for him, and now they had a child and were living happily ever after in a nowhere village in Cambodia.

She kept her eyes fixed on me.

"Just a story," I tried again. "Go anywhere in the East, and you'll hear dozens of stories just like it."

"But I didn't go anywhere in the East," she said, her look becoming even more piercing.

"Is he talking about us?"

A voice as melodic as a songbird issued from inside the house. I rose and stretched my arms out to Margarit, who cuddled up in my embrace with a smile. Iris stood there, looking disconcerted. I opened my arms and introduced her, "This is Iris."

Margarit hugged her as if it was the most natural thing in the world. Anan stood in the doorway, grinning. Eden came onto the porch, and Margarit gathered him up in her arms and kissed him. They purred like two kittens. "I love you, little boy," Margarit said, putting the child down, "but now I'm going to make supper because our guests are hungry. Are you hungry, sweetie?"

"Yes, Mommy."

"Do you want to give me a hand?" Margarit asked Iris. In response, Iris got up and followed her inside. I trailed after them and saw that despite her misery, Iris was being caught up in the harmony of the household. Eden took Iris's hand to show her the way. I could see how much she needed that. For a brief moment, it seemed to ease her heavy heart.

The spacious living room was furnished with elegantly carved wooden gems, including a huge mahogany desk and a cabinet with legs shaped like Hindu nymphs. Silk tapestries on the wall depicted mountains and water, herons and pine trees. But the most striking features were the Buddhist sculptures. I went from one to the other, examining them closely.

"Most of them are from the Angkor Wat region," Anan Ben-Or explained. "Examples of the exquisite Khmer sculpture. This one, for instance, is a Buddha carved from wood and covered in gold leaf. It's from the ninth century, the golden age of Khmer art. That large bronze Buddha with eight arms," he said, pointing to a statue with a broken base, "comes from a different site, not far from here."

"I see you've become an expert," I said.

"And an art dealer. I discovered I have a knack for it. The money we earn goes back into Cambodia for aid and education. Margarit and I started the first Buddhist school after the Khmer Rouge era."

The table was set for supper on the porch. As we ate, Margarit told us about the restaurant she owned. The staff was made up entirely of young boys and girls from the area who never got an education. She trained them for work in the hospitality trades so they could find jobs in restaurants and hotels in Phnom Penh or Siem Reap, where the tourists are.

When we were almost done, Iris asked Margarit, "Did you study social work?"

Margarit laughed, Anan smiled, and I remained silent. Glancing at her husband, our hostess said, "Yes. When I was younger. In the brothels in Phnom Penh."

Iris blushed. "I'm sorry," she mumbled.

"No need. That's a normal, honest response."

"You were...?"

"A whore? Yes."

Iris's face went even redder.

"I was born in Cambodia, in Phnom Penh. My father was French. He met my mother in a local brothel. Families only had two options in those terrible years after the war: to starve or to sell their daughters. So that's what my mother did. It's what everyone did."

Iris caught her breath.

"You're shocked. Those are just the facts of life in a cruel, crazy world. When the hunger becomes unbearable, families sell their daughters. Sadly, today, the practice has expanded. Children are sold to pedophiles who come to our wretched, broken country from all over the world. Do you know what we call these children? We call them children of dust. That's what they are, children of dust."

Iris muttered something unintelligible.

"Do you want to know how much I was worth?"

Iris shook her head.

"Two bags of rice. It's not a lot, but it meant the world to my family. They could survive on it for a whole year, another year of the atrocious life Pol Pot's crimes against humanity brought down on Cambodia. I was a virgin. That little piece of unbroken tissue was worth its weight in rice. Nothing more than a bit of hidden skin. But in their screwed-up heads, men, especially Asian men, think that deflowering a virgin will buy them potency and long life. The first thing I learned to say in English was, 'Hello, you want to fuck?' And I always said it with a smile. You know why? Because if I didn't, they would lock me up and beat me. Their favorite form of torture is electric shock. They tie you up, pour water over you, and attach bare 220-volt wires. It's very effective. It frightens the girls, and it's painful, but it doesn't detract from their appearance, and most importantly, it doesn't reduce their market value. They're all experts in torture techniques, all ex-Khmer Rouge. A twelve-year-old kid who doesn't want to fuck white pigs is nothing to them." Margarit fell silent. Finally, she said, "I'm sorry for ruining your evening."

Anan went to her and stroked her hair. Bending down to kiss her head, he said, "Don't ever apologize for what you were forced to go through."

He got a bottle of red wine and poured out glasses. Then he rolled cigarettes for me and himself. We puffed on them in silence, blowing the smoke toward the ceiling, each of us sunk in his own thoughts.

"You could say my life is an open book," Margarit said. "Not a lot of pages, and many of them simply repeat themselves almost word for word."

"How did you escape?" Iris asked.

"One day, the police raided the brothel. The owner probably didn't pay them enough. I didn't hesitate. In the midst of the commotion, I ran. I found a safe haven in a women's shelter, one of the first in Cambodia. A few months later, I started working there. Then I met Anan. I didn't think I'd ever want to look at another man, but somehow, I knew he was my redemption. And I was his. You already know that part of the story."

When Iris spoke, her pain was apparent. "You heard about my daughter, my Eden. I can't believe she's in that hell. It's inconceivable. Simply inconceivable."

Margarit got up and placed her hand on Iris's shoulder. "They're holding her for ransom. I don't think they'll do her any harm. And don't ever forget that all of us here will do whatever we can for you and for her."

Embracing Iris, she led her out to the yard. Gradually, her crying settled into a quiet keening.

Anan brought out a bottle of whiskey. "One of the few pleasures left," he said.

"Like old times," I replied.

"I'll start making calls tomorrow," he promised. "There are still a couple of people I can trust. If they've heard anything, they'll tell me, even if it's no more than a hint or a rumor. But our chances...," he sighed. "Do you know the kind of numbers we're talking about?" He didn't wait for an answer. "Thousands. They're not all Cambodian, either. There are Vietnamese girls who were abducted from their villages, girls from the Hmong, Yao, and Miao tribes in southern China. It's not going to be easy. The fact that she's a white girl may give us a certain advantage. She'll stand out. People will notice her, they'll remember. But whether or not they'll talk is another matter."

The whiskey bottle steadily emptied out. Finally, Anan stood up. "I'm going to bed. See you in the morning."

Nodding, I mumbled, "Good night." Beyond the covered porch, the nightly orchestra of cicadas and frogs was playing. Hundreds of moths banged into the screen, attracted by the light, its power too strong for them to resist. I continued to sit there, drinking and staring into the dark, struggling to drive away the ghosts that were haunting me that night.

Chapter Forty-Five

When I went to my room, I heard Iris weeping. I knocked softly on her door, but she didn't answer. I cracked it open, peeked in, and then pulled it aside and went in. She was curled up tightly on the bed, intermittently crying and wiping her eyes, a pile of tissues beside her.

"Hey," I said, setting off another burst of tears.

I took her hand and pulled her up gently. "Let's go get something to drink in the kitchen."

She got up, her whole body shaking uncontrollably. She needed a hug. I opened my arms, and she literally fell into them. Wrapping them around her, I soaked in her tension and granted her my warmth. "I feel like an animal trapped in a dark hole. There's nothing for me to grasp hold of," she said.

I stroked her hair.

"I'm falling apart. I'm furious with myself and furious for feeling so guilty. I know it isn't rational, but I can't control it. Do you understand?"

I didn't reply. I just kept stroking her hair.

All of a sudden, she grabbed my hand and moved it away. "You don't understand anything," she said angrily, but she continued to grasp my hand until the pressure she was applying to it gradually subsided.

"I'm sorry," she said, resting her head on my chest as if to acknowledge that I was her source of protection and comfort. Settling her head into the hollow of my shoulder, she whispered, "Kiss me."

Gently, I touched my lips to hers. Mine were on fire. She took a deep breath. Our lips remained pressed together. Her fingers dug into my flesh, clawing at it. I passed my hand down the side of her extraordinary body. When it reached the mound of her breast, she froze, arched her back like the string of a bow at its tautest the instant before it sends the arrow flying. Then she exhaled, the air escaping in a heavy sigh, and her body trembled and went limp.

I stroked her fondly, moving down her neck and along her back. She pressed closer to me. My fingers fluttered over her breasts, barely touching, and descended to her stomach. She began planting tiny kisses on my face, on my cheeks, the corners of my mouth, my eyes, and then pressed her lips to mine in a deep kiss. Her fingers danced across my chest, scratching it slightly in an effort to transfer her pain, until the marks gleamed like magical gemstones in the dark. I licked the curve of her neck and nibbled on her earlobe. She let out a sigh. The fire had been lit. We felt our way back to the bed. She held off for a moment, staring into my eyes, looking for approval. The heavy burden of emotions and guilt still threatened to trap her under its weight. But when she pulled off my shirt, her eyes conveyed something else entirely. She unbuckled my belt, opened my trouser buttons, and then pulled me decisively after her onto the bed.

Her lips were slightly open. I leaned over and kissed her, but she turned her head away, crawled out from under, and sat on top of me. I lay on my back, watching as she removed her blouse and bra without taking her eyes off me. Slowly, she leaned over until her nipples were touching my chest. Moving very slowly, her body rose and fell again and again, her mouth on my neck, kissing and biting, generating a perfect storm that held us both in its thrall. It was as if we were preparing for battle, except that our goal was not to win. She wailed and flailed at me like a trapped animal, turning the eventual penetration into a titanic clash. She twisted her body, pulling herself away and leaving behind an emptiness. But she continued to hold me tightly. I exhaled, sighed deeply, and she moved toward me, burying herself under me, until that longed-for moment when her body arched, her nails pierced my arms, and she let out a painful gasp. I let go inside of her, crying out in a sense of exaltation.

Finally, we lay quietly side by side, her arm resting on my chest. Staring at the ceiling, she said, "I don't feel guilty. Should I?"

"No." The word hung in the air. I hoped I sounded convincing. "You didn't break anyone's trust," I whispered in her ear. "Wherever Eden is, she believes in you, and she's waiting for you. We'll find her." She squeezed my hand. That was enough. I knew she trusted me. Now, I had to justify that trust.

Chapter Forty-Six

I awoke to the sound of the young monks chanting the mantra in the ancient Pali language: "I honor the supreme deity who has achieved the perfect self." I looked at my watch. Four-thirty a.m., and they were already reciting the age-old lessons, learning how not to get caught on the hook known as life and suffering. The sound of Iris's regular breathing brought a smile to my face. I tiptoed back to my room and fell asleep again. This time, I awoke to the sound of dishes rattling in the kitchen and Ben-Or calling, "Time to get up, lazy bones. Breakfast is ready."

The table was set for four. A vase in the center held fresh blue hyacinths picked early that morning. A single lotus flower occupied another slim Chinese vase. Next to it, sandalwood incense sticks were burning, filling the room with a pleasant scent.

"We're going into the city," Anan said. "Margarit has made arrangements for someone to stay with Eden in case we don't get back tonight."

Iris froze again at the sound of the child's name. Margarit looked at him quizzically. The boy waved goodbye as we left, and I took it as a good omen. I waited until we were in the jeep before asking Ben-Or where we were going.

"There are rumors of a white girl who was seen in the area recently. My friend tells me that something's going on. There's too much activity, he says. Too many unfamiliar faces, Westerners, Asians, Arabs. Too much money is being passed from hand to hand. The whole region is tense. To answer your question, we're going to a shelter for girls run by one of the aid organizations I know. There's a new girl there who's willing to talk."

"I was frightened," said the girl, about fourteen years old, her face partially hidden by her hair. Margarit translated from Khmer for us.

We were crammed into a small shack, forced to bend over because of the low ceiling. The window was open, and the sound of girls giggling came from outside. The new girl sat cross-legged on a mattress on the floor, her pregnant belly protruding outward. Aside from the mattress, the Spartan shack was almost bare, with no more than a single stool holding a plastic box of soap and a small towel. Laundry hung from a wire strung between two corners. The girl was only two years older than Eden, but she seemed to have lived a hundred years of torment.

She went on telling her story through the veil of hair over her face. "There was a guard outside the door all the time. He watched us and laughed at us. If he saw us trying to resist, arguing, or even saying a word he didn't like, he would plug in his device and give us a shock."

Iris covered her face with her hands. "Why did they let you go?" she asked.

"Because I got pregnant." She stroked her belly. "It was too hard for me. I said I couldn't sleep with men anymore. That's when they did this to me." She pushed her hair aside and showed us her eye. As white as an eggshell, the pupil pointed permanently downward. "With a hot iron. Then they threw me into the street. I wasn't worth anything to them anymore, so they made sure I wouldn't be worth anything to anybody."

I took out Eden's picture. The girl moved ponderously toward me. Her belly was the largest part of her scrawny body. Then she recrossed her legs under her and gently passed her hand over the picture.

"She's beautiful. Is she your daughter?" she asked Iris.

Iris nodded. The girl carried on a rapid conversation with Margarit. I didn't understand a word, but there was something in their expressions and gestures that prompted me to ask, "Did you see her?"

The girl looked at Margarit. "She asked me if she should tell you," Margarit said. "She says she's scared. I told her she had nothing to be afraid of; the worst was already behind her. No one here would hurt her. She said everyone knows a white girl is being hidden in Swamp Pak, but she didn't see her. Nobody she knows ever saw her. But she thinks it's your daughter because they say she has glowing hair like white gold. They know she's in Swamp Pak, but they're too scared to say anything."

"She's here. She's alive," Iris exclaimed. At last, there was a tiny glimmer of hope in her eyes.

"Where's Swamp Pak?" I asked.

"On the edge of Tonle Sap Lake. The houses are built on stilts on a narrow strip of land that's above water in the dry season. It's a hive of crime and prostitution. It's very hard to reach. You have to go through a web of canals, floating islands, quicksand. The village is a safe haven for people on the run from the law."

"When did she get here?" Iris asked, pointing to the girl. "How recent is her information?"

Margarit spoke with her and then translated. "She got here two days ago. Aid workers picked her up. She says she was on the street for three or four days. So what she knows is probably about a week old."

"I'm so sorry you had to go through all that. You're very brave," Iris said, embracing the girl. In just a few months, this girl who was still a child would be a mother to her own child.

We went outside.

"What are our chances of finding Eden?" Iris asked.

"We can't lose hope," Margarit said. "For years, Cambodia suffered unimaginable anguish. Maybe that's why we know there is always hope. It's out there, waiting for us, although we don't know where. All we know is that there's nothing worse than where we are now, so there must be something better."

Iris smiled. "How can I help that girl?" she asked.

"You can give her money, or give it to the aid organization. They're in desperate need."

Without a word, Iris walked to the small room that served as an office. When she came out, she was still smiling. We were standing in the middle of a compound of shacks. All around, barefoot girls in shorts and colorful T-shirts sat on the wooden steps in front of the buildings, chattering and giggling. They were all fascinated by us, particularly by Iris.

"What now?" Iris asked when she rejoined us.

"I'm going to talk to a police officer I know," Ben-Or said.

"I set up a meeting with an Israeli woman who works with a human rights organization," Margarit said. "Iris, why don't you come with me? The woman might be more forthcoming if you're there."

I know how suspicious aid workers are. They're wary of strangers who don't understand the complexity of the Third World reality they function in. They often have to contend with a hostile establishment and police force, as well as with frequent threats to their lives. Any meeting, any misplaced word, could spell disaster for them. The list of aid workers who have been killed in distressed regions is intolerably long.

Chapter Forty-Seven

Hundreds of stalls selling food, drinks, toys, and Cambodian flags had been set up along the Mekong River. The crowd was milling about, looking for a good spot on the bank from which to watch the boat race that was scheduled to begin shortly.

Ben-Or stopped the jeep at the top of 54th Street, which ran parallel to the river. "I'll make the rest of the way on foot," he said. "It'll be faster. Otherwise, I'll never get there in time. My friend is a stickler for punctuality and very cautious. If I'm even a minute late, he won't wait." He got out, waved goodbye, and started walking down the dusty street.

I got behind the wheel. I let Iris and Margarit off at the Almond Hotel. They were meeting with the Israeli aid worker in the hotel café.

"Don't lean on her," I advised. "Give her time to take it all in. She'll only talk to you if she's sure you'll keep every word of your conversation confidential. She won't want to put you, or herself, in any danger."

We agreed to meet up later at an isolated hotel on the riverbank, Villa de Angkor. I found the place without any trouble and sat down at a table in the garden café. The hotel had been built way back at the dawn of the French dream of an enlightened colony in Southeast Asia they called Indochina. All that was left of that dream was a beautiful building and a pleasant garden. Bougainvillea in blossom surrounded a small pond dotted with water lilies. It is usually hard to resist the tropical colonial charm, but all I saw now were the shadows and the rot and corruption beyond them.

Three Buddhist monks with shaven heads occupied a nearby table. Two of them were deep in conversation. The eldest one was fingering a chain of prayer beads, staring into the distance. I took my laptop out of my shoulder bag and hooked up to the hotel Wi-Fi.

The first email that came up was from Barnea. "Where are you? You leave behind a pile of shit and at least one body and disappear."

I smiled and pressed 'reply.' "Calm down," I wrote, "I didn't disappear. I'm still doing what I came here to do, remember? To find the girl."

He responded immediately, as if he had been waiting to hear from me. "Where are you? Cambodia?"

The was no reason not to tell him. "Yes."

I waited. Finally, the next message came up on the screen. "You know I could have given the border police a picture of your pretty face. You can thank me by feeding me some information now and then. I hear our fellow countrymen have started reaching their dirty claws out to Cambodia too. They say that gang whose mess I'm cleaning up here, the F Brigade, traveled back and forth between Koh Samui and some place called Swamp Pak. Ever hear of it?"

"Yes," I typed. "A flesh market."

"Women?"

"Women. Mostly young girls."

"You know we don't have a liaison in Cambodia. I can't keep an eye on everywhere Israelis go on my own. I'm getting hints from Interpol that something big is in the works in your neck of the woods. Keep your eyes open. Call me if you need me. I'm still on Koh Samui. I'm making arrangements for Eli Mazor to be transferred to a hospital in Israel."

"Gotcha," I wrote, although I knew the odds of me asking him for help were very slim.

His last message read: "Look out for Iris."

Since when did he give a damn? The guy was starting to get soft.

I sent an email to Jacob and got a reply almost instantly. "You won't believe what's going on here. Everyone's frantic. There are a lot of rumors going around about how the F Brigade met its end. They say the hitman was taken out, too. I suppose you don't know anything about that."

He waited for an answer. When it didn't come, he went on. "There's zero tolerance for Israelis here right now. The police are going after every one of us. They're just looking for someone to lay into. It's like the apocalypse. It's no paradise for Israelis anymore. We sucked all we could out of it. They're sick and tired of us and the criminal activity we brought with us."

"Have you heard anything about Sammy Ben-Lev?" I typed in response.

"He's on Koh Samui. I saw him at Shiloh's place."

"And...?"

"And there's more. I'm just getting to the good part. He's missing. A little bird told me he got his hands on the F Brigade's money. We're talking millions. He cleaned out their accounts. Do the math. Subtract the cost of the hitman, since it's a pretty safe bet that he's the one who ordered the contracts on them. Add to that the bribes he paid out, mainly to the cops who are now making noise so people will think they're doing something, and probably around fifteen percent to the bank for giving him access to the accounts. That still leaves him with a pretty piece of change. I'm guessing about close to a million in cash. A couple of Russians also showed up. They spit fire whenever they hear Sammy's name. They're on the hunt for him. Especially since they heard he's walking around with a suitcase cuffed to his wrist."

"Where do you think he is?"

Jacob didn't answer immediately. He preferred facts to theories or opinions.

"I think he's coming for you," he wrote after a long pause. "I think his obsession has taken over. He's ready to bring everything crashing down if it means he gets to settle the score with you."

That's pretty extreme, I thought. What was Sammy planning? If Jacob was right, what were the million dollars for? Ransom? Revenge? What ran through his veins wasn't blood, but I didn't know if it was fiery lava or ice water. Iris's smile swam up before me, and I thought of her innate compassion and warmth. I found it hard to imagine a meaningful relationship between two such complete opposites. Maybe Sammy hadn't always been like this; maybe he was once a loving father and husband who cared about more than his personal interests and wealth. Something must have awoken this evil in him. No, evil was the wrong word. I don't believe that people are inherently evil. I pictured Sammy in my mind, tried to sense him, to let my heart guide me. And then all of a sudden I knew. Sammy had a fear of failure. That's what motivated him to strive for success any way he could, at whatever cost. He had to prove himself to the world, and as far as he was concerned, Iris was the world. The compulsion was so strong that it broke through any moral barriers. For him, there was no such thing as a red line. The only piece of the puzzle still missing was how this meshed with what happened to Eden. I couldn't understand why he didn't protect his own daughter.

Chapter Forty-Eight

The café on the patio of the Almond Hotel is the best place in Phnom Penh to sit and watch the world go by. The tables were filled with tourists sipping cold lemonade to relieve the heat. In the shade between two teak columns sat a young man in light cotton trousers and a black T-shirt. Buddhist prayer beads were twisted around his right wrist and his long blond hair was pulled back in a ponytail. His pale face and the dark circles under his eyes suggested that he hadn't slept in a long time. There were white earbuds in his ears, and he was swaying slowly to the music, his eyes shut. From time to time, he opened them lazily, reached out for the large bottle of cold beer in front of him, and drank it thirstily.

Iris and Margarit made their way to a table on the shady side of the patio. Through the music playing in his head, the young man registered their presence. It was the same music that had accompanied him throughout the past few months whenever he thought he was going mad. A young woman suffering from a bad case of acne was nursing a large bottle of mineral water. She was obviously very tense. The man smiled to himself when he saw her wave to the new arrivals. He pulled the earbuds out of his ears.

Although Valium's brain was wiped clean by the hallucinatory drug derived from the datura inoxia flower, his hearing was exceptional. He closed his eyes and listened in on the conversation at the nearby table, totally oblivious to the ambient noise: Bob Marley playing on the café speakers, trucks honking in the street below, bells tinkling in the Buddhist shrine, beggars on the sidewalk holding their infants in their arms and pleading for alms.

Iris and Margarit sat down at the young woman's table.

"Thanks for agreeing to meet with me, Tamar," Margarit said.

Tamar looked around warily. Her eyes passed over the man with the ponytail staring into space. Another lost soul, she thought to herself. "I can't stay long," she said. "Someone's always watching. I'll be recognized."

Looking out from their shady corner toward the street, she pointed to a skinny woman pushing a wooden cart filled with mandarines. The woman stopped in front of a bar and exchanged a few words with two girls standing outside. "That's Joy," Tamar said. "She has maybe three, four months to live, but she's still doing everything she can to get food for her baby."

She could see the women wanted her to go on.

"She came here when she was around ten without a penny to her name. She couldn't read or write, but she had two features that are very valuable in this world. She was young, and she was pretty. Her family got two hundred dollars for her. In exchange, she got ten clients a day. She even got a bonus—AIDS. She doesn't work as a prostitute anymore. Not because some guardian angel came and rescued her, heaven forbid. Because she's dying. The bar she was working for threw her to the curb because she got too scrawny for the customers."

The three women sat in silence. "It's almost a cliché. We hear these stories all the time," Tamar said. "Women who sell their bodies or who are sold into the sex trade. It's shocking. You never get used to it."

A waiter came by, and Margarit ordered lemonade. "Can I get a large coffee?" Tamar said. Her hands were shaking. "I'm nervous," she explained. "No one here likes what we're doing. They look for reasons to make trouble for us."

She saw the worried look on Iris's face. "They haven't done us any physical harm yet, but it won't be long. I've felt the noose tightening around our necks recently." She took a gulp of the coffee the waiter had brought. "I know what it is you want to know."

Iris and Margarit nearly jumped out of their chairs.

"I'm sorry. I didn't phrase that right." She placed her hand over Iris's. It was shaking wildly. "I didn't mean to say it like that, as if I know where your daughter is."

Nodding, Iris chewed on her lip.

"When Margarit called, we tried to piece together what we could get from all the sources of information we have. And we have quite a few." There was a hint of pride in her voice. "Look, there are dozens of people here who are devoted to saving Cambodian girls from their horrendous fate. I'm just one of them. What I'm going to tell you is shocking. We're starting to understand that prostitution isn't just a feature of local society that attracts Westerners, sex tourists, and pedophiles. It's even worse than that now."

She took another sip of her coffee. Nervously, she wiped the foam off her upper lip. Iris noticed the sunburns on her long, thin arms. "It's clear to us that the girls are getting younger and younger. The prostitutes aren't women; they're adolescents and little girls. More and more men are coming to Cambodia for cheap sex with meek young girls. It's become a huge industry. There are thousands of people involved, including organized crime. It's an easy source of income for them." She looked back out at the street. Iris and Margarit followed her glance. The skinny young woman was pushing her small cart again. They watched until she disappeared up the street.

"The endless supply and unlimited resources of the clients created an appetite for something out of the ordinary, something exotic. Refined tastes can easily become malevolent when they get out of control and turn into an obsession. And boredom breeds cruelty. I think that's where they got the idea to hold public auctions of young girls. They collect the rarest ones, the most beautiful, like butterflies or exotic animals. Without an ounce of humanity. That's the latest fad. Humankind is once again proving just how low it can go. If you're looking for proof that the clients are all potential rapists, you've got it. Men stream to the auctions from the Persian Gulf, Japan, Russia, Ukraine, Israel, even China. Wherever people got rich too quickly and too corruptly. There aren't many Europeans. Not because there's less demand or less money, but because they're cracking down on pedophiles and the trafficking of minors in Europe. I have a source who says that more and more Arabs are showing up. The sheiks seem to enjoy it." Tamar's voice broke. The other two women waited until she was able to go on.

"It doesn't make me sad or angry anymore. All I feel now is despair. I never thought of myself as a feminist. Labels like that didn't interest me. But what I see here every day is making me hate men."

"When and where do the auctions take place?" Margarit asked.

"Have you heard of Swamp Pak?"

The women nodded.

"None of us has ever dared to go. It's too dangerous. A white girl shows up and starts asking questions; chances are she's not going to leave there alive. And they'll never even find her body in the marsh."

"So how can we find out when there's an auction?"

"We think they deliberately chose the time of the water festival when there are crowds in the city. We've been secretly following a few men who showed up here in the past few days. They came from Japan, China, Saudi Arabia." Tamar paused and surveyed the café. The tourists had already left, on their way to visit the palace and the museum. The women were alone, save for the Western boy with the ponytail. His earbuds were around his neck, and he was gazing idly out at the street. He didn't look threatening. Tamar went on. "Suddenly, all the men in the world belong to a secret brotherhood. Nobody's talking. The minute one of us asks a question, they shut down. Even the girls in the bars are more wary, more cautious. They're not willing to talk to us either."

"Aren't you scared?" Iris asked.

Tamar looked down at her coffee, unconsciously chewing on a fingernail. Iris saw her nails were stained yellow, the sign of a heavy smoker.

"You're asking me if I'm scared? I'm scared to death. Every minute of every day. I'm almost certain we've got a target on our back. We're messing with a well-oiled industry worth billions of dollars. It's as profitable as the arms trade. There's no doubt in my mind that we're a nuisance to a lot of people."

"Does your family back home know what you're doing here?" Iris asked. She admired this slender young woman, wrung out by exhaustion and fear.

Tamar laughed uneasily. "All they know is that I'm in Cambodia. They know I went to volunteer at an orphanage, and then I started working for a local aid agency. Which was true, until three months ago. If they knew I'm working for a human rights organization that's trying to catch human traffickers, my dad would be here in a second. He'd pack me up and take me home." Nervously, she fingered one of the pimples on her face.

"How many of you are there?" Iris asked.

"In our organization, we're only five. Another Israeli girl, an Australian, a Brit, and a Japanese woman. We're a bunch of weirdos."

"What do you mean?" Margarit asked.

Tamar hesitated before answering. Then she looked straight at the women and said, "Because we're all victims of sexual abuse. That's what unites us and gives us the strength to keep going even though we're scared."

They had nothing to offer her, neither protection nor assistance. Tamar was well aware of the danger, and she was facing it head-on. They sat in silence, listening to the noise from the street. Finally, Iris asked, "How can we stay in touch?"

"You have my number."

"We're using the Villa de Angkor as a sort of home base," Margarit said. "If for any reason you can't call us, you can leave a message there. Our contact is an Israeli investigator who's helping us. His name is Dotan Naor. If you can't reach us, you can talk to him. He's a good man."

"Are there any good men?" Tamar asked bitterly.

They didn't reply. Iris thought of Sammy, and her heart felt like ice. Margarit pictured Anan playing in the mud with their son and smiled to herself. "I'm staying at a guest house called Je t'aime," Tamar said. "An ironic name in a place where love died long ago. All that's left of what we used to call love are the bodies of molested girls. I move around a lot. It's too dangerous to stay in one place. Nobody greets us with a smile anymore." The desperation in her voice was painful to hear. She rose.

Iris wanted to tell her to be careful, but Tamar was already on her way out, not even waiting to say goodbye.

Valium put the earbuds back in his ears and began swaying to the music again.

Chapter Forty-Nine

They were sitting in a small bar on 54th Street, one of the many places where you can buy sex or drugs without getting up.

"Are you willing to pay the price?" Niccolo asked. The police officer was a broad, tall man with a hint of Italian blood in his veins. Ben-Or thought about what he had said. You start walking down this road, and you never know whose toes you're going to step on or how much it will cost you. What he did know was that if he kept digging, it would mean the end of his life in Cambodia. He was there without a valid passport or visa. His live and let live existence would be over, and who could tell how many demons would rise up from his past. Not only his past. He was primarily worried about Margarit. Everything they had worked so hard to create for the past seven years, the Buddhist school, the restaurant, the occupational training—it could all go up in smoke. No one would take pity on the young souls they cared for. They would all be thrown out into the street, would become children of dust.

"I owe him my life," he said.

"How dramatic."

"But it's true."

The waitress started clearing the table. The remains of the yellow curry were already drying out, and all that was left on the large plate of shrimp were the tails. Niccolo poured the last of the Angkor beer into their glasses.

"You're putting me in a very uncomfortable position," he said.

"I know."

The police officer fiddled with a toothpick. "Why do you Westerners have to ruin an ancient practice that works so well? When it comes right down to it, what have we got? Women selling sex and men buying sex. So what if it's against the law? What difference does it make? And that's the law talking."

"I'm not trying to change the way of the world," Ben-Or said. "I stopped doing that a long time ago. I just want to find one little girl."

"Yes. And Menelaus just wanted to find Helen, and that's how one of the worst wars in history began. It left one of the biggest cities in the ancient world in ruins. You want to start a war; that's what you want."

Ben-Or knew Niccolo was right.

"You can start a war," Niccolo went on, "but I'm not sure you'll know how to end it."

"Can't we find the girl without getting our hands dirty?"

Raising his eyes, Niccolo gave him a stern look. "Don't forget, hatred is gained as much by good works as by evil," he said, quoting his beloved namesake Niccolo Machiavelli.

Ben-Or could see the murky wave about to wash over them. He knew that Tunle Sap, the great lake, would change direction. It changed direction every rainy season. The question was how many bodies would come floating up, how much blood would be spilled into it. There was no way to know.

"What do you want from me?" Niccolo asked.

"I want to know if she's here."

Niccolo laughed. "I'm just a simple policeman. I may be in charge of the Swamp Pak region, but do you really think I know every girl who passes through? Do you know how many there are? How many disappear? How many we find dead in the corner of a shack with a needle stuck in their arm? Come spend a day with me at the precinct. Just one day. And you're asking about a particular girl?"

Ben-Or didn't answer. Despite the unusual friendship that had grown up between the two men, he knew he had to be careful. "You know about every new girl who turns up. Not a lot happens in the brothels here that you don't know about."

"Okay, you're right." Niccolo wasn't laughing anymore. "Our low-ranking officers have to make a living somehow. Do you know how many

Cambodian riels there are in a dollar and how little they're worth?"

"I know," Ben-Or said. "That's why they come in uniform at noontime to collect their money. Or they take a few girls into custody. Then they come back at night in plain clothes and demand a discount."

This time, Niccolo did laugh. "People can be bought for so little."

"This girl is different."

"None of them are different," Niccolo said drily. "They're all the same."

"She's white."

"Anan, my friend, you're either naïve or stupid. She's not the first white girl to turn up here. It's just like pigs. Most of them are black, and they all wallow in mud. Then suddenly there's a pink one, and they put it in a special pen. Why? Doesn't it eat the same swill? Of course, it does. But everyone thinks it tastes better because it's pink. The white girls come, and then they disappear. Only sooner."

Ben-Or was getting up to leave when the phone in his pocket vibrated. He read the message from Margarit and turned to Niccolo. "Where's the next auction?" he asked.

Niccolo sighed deeply. "I wish there never were any auctions. But you know the saying, if the sky could cry, there would never be a drought in Cambodia."

Ben-Or smiled.

"Sometimes I think things were simpler in Pol Pot's time, no matter how terrible that period was," Niccolo continued. "At least we fought. We didn't always know exactly what we were fighting for, but we were always sure it was a just cause. There are no ideals today. There's something posing as law and order, but at the end of the day, only money talks."

"You still haven't told me where they're holding the auction," Ben-Or said.

Niccolo stared at him for a long time, playing with a breadstick. "In Swamp Pak itself," he said finally. "It's a nasty mud pit, an independent territory run by the mob. Nobody comes or goes through the canals without their knowing about it. I know what you're thinking. Forget it. The only way to get past the mob is to go in with a commando unit that can fight on land and sea. I don't suppose you have such a unit up your sleeve?"

"When is it happening?"

Niccolo stood up and leaned his hands on the table. "If I find out, I'll let you know."

"You don't know?"

The police officer gave him a piercing look. "I'm sick and tired of the sky crying. I want people here to smile again. I want to hear the children laughing. The only thing I see is the profound sadness that overcomes everyone from the moment they come into the world along the Mekong. So I'm going to tell you—it's happening tonight."

Chapter Fifty

I did something I hadn't done in a long time. I took out the pack of Camels, lit a cigarette, and inhaled deeply, attempting to break through the wave of dark thoughts that was washing over me like a monsoon. But there was one image I couldn't erase. It kept rising up before me, as vivid as ever: a young girl on the beach on Koh Samui. I was frustrated knowing how close I was getting, but I still couldn't find her. I knew the time had come to settle the score, but I wasn't sure how or with whom. I looked up. Ben-Or was standing in front of me. Giving me his familiar warm smile, he sat down beside me.

"What?"

"There's an auction tonight," he said.

The rage I felt nearly overwhelmed me.

"Where and when?"

"Sometime tonight in Swamp Pak."

"What do you know about the place?"

"In all the time I've lived here, I've never dared go near it. There have always been rumors about what goes on there in the marsh. In the Pol Pot era, it was said to be home to one of his infamous prisons. Later, there was talk of girls being held there by the Cambodian-Russian mafia. There's a place like it outside every major Asian city."

"We have to get there."

"How?" Ben-Or asked. "We go in with guns blazing, like a pair of cowboys?"

"Something like that."

"Sounds like a plan."

I knew he wasn't joking. In fact, we both knew where he was coming from.

"We need weapons," he said.

"Auctioning off little girls? What the hell has the world come to? I used to love Asia, but now there are times when I despise it."

Anan didn't reply. He understood what I meant even better than I did.

At that moment, Iris and Margarit walked into the café. There was something in Iris's eyes that I hadn't seen in a long time—hope. Margarit kissed her husband on the cheek. I saw the look they exchanged. It spoke of true love that had overcome all the obstacles the world placed in its path and survived, stronger than ever.

Margarit gave us a report of their meeting with Tamar. Anan repeated what he had learned from Niccolo.

"What now?" Iris asked.

That was the million-dollar question. A light breeze blew in from the river, bringing with it the noise of the boat race, the loudspeaker announcements, and the thunderous roar of the crowd. I knew they were waiting for an answer from me, expecting me to lay out the details of a carefully plotted scheme. But I hadn't devised one yet.

A hotel clerk was moving through the café with a bell. "Mr. Naor? Mr. Naor?" I raised my hand. "There is a young lady in the lobby who is looking for you," he said.

The nervous, redheaded woman was standing by the reception desk, her whole body conveying apprehension and desperation. Impatiently, she asked, "Are you Dotan Naor? The Israeli investigator?"

I nodded.

"Tamar is dead."

"What?" I was in shock.

"She's dead," she repeated as heavy tears began rolling down her cheeks. "They killed her."

"Did you notify the police?"

"Of course we did. I waited for them to show up before I came here. I don't have phone numbers for you people, but Tamar…" Her voice broke. Wiping away her tears, she went on. "Tamar said you're staying here. She said if anything went wrong, I should contact you. We know why you're here, so we thought you should know what happened."

"Who's 'we'?" I asked.

"Me and the other girls in our human rights organization. I'm the only other Israeli, so I was the obvious choice to come talk to you."

"I'm sorry to hear about Tamar."

"She was a danger to them. She knew too much. She knew the names of people involved in trafficking little girls, both in the government and in the mafia. She was going to expose what she found out in the international press. She was just waiting for the auction today. She was planning to film it secretly. She wanted the whole world to know what's going on here. They couldn't let that happen."

What courage, what devotion, that young woman had.

"I have the information you need," the redhead said.

I stared at her, waiting.

"The auction is being held in a place called Swamp Pak."

"That much we know."

"They scheduled it for the same time as the finals of the boat race, around eight o'clock tonight. There'll be hundreds of boats on the river with people partying and getting drunk. The police will have their hands full. No one will notice a few boats slipping into the marsh with young girls on board. One of them might be the girl you're looking for."

"Are the buyers already there?"

"I've told you everything I know. I wish I could be more help."

"It's more than I hoped for," I said.

Taking my hand, she said, "God be with you."

That was unexpected, but it sounded genuine. She turned on her heels and disappeared out the door, her long red hair gleaming in the late afternoon sun. I deliberated with myself as I went back out to the café, but I had no choice. "Tamar was murdered," I announced.

Iris went white. In shock, Margarit reached for Anan's hand and held it

216

tight.

Iris was the first to find her voice. "What now?" she asked. "Where do we go from here?"

By now, the answer was clear. "I get a gun, find a boat, and go. Just me. It's less risky that way."

"No way you're going alone," Ben-Or said. "Just you against all the bad guys? Don't forget that every syndicate boss has armed bodyguards with him. I'm coming too."

"I'm going alone," I repeated. "I can't let you come. You've got Margarit and Eden to worry about."

As always, Ben-Or read me like an open book. He placed his hand over mine, knowing as well as I did that blood would be spilled that night.

But it was Margarit who said, "That's not your call, Dotan. Anan has to go with you."

"So do I," Iris said firmly.

"I don't want to sound like a macho pig," I said, "but it's not a job for a woman."

"Give me an M-16, and you'll see what I can do with it," Iris said, angry. "I was in the infantry in the army. I did everything the men did: patrols, ambushes, manning observation posts, catching infiltrators at the border, chasing drug runners, and arms smugglers. But forget all that. It's *my* daughter out there. Mine, not yours."

Finally, it was agreed. Only Margarit would stay behind as backup, maintaining contact with us. If we got in trouble, she would go to Niccolo.

"We need a blessing," Margarit said. "We're doing the right thing," she said. "I sincerely hope it ends well and you come back with Eden, but even then, your souls will be stained with blood and death. I can't let Anan come home like that to our child, the fruit of innocence and purity, or to the children in our school. It will cast a dark shadow over everything, destroy all we've created."

Margarit got up and went to the table where the three monks were still sitting. Pressing her hands to her heart, she spoke to them briefly. The oldest monk smiled broadly. He turned to look in our direction, moving his compassionate eyes from one of us to the next. Then he rose and motioned for us to follow. He led us to the small shrine at the edge of the garden.

We knelt before Buddha. The monk dipped the fingers of his right hand in a small bowl by the shrine. The blue sky was reflected in the water. Sprinkling a few drops on our heads, he said, "Water is a symbol of the purity Buddha wishes for you. The rest is in your hands, for in the heart in each of you sits the holy throne of virtue."

Chapter Fifty-One

Something out of the ordinary was happening at Phnom Penh's international airport. It's not every day that a white YAK-40 arrives on a direct flight from Moscow, the red letters on the fuselage spelling out Air Russ. The door opened, and the stairs were quickly wheeled in place. The man who emerged was short and stocky. He was dressed elegantly in black trousers and a tight striped shirt, each stripe like polished nickel. His face was flushed, his nose aquiline, and his bald head surrounded by a carefully groomed ring of gray hair that might, from a distance, be mistaken for a silver crown.

His name, Cezar, suited him very well. He was the *Bolshoi Načelnik*, the grand chief of the Russian-Israeli mafia that operated between Moscow and Tel Aviv. Its tentacles reached as far as Pattaya in Thailand and Phnom Penh in Cambodia.

The two bodyguards who followed him out were nearly double his size, yet they still seemed to walk in his shadow. The last to exit the plane was a blond woman who stood on the top step in heels that added another four inches to the five foot nine that nature had given her. She teetered precariously, either because of the weight of the fur coat on her shoulders or the effect of the drinks she had downed during the boring flight.

"Yuri, it's hot here," she called out petulantly.

Yuri Cezar didn't bother to turn around. "Galina, darling, I told you. You didn't listen."

She made her way haltingly down the flight of steps. At the bottom, she muttered, "You didn't tell me we were going into hell."

"I told you to leave the cat fur at home." Snatching the mink coat off her shoulders, he flung it in the direction of the Cambodian cleaning crew waiting to board the plane, their eyes lowered and trash bags, buckets, and brushes at the ready. "Go to the Russian market and buy it back before we leave. You're not the first to suffer from the heat here."

"I still don't know why we had to come here all the way from Moscow. They're launching a new Dior boutique, and I'm missing it."

"The less you know, the better you'll sleep."

The head of airport security and the district police commander came to greet them.

"Is everything ready?" Cezar asked in English in a heavy Russian accent.

The more senior official nodded.

"Close the airport. I'm expecting some very important guests."

The head of security looked at the police commander, who responded with no more than a slight nod. The security chief had no choice. And whatever the consequences, he'd never be able to claim that he'd been given a direct order. Speaking into his radio, he ordered the closure of the airport. Throughout Asia, in Singapore, Bangkok, Hong Kong, Ho Chi Minh City, and everywhere else where flights to Phnom Penh were scheduled, the boards lit up with the word "delayed." At the check-in counter, passengers were informed that there was a typhoon warning in the city, forcing the closure of the airport until further notice.

One of Cezar's bodyguards pulled out four passports. Yuri and Galina climbed into a limousine with darkly tinted windows while the head of airport security stamped the passports with a business visa. The limousine sped to the pier on the Mekong River, where a long snake boat was waiting for them. Hundreds of others just like it were on the water, except that this one wasn't being rowed by revelers. Instead, the men at the oars had stern faces and machine guns at their feet.

Chapter Fifty-Two

S undown comes suddenly in Southeast Asia. In the last light of day, a fleet of private jets began landing at Phnom Penh's international airport. The first to arrive came from Kunming, a center of the heroin trade in and out of China. A group of Chinese men in black suits emerged and was swallowed up by three Mercedes that headed for the river and the long boats that sat bobbing on the water, rubbing up against the pier, as they awaited their passengers.

The second plane belonged to Gulf Arrow, a private airline from the UAE. Two muscular bodyguards with short beards and suit jackets bulging with the weapons they concealed flanked a sheikh in a gleaming white jalabiya and a black ikal securing the matching keffiyeh on his head. The three disappeared into a white limousine that also set off for the pier.

The third plane, arriving from Osaka, was delayed. The airport manager in the control tower rang the head of security to complain that he couldn't keep the airport closed for much longer. "The problems will snowball, and we'll all pay the price," he warned.

The implication was clear. The security chief quickly calculated the effect on his cut and the chances he could raise his fee. Not likely. "Give it ten more minutes," he instructed.

A few minutes later, the executive jet landed, bringing several graying members of the Yakuza, the Japanese crime syndicate, who handed their passports to the security chief. Stamping them with a business visa, he said in broken English, "One hundred dollar, each man."

"Aah," said the youngest of the three, speaking to the others in what sounded like a tone of annoyance. The eldest man responded calmly and took out a leather wallet from which he drew three ten-thousand-yen notes. Taking back the passports, he said drily, "No ask again."

Flinching, the head of security hurried to open the door of a black Mercedes. The Japanese driver was in full uniform, down to the cap and white gloves.

Chapter Fifty-Three

That same afternoon, a cab turned onto a side street parallel to the river and made its way to the pier where a boat was waiting. Inside was a barefoot lad dressed only in shorts and a cap. Sammy got out of the cab and eyed him in surprise. It wasn't what they had agreed on. Not giving it too much thought, he climbed in.

He had a bulging attaché case in his left hand. He'd counted the contents again back at the hotel. It was the same amount as before: seven hundred twenty-five thousand and six hundred dollars. Every last cent he had, all that remained of the money he had managed to get his hands on from the accounts of the F Brigade. He didn't have another penny to his name. The hotel on Koh Samui and the apartment in the Herzliya marina had long ago been repossessed by the banks and loan companies. Everything he had in the world was here in this case. And in his pocket. With his right hand, he fingered the warm grip of the loaded semi-automatic Jericho pistol in the pocket of his windbreaker. He released the safety.

Chapter Fifty-Four

Valium was pedaling like mad. He'd never ridden a bike so fast before. He was there when the Israeli girl, Tamar, was murdered. They were staying at the same guest house, Je t'aime. He was sitting on his balcony smoking a joint when two Cambodians came into the large garden. All sorts of shady characters came and went at Je t'aime, ganja dealers, street kids, hookers picked up by Western guests. No one gave a second thought to the two young men; no one asked what they were doing there. They simply sat down at a plastic table, presumably waiting for someone. Only Valium, from his vantage point above, saw the outlines of the guns in their pants pockets. He was already half-stoned when he saw Tamar enter the garden. He wanted to jump up and shout a warning to her, but he could barely move. It felt as if his feet were nailed to the floor. He watched as one of the Cambodian thugs took out his gun and shot her, right there in the garden. He saw her fall and saw the two hoodlums take off. One of them kicked her body as he passed. Sensing there was still life in it, he shot her again, making sure she was dead. They exited the garden and disappeared among the thousands of revelers filling the streets.

The scene brought Valium to his senses. Befuddled, stoned Valium was gone. His eyes were no longer cloudy. Everything was suddenly clear to him. He knew what he had to do. He jumped up, rushed downstairs, and leapt over the guest house fence into the street. He could still see the back of one of the murderers. Running, he collided with him at full speed. The killer fell to the ground. His army training kicking in, Valium pinned him down and twisted the gun out of his hand. Hidden from view by the crowds, he brought it down hard on the Cambodian's head. His partner pulled out his gun, but Valium was quicker. The sound of the shot was swallowed up by the noise of the firecrackers set off to mark the end of the boat race. In the midst of the celebrations, an inconsequential street fight didn't attract any attention.

Valium ran toward the river. He saw a bicycle leaning against a doorway, jumped on it, and pedaled as fast as he could. He knew time was running out.

He rode madly through the city filled with revelers in high spirits. The street was dotted with huge potholes, so big that even rats occasionally fell into them as they dashed from one side of the street to the other. The bike was rusty, the gears barely worked, and the chain threatened to fall off at any minute. But Valium kept going. He poured all his energy into the effort, more clear-headed and focused than he had been in a long time.

A cab passed him, also heading to the river. He recognized the passenger, and his heart started pounding. Sammy Ben-Lev. What on earth was he doing here?

And then everything fell into place: the conversation he'd overheard in the hotel café, the realization that the Israeli girl who went missing was the daughter of Iris and Sammy Ben-Lev, the fact that Iris was here, along with Dotan Naor, his guardian angel. All the pieces locked together to create a picture, just like the puzzles he did on his better days at Hope House when he'd take the earbuds out of his ears and hum to himself. It was all clear to him now. The father of the missing girl, Eden, was the same Sammy Ben-Lev who had been his commanding officer in the army.

The darkness began to overtake him again, but Valium fought it off before it could muddle his brain. He reminded himself that he was racing to help Dotan and rescue the girl. But what was he going to do about Sammy? The motherfucker had screwed with his life, turning him into the quivering spaced-out junkie he had become.

Sammy had to pay for what he did. He'd made a laughing stock out of him in front of everyone, and they'd mocked him and passed the story on. The laughter followed him wherever he went, marking him. They'd returned from a mission and were cleaning their weapons, their hands still trembling from the adrenaline that ran through their veins instead of blood, and Sammy had singled him out and said, "Tell them you're a fucking queer." In front of all his brothers-in-arms in the special forces. He heard the laughter, and he felt the knives in his back. But Sammy's laughter was the loudest, and his knife was the sharpest. He hounded him mercilessly, constantly referring to him as the queer.

Valium hadn't laughed since then. It broke him. Everywhere he went, there were rumors and sideways looks. He couldn't sleep. The mental health officer diagnosed him as suffering from anxiety as a result of mental abuse and prescribed valium, five milligrams three times a day, earning him his nickname. When he got to Bangkok, he didn't need a prescription anymore, just cash. Everyone around him knew to look through his pockets for one of the pills and shove it in his mouth when he started to scream. It went on like this for days, or maybe weeks, or even years. Until one day, Dotan Naor showed up and took him under his wing. He put his warm arms around him and led him away, out of the darkness, to a better place.

Now, the puzzle was complete. Even better, something heavy was weighing his trousers down: the Glock 19C pistol he had taken from the Cambodian. And he was ready to use it. It was time to settle the score.

Chapter Fifty-Five

In the heart of the marshland outside Phnom Penh, in a clearing in the sea of reeds, preparations were underway for the special event orchestrated by Yuri Cezar: the public auction of little girls. Cezar was dressed in a safari suit with a wide leather belt and a colorful silk scarf around his neck. In his highly polished shoes, so inappropriate for the surroundings, he looked like a caricature, but no one was laughing. Anyone with eyes in their head could see that it was wise to keep their distance from the man, even now when he was lounging in a plush chair calmly smoking a Gitane.

He gave the orders in French to Major Joe, who in turn passed them on to the Cambodia crew. Major Joe, ex-Khmer Rouge, had a long litany of war crimes to his name, including murder, torture, and rape, for which he had never been brought to justice. The Cambodian was a short man with black rotting teeth and an oily yellow complexion spotted with pockmarks. His hair was slicked back with a generous dose of gel.

Cezar went on issuing orders. With a broad, authoritative motion, he gestured to the whole circumference of the clearing. "Put the seats here. I want two large spotlights on the center of the arena and flaming torches all around it. Stand three poles in the middle. Place the cages behind them in a horseshoe, at least four feet apart. And make sure they're entirely covered in black sheets. I don't want anyone getting even a glimpse of what's inside."

Major Joe barked orders to his two Cambodian assistants. They carried in large cages mounted on boards. "You heard the white asshole. Put them over there." Walking to the center of the clearing, he marked with his heel the exact spots where holes were to be dug for the poles.

Other members of the crew began spreading carpets on the sand and arranging comfortable chairs and sofas around small tables, each of which held an ashtray, an array of cigarettes, cigars, and drinks, and small ornate boxes of cocaine. Cezar got up and stood in the middle of the arena, overseeing the operation.

"How many have confirmed?" he yelled to Major Joe.

Major Joe took a notepad out of his pocket. "Bo Xi Gia, Kunming, China; the 'Big Spender,' Kung Dje Chung, Hong Kong; Kenta Koyabashi, Yokohama, Japan; Valerie 'Globe' Golgachek, Novosibirsk; Majjid Abdul Latif Al-Sheik, Bahrain; Nicholas Holerman, 'the Stick,' Frankfurt..."

"Hold on. Who's that?" Cezar asked. "He's new. Never heard of him before. How did he find out about us? Who recommended him?"

"Gerard Liszt. He says he's okay," Major Joe replied.

"And what about Gerard? Does he want in on the action?"

"No," Major Joe said. "He's getting a private shipment."

"I'm going to take a nap. Wake me up before our guests arrive," Cezar ordered.

He lay down in a hammock tied up just beyond the clearing. A young Cambodian girl with a small bowl and towel began massaging his feet. Cezar purred in pleasure. "Pussan, mon cherie," he called to one of the boys working in the arena. "Polish my shoes the way I like them."

Coming over, the boy picked up a shoe, drew a handkerchief from his pocket, spat on it, and set to work polishing it to a high shine.

Chapter Fifty-Six

The shopkeeper, a freak with a chiseled face and too many earrings and tattoos to count, gazed at us with expressionless eyes.

"What's up, pal?" Ben-Or asked. "Planning to shoot somebody?"

The Cambodian smiled, revealing crooked yellow teeth. "Sure, bro. There's always somebody who needs shooting."

He pointed to a table loaded down with weapons, including assault rifles and pistols, all thrown together like a pile of scrap metal.

"What is this place?" Iris asked, looking from me to Ben-Or.

Anan suppressed a smile. "What you see here," I said," is the legacy of Cambodia's bloody history. Mother Russia left behind thousands of AK-47s, the Communist neighbor to the north contributed bazookas, and even Uncle Sam did his part with M-16s that saw a lot of water and mosquitos in the Vietnam War. The grenades are eclectic artifacts."

Meanwhile, Ben-Or was casting his eyes over the table, picking up a weapon here and there to examine it more closely. "What are these, souvenirs for tourists? Show us some bon-bons," he said to the Cambodian.

The man moved farther back into the shop. Without a word, we followed. He pulled off the army blanket covering the goods on another table.

"Now you're talking," I said, picking up a Chinese AK-47 with a wooden grip. Ben-Or chose the Russian version with a folding grip. We tried on a couple of light bulletproof vests.

"With those on you, the only way you can die is from a bullet to the head," the shopkeeper said with a twisted smile.

"They come with a guarantee?" I asked, playing along.

"It's an international guarantee. But it's no good in Cambodia," Anan chimed in.

We counted out a few grenades that fit in the vest pockets and added extra magazines, flashlights, black balaclavas, and face paint. It was only when we were done that I noticed Iris staring at the stockpile of weapons—and the Cambodian staring at her.

"Something for the lady?" he asked.

Iris pointed to a short-barreled M-16, two double magazines, and a Beretta pistol. She put on a short vest and slipped two grenades into the pockets.

The Cambodian fawned over her.

"I'm paying for those, too," she said, gesturing to the small but carefully chosen pile of merchandise we had gathered up. Taking out a wad of hundred-dollar bills, she placed them, one by one, on the table. The shopkeeper took the money, counted it again, and then moved some of the items aside. Obviously, he wasn't satisfied by the amount Iris had offered.

I pushed the items back onto the pile. "How much for all of it?" I asked.

He pointed to Iris's jewelry, the large diamond ring, diamond earrings, and diamond pendant she had worn since the day I met her.

"I'll make up the difference," I said.

Iris shook her head. She took off the ring and earrings. Finally, she undid the necklace.

"He can have whatever he wants," she said matter-of-factly.

Smiling, the Cambodian threw bullets for the weapons on top of the pile. We packed it all into three green duffel bags, threw our purchases into Ben-Or's jeep, and sped toward the river.

The city was packed with partygoers. Thunderous cheering came from the river as the boat race reached its climax. The street lamps came on, casting yellow beams of light on the long river boardwalk. An extensive pop-up market lined both sides of the street, with stalls selling food and souvenirs. Thousands of people filled the street, chewing and drinking, the kids holding kites and balloons. The rowers were easy to spot. They walked in groups in their official team uniforms, grinning at everyone they passed, regardless of whether they'd won or lost. What difference did it make? It was just a contest, not a matter of life or death.

A long boat with six rowers was waiting for us on the river. Time was running out. We had to hurry if we were going to arrive at the very moment between dusk and darkness before the eyes had adjusted to the dark and the senses were not yet alert to the dangers of the night. It was a time when even experienced bodyguards were vulnerable.

Chapter Fifty-Seven

The men were in high spirits. They'd stayed at the finest hotels in the world, but in the end, they were all the same: a room, a bed, a private valet, champagne, a line of coke, an opium pipe, sex in the jacuzzi. Nothing to get excited about. But now Yuri Cezar was giving them a new experience. All of them—the Chinese, the Japanese, the Russians, the German, and the sheikh— knew they could count on Cezar to come through for them.

Dozens of Afghan and Persian rugs had been spread out on the soft sand in the clearing in the marsh. They could lie back on the plush chairs and sofas and relax from the long flight and the burdens of everyday life and enjoy the pleasures laid out for them on the tables in front of them: cigarettes, cigars, and joints; ice buckets alongside bottles of whiskey, vodka, and even baijiu, the Chinese liquor whose odor brings to mind a mix of ammonia and sheep dung; finely carved little boxes of cocaine.

Arms reached out from the bamboo cages. One of them was white. There was no mistaking what they were doing there. They were caged like animals for sale, for slaughter, and the men waited impatiently for the auction to begin so they could buy themselves a little girl.

Chapter Fifty-Eight

That was the scene that greeted Sammy when he burst into the clearing, his whole body covered in deep scratches and abrasions. Time and again, he had stumbled as he struggled to make his way from the river through the slippery marsh, the sharp, dry bamboo digging into his skin. But no matter how many times he landed in the mud, he kept going until he saw the lights. And he never let go of the briefcase. In his mind, he saw Eden's laughing eyes and repeated to himself over and over that she was alive. She had to be alive, and this time, he was doing the right thing. It had been so long since he had weighed his actions in terms of right and wrong, justice and injustice, truth and lies. The last time was probably when he was still a kid. Amazingly, that young Sammy, the one he was sure had disappeared long ago, had come back to life here, in this terrible place. That Sammy had principles. He would never allow himself to believe that the ground had opened up and swallowed his daughter forever.

With his sudden appearance in the clearing, everyone froze. Only Yuri Cezar broke into a broad, cruel grin as if nothing out of the ordinary had happened. His bodyguards put down their glasses and felt for their weapons. They weren't sure how to respond yet.

"I've been expecting you," Cezar said, laughing at what seemed to be a private joke. It made his whole body shake, even his budding potbelly.

"Where's my daughter?" Sammy demanded from the edge of the clearing. Mud was dripping from his clothes onto the expensive carpets, and he was panting heavily.

Cezar still didn't move. He drew deeply on his cigarette, letting the ashes fall on the rug. Then the grin vanished.

"What did you bring me?"

"Seven hundred and twenty-five thousand six hundred dollars," Sammy answered. "Everything I have. I'll get the rest; you have my word. Where's my daughter?"

"Let me tell you something, Sammy," Cezar said, no longer laughing. "How much did you say? Seven hundred and twenty-five thousand and six hundred? That's a lot for a lousy effort. Two million isn't a lot for a serious effort."

"What are you saying?"

"What you've got in that case, there's not enough in it for me. I'm sure you understand. I'm a businessman."

He turned to the sheikh. "Would you like to make an offer?"

"I'll match his offer," the sheikh said, "and I'll throw in some oil stocks. I'll admit they haven't been doing too well lately, but oil is a very dynamic commodity."

"You see, Sammy?"

Sammy didn't reply. Slowly, he reached for the pistol in his pocket.

"You don't get it, Sammy," Cezar went on. "I loved you like a son. But you didn't understand rule number one. Doing business with Russians is like playing Russian roulette. You should have rescued your daughter a long time ago. A real father would give his right arm for his daughter. You didn't. So tell me, right here and now. Are you in or out of the game?"

Sammy still remained silent.

"You think I'm going to turn my back on the sale of a pretty little white girl to the sheikh just because you give me your word? You're offering me seven hundred thousand and change for her when you owe me two million? Not only can't I trust your word, but you're a shitty father as well."

Sammy tightened his grip on the gun.

Cezar gave the signal to Major Joe, who raised the corner of the sheet on the third cage. Eden was hunched up inside, her eyes closed.

Lying in the marsh, Iris raised her body to get a better look. I grabbed her arm and pulled her back down. "You're staying here," I whispered.

"Not on your life," she whispered back furiously, "My daughter's in there."
Ben-Or glanced in my direction and started crawling to the right.

"Stay close to me." It was all I could say.

Out of the corner of my eye, I saw Ben-Or take out a Chinese bodyguard
without making a sound. Iris screwed the silencer onto her Beretta. The
only noise it made when she shot one of the Japanese bodyguards was a soft
ping. But it was enough to set off a commotion that erupted like a volcano.
That was my signal. I shot an Arab minder at close range. He collapsed onto
the ground, but the sheikh drew a gun and began firing in my direction. I
switched to automatic, working the machine gun as I ran into the center of
the clearing. I saw people falling all around me. Then, I caught a glimpse of
two chubby Yakuza running toward Ben-Or with their guns drawn. It was
a fatal mistake on their part. He stood his ground, calmly taking aim as if he
were on a firing range, bringing them down one after the other. They each
fell like a sack of potatoes.

At this point, Cezar's gulag soldiers joined the fray. It must have taken
a while for their heads to clear. One headed for Ben-Or, looking to attack
him with his bare hands. Anan put down his weapon, leapt toward the
Russian, and punched him in the head. A blow like that could have fractured
a telephone pole, but the oversized Russian just bent over, shook his head
from side to side, and straightened up again. Within a split second, he was
crushing Ben-Or in his two massive arms covered in the infantile tats of
Siberian prisons. It was no time for games. I knew Ben-Or would never
forgive me for not letting him get to the fun part, but still, I picked up a large
stone ashtray from a table and brought it down on the giant's head. A few
cigarette butts flew into the air. It's odd how the brain registers meaningless
details like that, even in the midst of a battle. I saw the Russian's mouth
open in a twisted smile, revealing his teeth and protruding tongue. Then he
went to sleep.

The other gulager moved toward us, armed with a short metal pipe. That's
a great weapon if you like to break bones, and from the cold grin on the
degenerate's face, it was obvious that was his recreation of choice. What
the goon didn't know was that I trained at the Shaolin Temple, where they

tattoo on their foreheads in invisible ink the motto, "Soft as cotton, light as a swallow, hard as steel."

In the style of a drunken boxer, I executed a kick that sent the pipe flying out of his hand. He didn't get the chance to see it roll on the ground, where it lay like nothing more than a piece of scrap metal. Like the black dragon spreading its claws, I struck him on both sides of his head. Then I turned sideways and grabbed him under the chin, just above the Adam's apple, and swung him around. I heard his windpipe break. That was all it took. His 290 or so pounds of muscle mass didn't do him any good. That's the problem with chumps like him. In the end, muscles alone aren't enough.

The Chinese were a tougher bunch. The three of them teamed up by the sofas, firing at Iris and pinning her in place as they leapfrogged closer to her, taking advantage of the dark and any furrow or table along the way to protect them from return fire. "Grenade!" Iris shouted. I stretched out flat on the expensive rug, already soaked in blood, and saw Anan do the same, taking cover behind one the many bodies on the ground. The grenade exploded. I raised my head. There was no sign of the Chinese. Iris's head popped up, followed by Ben-Or's.

The Cambodian and the German were trying to flee through the thick reeds. The sound of sirens could already be heard from the direction of the river. Apparently, Margarit hadn't wasted any time. Sammy and Yuri Cezar were standing face to face in the center of the clearing, guns drawn. They were both wounded and smeared with blood, but each of them seemed totally oblivious to anything except the man in front of him. Sammy was quicker and more practiced. It must have been years since he'd held a gun in his hands, but it's something you never forget.

"You should have taken the money, Yuri," Sammy said, squeezing the trigger. The bullet hit Cezar in the middle of the forehead. A thin trickle of blood began dripping down his face as he collapsed.

Iris started toward the cages, but I held her back. I'd heard a sound I couldn't identify, something like the noise of a wild elephant stampeding through the marsh. A scrawny man with crazed eyes burst into the clearing, waving a gun.

CHAPTER FIFTY-EIGHT

"Valium," I shouted, "what the hell are you doing here?"

But Valium was focused on only one man: Sammy. In a voice filled with anguish, he shrieked, "You fucked with my life. You fucked with the life of everyone you ever touched. Now you're going to pay."

"No, no!" Iris screamed as I started running toward Valium. Sammy tried to aim his gun at his accuser, but his hand was shaking too much. A strange look came into his eyes, as if they realized that his day had come even before his brain did. But he still didn't understand why now. Before the bullet entered his chest, he managed to ask quizzically, "How come you suddenly show up in my life again?"

Sammy grabbed his chest with his left hand. The gun was still in his right, but it wasn't pointed at Valium. It was pointed at me. His eyes burning with hatred, he gasped, "If she can't belong to me, she can't belong to anyone." He squeezed the trigger. But Valium's second shot, a split second sooner, hit him in the shoulder. Sammy's bullet passed less than an inch from my cheek. The third shot Valium fired penetrated Sammy's neck. He collapsed to the ground.

Valium dropped the gun but remained frozen in place. I saw his eyes looking blankly at Sammy spread out on the rug, bleeding profusely.

Iris knelt beside her husband. The life was draining out of him, but he was still conscious. He reached out for her. She took his hand, but there was no love in the gesture. Only profound pity.

"I don't regret anything," Sammy whispered.

Iris tried to pull away, but he held on tight. "Except what I did to Eden," he went on. "That was unforgivable. Look out for her. You're her mother. You're all she has left." His hand went slack. Iris sat up. Her hands were covered in blood. Sammy Ben-Lev was dead.

I saw Anan gesture to me and I got the message. "Come," I said to Iris, helping her up. Her only response was a single word: "Eden."

I understood that Anan wanted the final act to be played out as far as possible from the blood-soaked arena and the bodies scattered around it. And as far as possible from Sammy's body. "Eden, Eden darling," Iris shouted, running toward the cages without waiting for an answering call. Ben-Or

237

moved quickly, pulling the sheets off and opening the cages. From the third came the heart-wrenching cry of a young girl, "Mommy!" Ben-Or helped her out. She took one hesitant step and then started running, falling and crying as she ran, but not giving up. A young body has incredible resilience. Iris ran toward her and took her in her arms. Finally, they were together again, bound in the embrace of mother and daughter. But it was also more than that. I realized that Sammy was right. For both of them, they were all they had left.

I had no idea how their life would go forward from this point. Would the wounds ever heal and the scars on the heart fade away? How long would it take for love and tenderness to compensate for months of terror and abuse? For Sammy's death? For what he had done? But at that moment, the embrace seemed to be their whole world, as if Iris and Eden would never let go of each other again. There was only one thing I knew for certain: I would never forget that sight.

I stepped back and gestured to Anan. Valium was sitting, frozen, staring at the sky. We stood there above him in silence, knowing without having to put it in words: Whatever happens is meant to happen.

A Note from the Author

DOTAN NAOR is an ex-Mossad agent, bounced out of the agency not just for a fatal miscalculation in Palestinian Jenin but for his inability to live within the bureaucracy and submit to authority. Dotan is now a private detective who uses his immense skills of persuasion and violence to rescue Israelis who are in peril throughout the world. Through his extensive travels in Asia, Dotan has developed a love for Eastern philosophy and lifestyle; his enhanced spiritual existence also happens to be good for business, as many Israelis run off to exotic Asian locales to let off steam after their mandatory and often dangerous military service.

About the Author

Yigal Zur is a noted Israeli writer, journalist, and travel guide who has written 14 books to date. His thriller *Passport to Death* is the first to feature ex-Mossad agent Dotan Naor and takes place in Thailand (published November 2019, Oceanview). His second thriller, *Death in Shangri-la*, which was the first to be translated into English (published by Oceanview 2018), continues to feature Dotan Naor and takes place in North India. The third thriller in the same series is *Child of Dust*, which takes place in Ko-Samui, Thailand, and in Cambodia.

Zur also wrote travel books and guides to India and China, as well as a script for *Menelik—A Black Jewish Prince*, which was filmed in 1999 and won the Wolgin prize at the Jerusalem Film Festival.

Amongst his published works are the novels *Dark Prune, Spring of Almond's Blossom*, and *The Monsoon's End*. Yigal Zur has also hosted successful TV travel shows. He served in the military, spending time on the front lines in the Golan Heights during the 1973 Yom Kippur War. He is the only Israeli journalist ever to be embedded with the US Army in action during Desert

Storm 2003 in Iraq.

Zur has traveled extensively in 114 countries and is an expert on Southeast Asia.

SOCIAL MEDIA HANDLES:
https://www.facebook.com/yigal.zur
https://tinyurl.com/3w3rehxk

AUTHOR WEBSITE:
https://yigal-zur.com/

Also by Yigal Zur

The Dotan Naor Thrillers:
Death in Shangri-La
Passport to Death

www.ingramcontent.com/pod-product-compliance
Lightning Source LLC
Chambersburg PA
CBHW020719130726
47899CB00011B/504